"I need to leave," she said softly.

Reggie turned his head towards her on the pillow. He doubted he could move. He could barely breathe. It was close to morning. As soon as they had ended one session they'd been quick and eager to start another. Where in the hell did all that energy come from?

He knew she had to leave. So did he. But he didn't want their one and only night together to end. "You do know there is no reason why we can't –"

She quickly turned towards him and placed a finger on his lips. "Yes, there is. I can't tell you my true identity. It could hurt someone."

He frowned. As if reading his mind, she said, "I don't have a husband. I don't even have a boyfriend."

"Then who?" he asked. He probably had more to lose than her since his campaign for Senate officially began that day.

"I can't say. This has to be goodbye."

The Moretti Seduction
by Katherine Garbera

It was the only way to keep her mind off Antonio.

Work twenty-four hours a day.

When she was at home, she imagined him there with her. When she slept, he haunted her dreams, making love to her and speaking to her in that beautiful Italian voice of his. When she worked out in the gym, she heard his footfalls on the treadmill next to hers.

He was haunting her. Damn him.

As if she conjured him, he called her. "Nathalie, why haven't you returned my calls?" he asked.

"I'm not sure. I've been busy." Excuses. She knew better than that. "I guess I wanted a chance to get you out of my head."

"Did it work?"

No, she had to admit. *Not at all.*

Available in May 2010
from Mills & Boon® Desire™

TALL, DARK...
WESTMORELAND!
BY
BRENDA JACKSON

THE MORETTI
SEDUCTION
BY
KATHERINE GARBERA

All the characters in this book have no existence outside the imagination of
the author, and have no relation whatsoever to anyone bearing the same name
or names. They are not even distantly inspired by any individual known or
unknown to the author, and all the incidents are pure invention.

All Rights Reserved including the right of reproduction in whole or in part
in any form. This edition is published by arrangement with Harlequin
Enterprises II B.V./S.à.r.l. The text of this publication or any part thereof may
not be reproduced or transmitted in any form or by any means, electronic or
mechanical, including photocopying, recording, storage in an information
retrieval system, or otherwise, without the written permission of the publisher.

This book is sold subject to the condition that it shall not, by way of trade or
otherwise, be lent, resold, hired out or otherwise circulated without the prior
consent of the publisher in any form of binding or cover other than that in
which it is published and without a similar condition including this condition
being imposed on the subsequent purchaser.

® and ™ are trademarks owned and used by the trademark owner and/or its
licensee. Trademarks marked with ® are registered with the United Kingdom
Patent Office and/or the Office for Harmonisation in the Internal Market and
in other countries.

First published in Great Britain 2010
Harlequin Mills & Boon Limited,
Eton House, 18-24 Paradise Road, Richmond, Surrey TW9 1SR

The publisher acknowledges the copyright holders of the
individual works as follows:

Tall, Dark...Westmoreland! © Brenda Streater Jackson 2009
The Moretti Seduction © Katherine Garbera 2009

ISBN: 978 0 263 88167 7

51-0510

Harlequin Mills & Boon policy is to use papers that are natural, renewable
and recyclable products and made from wood grown in sustainable forests.
The logging and manufacturing processes conform to the legal environmental
regulations of the country of origin.

Printed and bound in Spain
by Litografia Rosés S.A., Barcelona

TALL, DARK...
WESTMORELAND!

BY
BRENDA JACKSON

Dear Reader,

I am pleased to present to you Reginald Westmoreland's story. At long last!

Reggie was introduced in my very first Westmoreland book, *Delaney's Desert Sheikh*, as Delaney's partner in crime. By the end of the story, he had earned a special place in readers' hearts because he helped Delaney outsmart her overprotective brothers. Now, fifteen books later, it is time for his story to be told. I knew he would be the one to wrap up my books on the Atlanta-based Westmorelands.

I also knew he would be the one who would eventually become the Westmoreland to enter politics. And considering everything, doing so would not be an easy task. Especially if the woman your heart desires the most is the daughter of the man you're running against.

Neither Reggie nor Olivia Jeffries expect the explosive desire their initial meeting brings, and together they face many challenges. But they discover that no matter what, true love conquers all.

I've received a lot of letters and e-mails asking if Reggie's book is the end of the Westmorelands. My response is a resounding "No." There are more Westmorelands to come, and I look forward to introducing you to all the Denver-based Westmorelands. They are men you will continue to fall in love with.

Thank you for making the Westmorelands a very special family. I look forward to bringing you more books of searing desire and endless love and passion.

Happy reading!

Brenda Jackson

Brenda Jackson is a die "heart" romantic who married her childhood sweetheart and still proudly wears the "going steady" ring he gave her when she was fifteen years old. Because she's always believed in the power of love, Brenda's stories all have happy endings. In her real-life love story, Brenda and her husband of thirty-six years live in Jacksonville, Florida, and have two sons.

A *New York Times* bestselling author of more than fifty romance titles, Brenda is a recent retiree who worked thirty-seven years in management at a major insurance company. She divides her time between family, writing and travelling with Gerald. You may write to Brenda at PO Box 28267, Jacksonville, Florida 32226, USA, by e-mail at WriterBJackson@aol.com or visit her website at www.brendajackson.net.

To the love of my life, Gerald Jackson, Sr, and to everyone who has ever sent me a letter or e-mail to let me know how much you've enjoyed the Westmorelands. This book is for you!

Withhold not good from them to whom it is due, when it is in the power of thine hand to do it.
—*Proverbs 3:27*

THE WESTMORELAND FAMILY

Scott and Delane Westmoreland

John (Evelyn)   **James (Sarah)**   **Corey (Abbie)**

②	③	④	⑤	⑦	①
Dare (Shelly) AJ, Allison	Thorn (Tara) Trace	Stone (Madison) Rock	Storm (Jayla) Shanna, Johanna	Chase (Jessica)	Delaney (Jamal) Ari, Arielle
					⑮

⑥	⑪	⑧	⑨	⑭	
Spencer (Chardonnay) Russell	Jared (Dana)	Durango (Savannah) Sarah	Ian (Brooke) Pierce, Price	Quade (Cheyenne) Venus, Athena, Troy	Reggie

⑫	⑬	⑩			
Clint (Alyssa) Cain	Cole (Patrina) Emilie, Emery	Casey (McKinnon) Corey			

① Delaney's Desert Sheikh
② A Little Dare
③ Thorn's Challenge
④ Stone Cold Surrender
⑤ Riding the Storm
⑥ Jared's Counterfeit Fiancée

⑦ The Chase is On
⑧ The Durango Affair
⑨ Ian's Ultimate Gamble
⑩ Seduction, Westmoreland Style
⑪ Spencer's Forbidden Passion
⑫ Taming Clint Westmoreland

⑬ Cole's Red-Hot Pursuit
⑭ Quade's Babies
⑮ Tall, Dark...Westmoreland!

One

There has to be another way for a woman to have fun, Olivia Jeffries thought as she glanced around at everyone attending the Firemen's Masquerade Ball, an annual charity event held in downtown Atlanta. Already she was gearing up for a boring evening.

It wouldn't have been so bad if she hadn't arrived from Paris just yesterday, after being summoned home by her father. That meant she had to drop everything, including plans to drive through the countryside of the Seine Valley to complete the painting she had started months ago.

Returning to Atlanta had required her to take a leave of absence from her job as an art curator at the Louvre. But when Orin Jeffries called, she hadn't hesitated to drop everything. After all, he was only the greatest dad in the entire world.

He had wanted her home after making the decision to run for public office, saying it was important that she was there not only for his first fund-raiser but also for the duration of his campaign. There would be a number of functions he would need to attend, and he preferred not to go with any particular woman on a regular basis. He didn't want any of his female friends to get the wrong idea.

Olivia could only shake her head and smile. Her divorced father had taken himself off the marriage block years ago. In fact, she doubted he'd ever allowed himself to be there in the first place. He dated on occasion, but he'd never gotten serious about any woman, which was a pity. At fifty-six, Orin Jeffries was without a doubt a very good-looking man. His ex-wife, who was Olivia's mom in genes only, had left a bad taste in Orin's mouth. A taste that the past twenty-four years hadn't erased.

Her two older brothers, Duan, who was thirty-six, and Terrence, who was thirty-four, had taken after her father in their good looks. And as in the case of their father, the thought of marriage was the last thing on their minds. In a way, she followed in her dad's footsteps as well. Finding a husband was the last thing on hers.

So there you had it. They were the swinging single Jeffries, although for the moment, nothing was swinging for her, Olivia thought. There were a few people at this ball who seemed to be having fun, but most, like her, were looking at their watches and wondering when proper etiquette dictated it would be okay to leave.

Whoever had come up with the idea of everyone wearing masks had really been off their rocker. It made her feel like she was part of the Lone Ranger's posse. And because all the money raised tonight was for the new wing at the children's hospital, in addition to the mask, everyone was required to wear a name badge on which was printed the name of a nursery rhyme character, a color of a crayon or a well-known cartoon or comic-book character. How creative.

At least the food was good. The first words out of her father's mouth when he'd seen her at the airport the day before had been, "You look too thin." She figured the least she could do was mosey on over to the buffet table and get herself something to eat. Hopefully, in a little while she could split.

Reginald Westmoreland watched the woman as she crossed the room, making her way over to the buffet table. He had been watching her for over twenty minutes now, racking his brain as to who she was. Mask or no mask, he recognized most of the women at the ball tonight. He knew almost every one of them because for years he had been immersed in the science of "lip-tology." In other words, the first thing he noticed about a woman was her lips.

He could recognize a woman by her lips alone, without even looking at any other facial feature. Most people wouldn't agree, but no two pairs of lips were the same. His brothers and cousins had denounced his claim and had quickly put him to the test. He had just as quickly proven them wrong. Whether you considered it a blessing or a curse, the bottom line was that he had the gift.

And there were other things besides her lips that caught his attention, like her height. She had to be almost six feet tall. And then he was struck by the way she fit into her elegantly designed black and silver beaded dress, the way the material clung to her shapely curves. He had noticed several men approach her, but she had yet to dance with any of them. In fact, it seemed that she was brushing them off. Reginald smelled a challenge.

"So, how is the campaign going, Reggie?"

Reginald, known to all his family as Reggie, turned to look at his older brother, divorce attorney extraordinaire, Jared Westmoreland. Just last week Jared had made the national news owing to a high-profile settlement he'd won in favor of a well-known Hollywood actor.

"It officially kicks off Monday. But now that Jeffries has decided to throw his hat into the ring, things should be rather interesting," he said, referring to the older man who would be his opponent. "With Brent, I have a good campaign manager, but I still feel it might be a tight race. Jeffries is well-known and well-liked."

"Well, if you need any help, let me know, although I'm not sure how much time I can spare now that Dana's expecting and all."

Reggie rolled his eyes. Just last month Jared had found out he was going to be a father. "Dana is going to be carrying the baby, Jared, not you."

"I know, but I'm the one who's been getting sick in the morning, and now I'm getting cravings. I never liked pickles until now."

Reggie couldn't help but smile over his wine-glass. "Sounds like a personal problem to me." At the moment, his attention strayed from whatever Jared was saying. Instead, his gaze focused on the other side of the room. He noticed the woman whom he'd been watching sit down at a table. He had yet to see a man by her side, which meant she had come to the party alone.

"Umm, I wonder who she is?" he asked.

Jared followed Reggie's gaze and chuckled. "What's wrong? Don't you recognize the lips?"

Reggie shifted his gaze from the woman to his brother and frowned. "No, she's someone new. I definitely haven't met her before. Her lips don't give her away."

"Then I guess the only thing left for you to do is go over there and introduce yourself."

Reggie grinned. "I know they don't call you the sharpest attorney in Atlanta for nothing."

"Don't you know sitting alone at a party isn't good for you?"

Olivia swung her head around at the sound of the deep, throaty masculine voice to find a tall, handsome man standing beside her. Like everyone else, he was wearing a mask, but even with it covering half of his face, she knew he had to be extremely good-looking. In the dim lighting, her artist eye was able to capture all his striking features that were exposed.

First of all, there was his skin, flawlessly smooth and a shade of color that reminded her of rich, dark maple syrup. Then there was the angular plane of a jaw that supported a pair of sexy lips. The same ones that bestowed a slow smile on her. Apparently, he realized she was checking him out.

"In that case, I guess you need to join me," she replied, trying to remember the last time she'd been so outrageously forward with a guy and quickly deciding never. But the way the evening was going, she would have to stir up her own excitement. And now was as good a time as any to start. Maybe it was the fact that the party was so unrelentingly boring that made her long for a taste of the wild and reckless. The other men who had approached her hadn't even piqued her curiosity. She had no desire to get to know them better. But this man was different.

"I don't mind if I do," he said, easily sliding into the chair beside her while his eyes remained locked with hers. Her nose immediately picked up the scent of his cologne. Expensive. She quickly checked out his left hand. Ringless. Her gaze automatically went back to his face. Beautiful. Now he was smiling in earnest and showing beautiful white teeth.

"You're amused," she said, taking a sip of her punch but wishing she had something a little stronger.

Whoever he was, he was certainly someone worth getting to know, even if she was returning to Paris in a few months. That made it all the more plausible. It had taken her two years to get on full-time at the Louvre, and the hard work was just beginning. Once she returned, she would be working long hours, with little time to get her painting done. That was why she had brought her paints to Atlanta with her. She was determined to capture something worthwhile on canvas while she was here. The man sitting beside her would be the perfect subject.

"Flattered more than amused," he said, his voice reaching out and actually touching her, although she barely registered his words in her mind, because she was too busy watching the way his mouth moved. Sensuously slow.

She couldn't help wondering who he was. She had been gone from Atlanta a long time. After high school she had attended Pratt Institute in New York before doing her graduate work at the Art Institute of Boston. From there she had made the move to Paris, after landing a job as a tour professional, a glorified name for a tour guide.

He had to be around her brother Terrence's age, or maybe a year or so younger. She wondered if he would give her his real name, or if he would stick to the rules and play this silly little game the coordinators of the ball had come up with. His name badge said Jack Sprat. No wonder he was in such fine shape, she thought. Even in the tuxedo he was wearing, she saw broad, muscular shoulders and a nice solid chest. All muscles. Definitely no fat.

"So, Jack," she said, smiling at him the same way he was smiling at her. "What is such a nice guy like you doing at a boring party like this?"

He chuckled, and the sound sent goose bumps over her body. "Waiting to meet you so we can start having some fun." He glanced at her name badge. "Wonder Woman."

The smile that touched the corners of her mouth

widened. She liked him already. "Well, trust me when I say, it's a *wonder* that I'm here at all. I really want to be someplace else, but I promised the person who paid for this ticket that I'd come in his place. And since it's all for charity, and for such a good cause, I decided to at least make an appearance."

"I'm glad you did."

And Reggie meant it. He'd thought she had a beautiful pair of lips from afar, but now he had a chance to really study them up close. They were a pair he would never forget. They were full, shapely, and had luscious-looking dips at the corners. She had them covered in light lip gloss, which was perfect; any color would detract from their modish structure.

"We've exchanged names, and I'm glad to make your acquaintance, Jack," she said, presenting her hand to him.

He grinned. "Likewise, Wonder."

The moment their hands touched, he felt it and knew that she did, too. Her fingers quivered on his, and for some reason, he could not release her hand. That realization unnerved him. No woman had ever had this kind of effect on him before, not in all his thirty-two years.

"Are you from Atlanta?"

Her voice, soft and filled with Southern charm, reclaimed his attention.

"Yes, born and raised right here," he said, reluctantly releasing her hand. "What about you?"

"Same here," she said, looking at him as if she could see through his mask. "Why haven't we met before?"

He smiled. "How do you know that we haven't?"

Her chuckle came easily. "Trust me. I would remember if we had. You're the type of man a woman couldn't easily forget."

"Hey, that's my line. You stole it," he said jokingly.

"I'll give it back to you if you take me away from here."

He didn't say anything for a minute but just sat there studying her face. And then he asked, "Are you sure you want to go off with me?"

She managed another smile. "Are you sure you want to take me?" she challenged.

Reggie couldn't help but laugh loudly, so loudly, in fact, that when he glanced across the room, his brother Jared caught his gaze and gave him a raised brow. He had five brothers in all. He and Jared were the only ones still living in Atlanta. He also had a bunch of cousins in the city. It seemed Westmorelands were everywhere, but he and Jared were the only ones who were here tonight. The rest had other engagements or were off traveling someplace.

A part of Reggie was grateful for that. He was the youngest of the Atlanta-based Westmorelands, and his brothers and cousins still liked to consider him the baby of the family, although he stood six-seven and was the tallest of the clan.

"Yes, I would take you in a heartbeat, sweetheart. I would take you anywhere you wanted to go."

And he meant it.

She nodded politely, but he knew she was thinking, trying to figure out a way she could go off with him and not take any careless risks with her safety. A woman couldn't be too trusting these days, and he understood that.

"I have an idea," he said finally, when she hadn't responded and several moments had passed.

"What?"

He reached into his jacket pocket and pulled out his cell phone. "Text someone you know and trust, and tell them to save my number. Tell them you will call them in the morning. When you call, they can erase the number."

Olivia thought about what he'd suggested and then wondered whom she could call. Any girlfriends she'd had while living here years ago were no longer around. Of course, she couldn't text her father, so she thought about her brothers. Duan was presently out of the city, since his job as a private investigator took him all over the country, and Terrence was living in the Florida Keys. She and her brothers were close, but it was Terrence who usually let her get away with things. Duan enjoyed playing the role of older brother. He would ask questions. Terrence would ask questions, too, but he was more easygoing.

Perhaps it was Duan's inquisitive mind that made him such a stickler for the rules. It had to be all those years he'd worked first as a patrolman and then as a detective for Atlanta's police department. Terrence, a former pro football player for the Miami Dolphins, knew how to have fun. He was actually the real swinging single Jeffries. He owned a nice club in the Florida Keys that really embodied the term *nightlife*.

Her safest bet would be to go with Terrence.

"Okay," she said, taking the phone. She sent Terrence a quick text message, asking that he delete the phone number from which the message was sent after hearing from her in the morning. She handed the phone back to him.

"Feel better about this?" he asked her.

She met his gaze. "Yes."

"Good. Is there any particular place you want to go?"

The safest location would be her place, Olivia thought, but she knew she couldn't do that. Her father was home, going over a campaign speech he would be giving at a luncheon on Monday. "No, but I haven't been out to Stone Mountain in a while."

He smiled. "Then Stone Mountain it is."

"And we'll need to go in separate cars," she said quickly. She had begun to feel nervous because she had never done anything like this in her life. What was she thinking? She got a quick answer when she met his gaze again. She was thinking how it would probably feel to be in this man's arms, to rub her hand across that strong, angular jaw, to taste those kissable lips and to breathe in more of his masculine scent.

"That's fine," he said in a husky voice. "You lead and I'll follow."

"And we keep on our masks and use these names," she said, pointing to her name badge.

He studied her intently for a moment before nodding his head. "All right."

She let out a silent breath. Her father was well-known in the city, and with the election just a couple of months away, she didn't want to do anything to jeopardize his chances of winning. Anything like having her name smeared in the paper in some scandal. Scandals were hard to live down, and she didn't want do anything that would be a nice addition to the *Atlanta Journal-Constitution*'s gossip column.

"Okay, let's go," she said, rising to her feet. She hoped she wasn't making a mistake, but when he accidentally brushed up against her when they headed for the exit, she had a feeling anything that happened between them tonight could only be right.

Reggie, as a rule, didn't do one-night stands. However, he would definitely make tonight and

this woman an exception. The car he was following close behind was a rental, so that didn't give
him any clues as to her identity. All he did know
was that she was someone who wanted to enjoy
tonight, and he was going to make sure she wasn't
disappointed.

She'd indicated that she wanted to go someplace
in Stone Mountain, and she was heading in that direction. He wondered if they would go directly to a
place where they could be alone, or if they would
work up to that over a few drinks in a club. If she
wanted a night on the town first, there were a number of nightclubs to choose from, but that would
mean removing their masks, and he had a feeling
she intended for these to stay in place. Why? Was
she as well-known around the city as he was? At
least after Monday he would be. Brent Fairgate, his
campaign manager and the main person who had
talked him into running for the Senate, had arranged
for campaign posters with his picture to be plastered
on just about every free space in Atlanta.

Returning his attention to the car in front of
him, he braked when they came to a traffic light.
Just then his cell phone rang. He worked it out of
his pocket. "Hello?"

"Where are you?"

He gave a short laugh. "Don't worry about me,
Jared. However, I do apologize for not letting you
know I was leaving."

"That woman you were with earlier isn't here, either. Is that a coincidence?"

Reggie shook his head, grinning. "I don't know. You tell me."

There was a pause on the other end. "You sure about what you're doing, Reggie?"

"Positive. And no lectures please."

"Whatever," came his brother's gruff reply. And then the call was disconnected.

The traffic began moving again, and Reggie couldn't help but think about how his life would change once the campaigning began. There would be speeches to deliver, interviews to do, television appearances to make, babies to kiss and so on and so forth. He would be the first Westmoreland to enter politics, and for him, the decision hadn't been an easy one to make. But Atlanta was growing by leaps and bounds, and he wanted to give back to the city that had given him so much.

Unlike his brothers, who had left town to attend college, he had remained here and had gone to Morehouse. And he had never regretted doing so. He smiled, thinking that the good old days were when he got out of college and, a few years later, when he opened his own accounting firm. At the time, his best buddy had been his cousin Delaney. They were only a few months apart in age and had always been close. In fact, he was the one who had helped Delaney outsmart her five overprotective brothers right after she finished med school and needed to get some private time. He had let her use his cabin in the mountains for a little rest and relaxation, without telling Dare, Thorn, Stone, Chase or Storm where she was. Lucky for him, his cousins hadn't broken his bones, as they had threatened to do, when they discovered his involvement. The good thing was that Delaney had met her desert sheikh and fallen in love at his cabin.

Reggie's attention was pulled back to the car in front of him when Wonder Woman put on her blinker to turn into the parking lot of the luxurious Saxon Hotel. He smiled. He liked her taste, but given that they were wearing masks, he wondered how this would work. And then he got an idea and immediately pulled his cell phone out of his jacket pocket to punch in a few numbers.

"Hello?"

Reggie could hear babies crying in the background. "This is Reggie. What are you doing to my nieces and nephew?"

He heard his brother Quade's laugh. "It's bath time, and nobody wants to play in the water tonight. What's up? And I understand congratulations are in order. Mom told me you've decided to run for the Senate. Good luck."

"Thanks." And then, without missing a beat, he said, "I need a favor, Quade."

"What kind of favor?"

"I need a private room at the Saxon Hotel here in Atlanta tonight, and I know Dominic Saxon is your brother-in-law."

"So?"

"So make it happen for me tonight, as soon as possible. And I need things kept discreet and billed to me."

There was a pause on the other end. "You sure about this, Reggie?"

He shook his head. It was the same question Jared had asked him moments ago. "Yes, Quade, I'm sure. And I don't expect any lectures from you, considering when and how my nieces and nephew were conceived."

"Go to hell, Reggie."

He smiled. "Not in front of the babies, Quade. And as far as going to hell, I'll go, but only after I get a night of heaven. So make it happen for me, Quade. I'll owe you. I'll even volunteer to fly in one day and babysit."

"Damn, she must be some woman."

Reggie thought about those lips he wanted so desperately to taste. "She is."

"I'll see what I can do." And then the call was disconnected.

Smiling and feeling pretty certain that Quade would come through for him, he watched as Wonder Woman parked her car, and then eased his car into the parking spot next to hers. As soon as she turned off the engine, he got out of his car and glanced around, making sure there weren't a lot of people about. She had parked in an area that was pretty empty, and he was grateful for that.

When he got to her side of the car, she rolled down the window and looked a little flushed. "Sorry. I guess I didn't think this far ahead."

He bent down and leaned forward against her door and propped his arms on the car's window frame and smiled at her. She smelled good, and she looked good. His gaze shifted from her eyes to her lips and then back to her eyes again. He couldn't wait to taste her lips.

"Don't worry. Tonight will end the way we want," he said, with certainty in his voice and all the while thinking that if Quade didn't come through for him tonight, he was liable to kill him. At her confused expression, he said, "I've made a call, and it will only be a few moments. I'll get a call back when things get set up."

Olivia eyed the man staring at her and tried to ignore the stirring in the pit of her stomach. She couldn't help wondering just who was he and what kind of connections he had. They had to be big ones if he was able to get them a room at the Saxon from the parking lot. Would they have to do the normal check-in?

One part of her brain was screaming at her, telling her that what she was contemplating doing was downright foolish and irresponsible. No good girl, certainly not one who'd been raised to be a proper young lady, would think about having a one-night stand with a stranger.

But then the other part of her brain, the one that was daring, as well as wild and reckless, urged her on. Go ahead, Libby. Have some fun. Live a little. You haven't been seriously involved with a man for almost two years. You've been too busy. You deserve some fun. What will it hurt as long as you've taken every precaution to make sure you're safe?

And at the moment she was safe. Terrence had this man's phone number, and the hotel was definitely a respectable one. And it was one she had selected, not him. But she had to admit, she felt a little silly with the two of them still wearing their masks. At least she had taken off her name badge.

"So, Wonder Woman, what's your favorite color?"

She couldn't help but smile. He evidently felt the tension and was making an attempt to ease it. "Lavender. What's yours?"

"Flesh tone."

She grinned. "Flesh tone isn't a color."

"Depends on who's wearing it," he said softly, and then his eyes flickered to her lips. She felt the intensity of his gaze just as if it was a soft caress. Suddenly, she felt the need to moisten her lips with her tongue.

"I wish you hadn't done that," he whispered huskily, leaning his body forward to the point where more of his face was in the window, just inches from her face.

A breathless sigh escaped from her lips. "What?" she asked in a strained voice.

"Tasted your own lips. That's what I want to do. What I'm dying to do."

"What's stopping you?"

Reggie thought that was a dare if ever he'd heard one. Deciding to take her up on it, he leaned his body in closer. She was tilting her head toward his face when suddenly his cell phone rang.

Damn. He reluctantly pulled back and pulled the cell phone from his jacket.

Olivia took that time to take a deep breath, and then she listened to his phone conversation.

"Yes?" he said into the phone.

She watched a huge smile brighten his face, and at the same time, she felt intense heat gather at the junction of her thighs.

"Thanks, man. I owe you one," he said. She then watched as he clicked off the phone and put it in his pocket. He glanced over at her. "Okay, Wonder Woman. Everything is set. We're on the sixteenth floor. Room sixteen thirty-two. Ready?"

She exhaled slowly. A part of her wanted to tell him that, no, she wasn't ready. She wanted to know how he'd arranged everything from a parking lot.

Another part of her needed to know how he was capable of making her feel things that no other man had ever made her feel before. How was he able to get her to take risks when she was the least impulsive person that had ever lived? At least she had been risk averse until she'd seen him at the party tonight.

She met his gaze, knowing this would be it. Once she got out of the car and walked into that hotel with him, their night together would begin. Was that what she really wanted? He was staring at her, and his gaze seemed to be asking her that same question.

She drew in a deep breath and nodded her head and said, "Yes, I'm ready."

He then opened the car door for her. "You go on ahead, and I'll follow within five minutes. The bank of elevators you should use is the one to the right of the check-in desk," he said.

"Okay."

He watched as she placed the strap of her purse on her shoulder before walking away. He smiled as she gracefully crossed the parking lot and headed toward the entrance to the hotel. He couldn't help but admire the way she looked in her dress, a silky number that swished around her legs whenever she made a movement. And she had the legs for it. Long, shapely legs that he could imagine wrapped around him, holding him inside her body during the heat of passion.

He was so into his thoughts that when she suddenly stopped walking, his heart nearly stopped beating. Had she changed her mind? Moments later he gave a deep sigh of relief when he realized she had stopped to remove her mask. He wondered if she would take the risk and turn around to let him see her face, voluntarily revealing her identity. He got his answer when she began walking again without looking back. He had a feeling that that was how the entire night would go. Identities and names would not be shared. Only passion.

He would respect her wishes, and when he joined her in the hotel room, his mask, too, would be back in place.

There was no doubt in his mind that this would be a night he would always remember.

Two

Olivia was grateful that no one seemed to pay her any attention when she walked into the huge lobby of the Saxon. It had always been her dream to spend a night in what had to be one of the most elegant hotels ever built. It was more stylish and extravagant than she had expected. There were only a few Saxons scattered about the country, in the major cities, and all had a reputation of providing top-quality service.

When she stepped onto the elevator that would carry her to the sixteenth floor, she couldn't help but again wonder about the man behind the mask and the connections he seemed to have. Reservations were hard to get because the hotel was booked far in advance, even as much as a year.

As she stepped out of the elevator and walked down the spacious hall, she studied the decor. Everything had a touch of elegance and class. With an artist's eye, she absorbed every fine detail of not only the rich and luxurious-looking carpet on the floor but also of the beautiful framed portraits that lined the walls. She would bet a month of her salary at the Louvre that those were original Audubon prints. If they devoted this much time and attention to the hallways, she could only imagine what one of the rooms would look like.

She wondered what Jack Sprat thought of her taste, since she was the one who'd guided him here. Of course, she would pay tonight's bill, since coming here was her idea. Connections or no connections, this place was her choice and not his, so it would only be fair. The last thing she wanted to do was come off as a thoughtless, high-maintenance woman.

Moments later she stood in front of room 1632. She didn't have a key and could only assume the door was unlocked. There was only one way to find out. She turned the handle and smiled when it gave way without a problem. She slowly opened the door and stepped into the room. Quickly closing the door, she glanced around, her eyes widening. This had to be a penthouse suite. She hadn't expected this, wasn't even sure she would be able to pay for it. She had figured on a regular room, which, though costly, would have been within her budget.

She was paid well, and loved Paris, but eventually she intended to return to the United States. She planned to open an art gallery in a few years, and that took money. Every penny she earned went into her special savings. Her father and brothers had promised to invest in the venture, but she felt that it was her responsibility to come up with the majority of the capital for her gallery. This little tryst was going to cost her. She would have to dip into her savings to pay for this suite. She wondered if just one night with a stranger could possibly be worth the sacrifice.

She crossed the room, drawn to the stately furnishings. She had stayed in nice hotels before, but there was something about a Saxon that took your breath away. Besides the elegant luxury that surrounded you, there was also the personalized service, culinary excellence and other amenities, which she had often heard about, but had yet to experience.

She walked through the sitting area to the bedroom. Her gaze moved from the plush love seat in the room to the bed. The bed was humongous and stately; the covering was soft to the touch. It felt as if you could actually lose yourself under it. The bedcoverings and curtains were done in an elegant red and a single red rose had been placed in the middle of the bed. Very romantic.

The connecting bath was just as stunning, with a huge Jacuzzi tub that sat in the middle of the floor, surrounded by a wall-to-wall vanity the likes of which she'd never seen in a hotel. Everything was his and hers, and the bathroom was roomy, spacious.

Nervously, she walked out of the bathroom and back into the bedroom and sat down on the edge of the bed.

When she was growing up, people had often said she was spoiled and pampered, and in a way, she had been. Being the only girl in the house had had its advantages. She had been only three years old when her mother left her father, ran off with a married man and destroyed not one, but two families. She would always admire her father for doing what had to be done to hold their family together. He'd worked long and hard hours as a corporate attorney and still had been there for her piano recitals and art shows and her brothers' Little League games. And one year he had even gotten elected president of the PTA. It hadn't been easy, and everyone had had to pitch in and help. And she could now admit that her brothers had made it easier for her.

Leaving home for college had been good for her. Against her father's and brothers' wishes, she had worked her way through college, refusing the

money they would send her. She'd needed to encounter the real world and sink or swim on her own
while doing so.

She'd learned how to swim.

She glanced at her watch. Chances were that
Jack Sprat was on his way up, so now was not the
time to get nervous. She had come on to him at the
party, and he had come on to her. They were here
because a night together was what they both
wanted. So why was she thinking about hightail-
ing it all of a sudden? Why were butterflies flying
around her stomach? And what was with the darn
goose bumps covering her arms?

She stood and began pacing. He would be here
at any moment, so she stopped and took the time
to put her mask back on. In a way she felt silly, but
at the same time mysterious.

Olivia glanced at her watch again. She felt her
body heating up just thinking about what would
happen when he did arrive. To say she was fascinated by a complete stranger would be an understatement. If anyone had told her that within less
than forty-eight hours of returning to Atlanta,
she, Olivia Jeffries, would be involved in an
affair to nowhere, she would not have believed
them. Usually she was very conservative, but not
tonight.

She caught her breath when she thought she
heard footsteps coming down the hall. An antici-

patory shiver ran down her spine, and she knew that in just a minute he would be there.

Reggie walked down the hallway, deep in thought. Some people engaged in casual affairs to pass the time or to feel needed. He was not one of them, and for some reason, he knew that the woman waiting on him in the hotel room wasn't, either. He would admit that there had been a few one-night stands in his history, back in the day at Morehouse, when he hadn't had a care in the world other than studying, making the grade and getting an easy lay. But now as a professional who owned a very prestigious accounting firm and as a political candidate, he picked his bed partners carefully. He hadn't been involved in any long-term affairs since right after college—and that disastrous time with Kayla Martin a few years ago, which he preferred to forget. He'd pretty much stuck to short-term affairs.

His family constantly reminded him he was the last Westmoreland bachelor living in Atlanta, but that was fine with him. Settling down and getting married were the furthest things from his mind. He was glad it wouldn't be an issue in his campaign, because his opponent, Orin Jeffries, was a long-term divorcé, and from what he'd heard, the man had no plans of ever remarrying.

Finally, he stood in front of room 1632. Only

pausing for a brief second, he reached out to open the door and then stopped when he remembered his mask. Glancing up and down the hall to make sure it was empty, he pulled the mask out of his pocket and put it on. Then, after drawing a deep breath, he opened the door.

The moment he opened the door, his eyes, that is, the portion of them that Olivia could see through his mask, met hers. They felt possessive, as if he was stamping ownership on her, when there was no way he could do that. He didn't know her true identity. He knew nothing about her other than that it seemed her need for him was just as elemental and strong as his need for her. It was a tangible thing, and she could feel it, all the way to her toes.

Yet there was something in the way he entered the room, not taking his eyes off her as he pushed the door closed behind him. And then giving the room only a cursory glance. Without a single word spoken between them, he swiftly crossed the room and drew her into his arms.

And kissed her.

There was nothing to be gained by any further talking, and they both knew it. And the moment his mouth touched hers, lightly at first, before devouring it with a hunger she felt deep in her belly, she moaned a silent acceptance of him and their night together.

This was sexual chemistry at its most potent. He was all passion, and she responded in kind. She kissed him, not with the same skill and experience he was leveling on her, but with a hunger that needed to be appeased, satisfied and explored.

The kiss intensified, and they both knew it wouldn't be enough to quench the desire waiting to be unleashed within them. Sensations were spreading through her, seeping deep into her bones and her senses. Urges that she had tried desperately to control were now threatening to consume her.

He reluctantly pulled his mouth away, and she watched as a sensuous smile touched his lips. "Tonight is worth everything," he whispered softly against her moist lips. "Not in my wildest imagination would I have thought of this happening."

Neither would I, Olivia thought. The masks were silly, but they had a profound purpose. So were the pretend names. With them, they were free to do what they pleased, without inhibitions or thought of consequences. If their paths were to cross again, after tonight, there would be no recognition, no recrimination and no need for denials. What happened in this hotel room tonight would stay in this hotel room tonight.

Reggie's gaze studied Olivia as he fought to catch his breath while doing the same for his senses. Kissing her, tasting her lips, had been like an obsession since the moment he'd laid eyes on her. The shape, texture and outline of her lips had a provocative effect on him. Some men were into the shape and size of a woman's breasts; others into her backside. He was definitely a lips man. The fullness of a pair, covered in lipstick or not, could induce a state of arousal in him. Just thinking of all the things he could do with them was enough to push him over the edge.

And then, losing control, he leaned down and kissed her again, and while his tongue dominated and played havoc with hers, he felt her loosen up, begin to relax in his arms. She wrapped her arms around his neck while her feminine curves so effortlessly pressed against him in a seamless melding of bodies. They fit together perfectly, naturally. There was nothing like having soft female limbs and a beautiful set of lips within reach, he thought.

The hand around her waist dipped, and he felt the curve of her backside through the gown she was wearing. A firm yet soft behind. He needed to get her out of her gown.

Pulling his mouth away, he swept her into his arms. At her startled gasp and with a swift glance, he met the eyes staring at him through the mask, and then his lips eased into a smile. So did hers. And with nothing left to be said, he walked to the bedroom.

Instead of placing her on the bed, he held her firmly in his arms and sat down on the love seat, adjusting her in his lap. She pulled in a deep breath and caught hold of the front of his jacket.

He smiled down at her. "Trust me. I'm not going to let you fall." She loosened her hold on him yet continued looking into his eyes, studying his features so intently that he couldn't help asking, "Like the part you can see?"

She smiled. "Yes. You have such an angular jaw. It speaks of strength and honesty. It also speaks of determination."

He raised a brow, wondering how Wonder Woman could tell those things about him from just studying his jaw. He stopped wondering when she reached out and her finger traced that same jaw that seemed to fascinate her.

"It's rigid, but not overbearing. Firm, but not domineering." She then smiled. "Yet I do see a few arrogant lines," she said, tapping the center of his jaw.

He had sat down with her in his arms, instead of placing her on the bed, so as not to rush things with her, to give her time to collect herself after their kisses. He refused to rush their lovemaking. For some reason, he wanted more, felt they deserved more. He was never one for small talk, but he figured he would take a stab at it. But now her touch was making it almost impossible not to touch. Not to undress her and give her the pleasure they both wanted. And then it came to him that the reason he was here with her had nothing to do with lust. He'd gone months without a woman warming his bed before. What was driving him more than anything was her appeal, her sexiness and his desire to mate with her in an intimate way. Only her.

He stood while cradling her tightly in his arms and moved toward the bed and gently placed her in the middle of it, handed her the rose and then he took a step back so she could be in the center of his vision. He wanted the full view of her.

Her shoulder-length hair was tousled around her face, at least the part of her face he could see. Her dress had risen when he'd placed her on the bed. She had to know it was in disarray and showing a great deal of flesh, but she didn't make a move to pull anything down, and he had no intention of suggesting she do so. So he looked, got his fill, saw the firmness of her thighs and the shapeliness of her knees. And he couldn't help but notice how the front of the dress was cut low, showing the top portion of her full and firm breasts. He was a lips man first and a breasts man second. As far as he was concerned, he had hit the jackpot.

Olivia wondered how long he would stand there and stare. But in a way, it reassured her that he liked what he saw. No man had taken the time to analyze her this way. She might as well make it worth his while. She placed the rose to one side and reached down and unclasped her shoes before slipping them off her feet. She tossed one and then the other to him. He caught them perfectly, and instead of dropping them to the floor, he tossed them onto the love seat they had just vacated.

She was surprised. He had recognized a pair of stilettos by Zanotti. They had been another whim of hers. Shoes were her passion, and she appreciated a man who knew quality and fine workmanship in a woman's shoes when he saw it. He moved up another notch in her book.

Now it was time to take off the rest. Because she never wore panties with panty hose, that would be easy. Instead of removing her panty hose last, she decided to take them off first. He wouldn't be expecting it, and the thought of catching him off guard stirred something inside of her. With his eyes still on her, she lifted her bottom off the bed slightly to ease down her panty hose, deliberately giving him a flash to let him know that once they were gone, there would not be any covering left. After she'd removed them, she rolled the hose up in a ball and tossed them to him. As with her shoes, he made a perfect catch, and then, while she watched him, he brought the balled-up nylon to his nose and took a whiff of her scent before placing it in the pocket of his jacket.

Her gaze had followed his hands, and now it moved back to his face. She saw the flaring of his nostrils and the tightening of his fists by his sides, and she saw something else. Something she had noted earlier, when he had walked across the room to her, but that now had grown larger. His erection. There was no doubt in her mind, unclothed and properly revealed, it would put Michelangelo's *David* to shame. Her artistic eye could even make out the shape of it through his pants. It was huge, totally developed, long and thick. And at the moment, totally aroused. That was evident by the way the erection was straining against the fly of his pants.

He shifted his stance. Evidently, he'd seen where her gaze had traveled, and she watched as his fingers went to the zipper of his tuxedo pants and slowly eased it down. She could only stare when, after bending to remove his shoes and socks, he stepped out of his pants, leaving his lower body clad only in a pair of sexy black briefs. She knew they were a designer pair; their shape, fit and support said it all. The man had thighs that were firm, hard and muscular. She didn't have to see his buns to know they were probably as tight as the rest of him. There was no need to ask if he worked out on occasion. The physical fitness of his body said it all.

And he looked sexy standing there, with a tux jacket and white shirt on top and a pair of sexy briefs covering his lower half. She figured he had decided to remove the clothes from the same part of his anatomy as she had. They were both undressing from the bottom up.

She held her breath, literally stopped breathing, when his hands then went to the waistband of his briefs. And while her gaze was glued to him, he slowly pulled the briefs down his legs.

Damn.

The man, thankfully, had no qualms about exposing himself, and for that she was grateful, because what her eyes were feasting on was definitely worth seeing. He was truly a work of art. And while her focus was contained, he went about removing the rest of his clothes. She wasn't aware of it until he stood before her, totally naked in all his glorious form.

Her gaze traveled the full length of his body once, twice, a total of three times before coming back to settle on his face. He was a naked, masked man, and she would love to have him pose for her as such. On canvas she would capture each and every detail of him. He was pure, one hundred percent male.

"It's your turn to take off the rest of your clothes, Wonder."

His words, deep and husky, floated around the already sexually charged room.

She forced her gaze from his thick shaft and moved it to his face as, on her knees, she reached behind herself and undid the hooks of her dress before pulling it over her head. It was simple, and she was naked, since she hadn't worn a bra.

Now he saw it all. And like she had earlier, his gaze moved to her lower part, zeroing in on the junction of her thighs. Suddenly she felt awkward. She wondered what he was thinking. She kept her body in great shape, and her Brazilian wax was obvious.

She met his gaze when he returned it to her face. She smiled. "I'm done."

"No, baby," he said in a tight and strained voice. "You haven't even got started."

Reggie pulled in a deep breath, meaning every word he'd just spoken. Never in his life had he been so hard and hot for a woman. Never had he wanted to eat one alive. As far as he was concerned, there would not be enough time tonight to do everything he wanted to do. So there was none to be wasted. But first…

"Is there anything you have an aversion to doing?" he felt the need to ask.

He watched how she lifted her gaze a moment, and then she said in a soft voice, "Yes. I'm not into bondage."

He chuckled. "Then it's a good thing I left my handcuffs at home." And because he saw the slight widening of her eyes, he smiled and said, "Hey, I'm just teasing. I would be crazy to tie your hands since I prefer you putting them all over me."

As far as Olivia was concerned, that was the

perfect invitation. She scooted close to the edge of the bed and reached out and splayed her hands across his chest. She smiled when she heard his sharp intake of breath. And she was fascinated by the way his muscles flexed beneath her hands and by the warmth of his skin beneath her fingers.

"You're into torture?" he asked huskily, his tone sounding somewhat strained.

"Why? Do you feel like you're being tortured?" she asked innocently, shifting one of her hands lower to his stomach.

"Yes." His answer was short and precise. His breathing seemingly impaired.

"You haven't seen anything yet, Jack Sprat."

And then her hand dropped to that part of him she'd become fascinated with from the moment she'd seen it. It was large, heavy and, for tonight, it was hers. Her hand closed up, contracted and then closed up again, liking the feel of holding it, stroking it.

Breathing at full capacity, Reggie could no longer handle what his mystery woman was doing to him and pulled back and reached down for his pants to retrieve a condom packet from his wallet. Ripping the packet with his teeth, he proceeded to put the condom on.

He glanced up to see her lying back on the bed, smiling at him, fully aware of the state she'd pushed him to. He moved so quickly, it caught her off guard, and then he was there with her in the bed, pinning her beneath him on the coverlet and immediately taking her mouth captive, devouring it like he intended to devour her. And when he pulled back, he moved down to her breasts, taking the nipples in his mouth, doing all kinds of things to them with his tongue until she cried out. She pleaded with him to stop, because she couldn't take any more.

But he definitely wasn't through with her yet. Intent on proving that she wasn't the only one with hands that could torture, he used his knee to spread her legs. He then settled between them, determined to fit his erection in the place where it was supposed to be.

There was so much more he wanted to do— devour her breasts, lick her skin all over—but at that moment, the one thing he had to do before his brain exploded with need was get inside of her.

He pulled his mouth away from her breasts, and breathing hard, he stared down at her, determined to see what he could of her eyes through the mask. "This is crazy," he said, almost choking for both breath and control of the words.

"Might be," she said, just as short of breath. "But it's the best craziness I've ever experienced. Let's not stop now."

He stared at her. "You sure?"

She stared back. "Positive."

And with their gazes locked, he entered her.

He felt her small spasms before he even got into the hilt, and when her inner muscles clenched him, he pressed deeper inside of her. She was tight, but he could feel her opening wider for him, like a bloom. "That's it. Relax, let go and let me in," he said.

And as if her body was his to command, it continued to open, adjust, until it was a perfect fit and curved around him like a glove. And at that moment, while buried deep inside of her, he just had to taste her lips again. He leaned forward, took her mouth and began swallowing every deep, wrenching moan that she made.

And then he began moving back and forth inside of her, thrusting, then retreating, then repeating the process all over again, each thrust aimed with perfect accuracy at her erogenous zone. He lifted her hips, and she dug her fingertips deep into his shoulders and cried out with each stroke he took.

It was at that moment that he actually felt her body explode. Then the sensations that had rippled through her slammed through him as well. He threw his head back; and he felt the muscles in his neck pop; and he breathed in deep, pulling in her scent, which filled the air.

Shudders rammed through him, and he squeezed his eyes shut as his body exploded. His orgasm came with the force of a tidal wave, and he continued to thrust inside her as his groans mingled with her cries of pleasure. And with their bodies fully engaged, their minds unerringly connected, together they left Earth and soared into the clouds as unadulterated pleasure consumed them.

"I need to leave," she said softly.

Reggie turned his head on the pillow and looked over at Wonder. He doubted he could move. He could barely breathe. It was close to morning. They'd made love all night long. As soon as they had ended one session, they'd been quick and eager to start another.

He knew she had to leave. So did he. But he didn't want their one and only night together to end. "You do know there is no reason why we can't—"

She quickly turned toward him and placed a finger on his lips. "Yes, there is. I can't tell you my true identity. It could hurt someone."

He frowned. She wasn't wearing a ring, so quite naturally, he had assumed she wasn't married. What if she…

As if reading his mind, she said, "I don't have a husband. I don't even have a boyfriend."

"Then who?" he asked quickly, trying to understand why they couldn't bring their masquerade to an end. He probably had more to lose than she, because his campaign for the Senate officially began Monday.

"I can't say. This has to be goodbye—"

Before the words were completely out of her mouth, he reached out and pulled her into his arms, knowing this would be the last time he would kiss the lips he had grown so attached to.

Moments later he released her mouth, refusing to say goodbye. She wiggled out of his arms and began re-dressing. He watched her do so, getting turned on all over again.

"I'm getting money out of the ATM to pay for the room," she informed him.

He frowned at her words. "No, you're not."

"I must. It was my idea for us to come here," she said.

"Doesn't matter. Everything has been taken care of, so they won't take any money from you at the front desk. Last night is on me, and I don't regret one minute of spending it with you."

Olivia slipped back into her shoes and gazed across the room at him. He was lying in bed, on top of the covers. Naked. So immensely male. "And I don't regret anything, either," she said, meaning every word. She was tempted to do as he wanted— cross the room, remove his mask and remove hers as well—but she couldn't. She couldn't even trust herself to kiss him goodbye. It had to be a clean break for both of them. "And you sure you don't want me to pay for the room?" she asked.

"Yes, I'm sure."

"At least let me give you something toward it and—"

"No," he said, declining her offer.

She didn't know how much time passed while they just stared at each other. But she knew she had to leave. "I have to go now," she said, as if convincing herself of that.

He shifted on the bed to take the rose, and offered it to her. She closed the short distance between them to retrieve it. "At least let me walk you to the door," he said.

She shook her head. "No. I'll see myself out."

And then she quickly walked out of the bedroom.

Reggie pulled himself up in the bed when he heard the sound of the hotel door closing. He sat on the edge of the bed, suddenly feeling a sense of loss that touched his very soul and not understanding how such a thing was possible.

He stood up to put on his clothes, and it was then that he snatched off the mask. It had served its purpose. He reached for his shirt and tie and noticed something glittering on the carpet. He reached down and picked it up. It was one of the diamond earrings that she had been wearing.

He folded the earring in the palm of his hand. He knew at that very moment that if he had to turn Atlanta upside down, he would find his Wonder Woman.

He would find her, and he would keep her.

Three

"So, Libby, how was the party?"

Olivia, who had been so entrenched in the memories of the night before, hadn't noticed her father standing at the bottom of the stairs. She glanced down at him and smiled. "It was simply wonderful." He didn't need to know that she was speaking not of the party per se but of the intimate party she'd gone to at the Saxon Hotel, with her mystery man.

It had been just before six in the morning when she slipped into her father's home, and knowing he was an early riser, she had dashed up the stairs and showered. She had also put in a call to Terrence, leaving a message on his cell phone that it was okay to delete the text message she had sent to him the night before. And then she had climbed into bed. By the time her head had hit the pillow in her own bed, she had heard her father moving around.

She had enjoyed the best sleep in years. She had awakened to a hungry stomach, and the last person she had expected to meet when she took the stairs to go pillaging in the kitchen was her father. Typically, after early morning church services on Sunday, he hit the country club with his buddies for a game of golf. So why was he still here?

Orin met his daughter on the bottom stair and gave her a hug. "I'm glad you enjoyed yourself. I felt kind of bad that I couldn't attend the ball with you, but I did have to work on that speech."

She looked up at him and, not for the first time, thought that he was definitely a good-looking man, and she was glad he took care of himself by eating right and staying active. "No problem, Dad."

Not wanting him to ask for details about the party, she quickly asked a question of her own. "So why are you home and not out on the golf course?"

He smiled as he tucked her arm in his and escorted her to the kitchen. "Cathy threatened me with dire consequences today if I left before she got the chance to come over and go over my speech."

Olivia smiled but didn't say anything for a moment. Cathy Bristol had been her father's private secretary for almost fifteen years, and Olivia couldn't help but wonder when her father would wake up and realize the woman was in love with him. Olivia had figured it out when she was in her teens, and when she'd gotten older had asked her brothers about it. Like her dad, they'd been clueless. But at least Duan and Terrence had opened their eyes even if her father hadn't. Cathy was a forty-eight-year-old widow who had lost her husband over eighteen years ago, when he died in a car accident, leaving her with two sons to raise.

"So when is Cathy coming? I'd love to see her."

Her father smiled. "Around noon. I'm treating her to lunch here first before I put her to work."

"To review your speech?"

"Yes," he said when they reached the kitchen and he sat down at the table. "She's good at editing things and giving her opinion. As this is my first speech, I want to impress those who hear it. It will be one of those forums in which all the candidates speak."

Olivia nodded as she grabbed an apple out of the fruit bowl on the table and sat down across from him.

Orin frowned. "Surely that's not all you're having for breakfast."

"Afraid so," she said before biting into her apple.

"You're so thin," he pointed out. "You should eat more."

Olivia could only smile. There was no way she could tell her father that she had eaten quite a lot last night. After making love several times, they had ordered room service, eaten until their stomachs were full and then gone back to bed to make love some more.

Deciding to get her father off the subject of her weight, she said, "So, tell me something about this guy who has the audacity to run against my father."

Orin leaned back in his chair. "He's one of those Westmorelands. Prominent family here in Atlanta. He's young, in his early thirties, and owns an accounting firm."

Olivia nodded. She recalled the name, and if she wasn't mistaken, Duan and Terrence had gone to school with some of them. They were a huge family. "So what's his platform? How do the two of you differ?"

"On a number of issues, we're in agreement. The main thing we differ on is whether or not Georgia can support another state-financed university. He thinks we can, and I don't. We have a number of fine colleges and universities in this area. Why on earth would we need another one? Besides, he's inexperienced."

Olivia couldn't help but smile at that, because her father didn't have any political experience, either. In fact, she and her brothers had been shocked when he'd announced he was running for a political office. The only thing they could come up with as to the reason was that his good friend and golfing buddy Senator Albert Reed was re-tiring and wanted someone to replace him whom he knew and could possibly influence. Not that her father was easily influenced, but he was known to give in under a good argument, without fully standing his ground.

"And young Westmoreland will run on his name recognition since he has a couple of celebrities in the family. One of his cousins is a motorcycle racer, and another is an author."

And your son just happens to be a very well-known former NFL player, she wanted to say. Who you have called upon to appear at a couple of rallies. So you are just as bad.

Olivia said nothing but listened as she took another bite of her apple. At least she tried to listen. More than once her mind took a sharp turn, and she found her thoughts drifting to breath-stopping memories of the tall, dark and handsome man she had met and spent a wonderful night with. She could vividly recall his kisses and the way he had been methodically slow and extremely thor-ough each time he'd taken her mouth in his, eating away at her lips, unrestrained, unhurried and not distracted.

And there were the times his mouth had touched her everywhere, blazing a trail from her nape to her spine, then all over her chest, tasting her nipples and making her intensely aware of all her hidden passion—passion he'd been able to wrench from her.

The only bad thing about last night was the fact that she had lost one of the diamond earrings she had purchased a year ago in Paris. The earrings had been a gift to herself when she landed her dream job. She would love to get it back, but knew that wouldn't be happening. But she would be the first to admit that the night spent in her one-time lover's arms had been worth the loss.

The ringing of the doorbell claimed her attention and brought her back to the present.

"That must be Cathy," Orin said. He quickly rose from the table and headed to the front door.

Olivia studied her father and couldn't do anything but shake her head. He seemed awfully excited about Cathy's arrival. Olivia couldn't help wondering if perhaps her father had finally awakened and smelled the coffee and just wasn't aware he'd been sniffing the aroma. She had been around her brothers long enough to know that when it came to matters of the heart, men had a tendency to be slow.

She turned in her seat when she heard a feminine voice, Cathy's voice. Olivia smiled when she saw the one woman she felt would be good for her father and again wondered why her father hadn't asked Cathy to be his escort for some of these functions. Cathy was very pretty, and Olivia thought, as she glanced at the two of them walking into the kitchen, that they complemented each other well.

Brent Fairgate waved his hand back and forth in front of Reggie's face. "Hey, man, are you with us, or are you somewhere in la-la land?"

Reggie blinked, and then his gaze focused on the man standing in front of him, before shifting to the woman standing beside him, Pam Wells. Brent had hired Pam as a strategist on a consulting basis.

"Sorry," he said, since there was no use denying they hadn't had his attention. "My mind drifted elsewhere for a moment." There was no way he was going to tell Brent that he was reliving the memories of the prior night. Brent was the most focused man that Reggie knew. Reggie was well aware that Brent wanted him to be just as focused.

"Okay. Then let's go back over the layout for tomorrow," Brent said, handing him a folder filled with papers. "The luncheon is at the Civic Center, and both you and Jeffries will be speaking. The order will be determined by a flip of a coin. You got the speech down pat. Just make sure you turn on your charm. Jeffries will be doing likewise. Without coming right out and saying it, you will have to make everyone see you as the voice of change. You will have to portray Jeffries as more of the same, someone who represents the status quo."

"Okay. Give me some personal info on Jeffries, other than he's the Holy Terror's father," Reggie said.

Early in his professional football career, Terrence Jeffries had been nicknamed the "Holy Terror" by sportscasters. Reggie understood that Terrence was now a very successful businessman living in the Florida Keys.

"He also has another son, who's a couple years older than the Holy Terror," Pam replied. "He used to be on the Atlanta police force, but now he owns a private investigation company. He's low-key and definitely not in the public eye like Terrence."

Reggie nodded. "That's it? Two sons?"

Pam shook her head. "There's also a daughter, the youngest. She's twenty-seven. An artist who lives in Paris. I understand she's returned home for the campaign."

Reggie lifted a brow. "Why?"

Pam smiled. "To act as her father's escort for all the fund-raisers he'll be expected to attend. From what I understand, he hasn't dated a lot since his wife up and left him."

Reggie frowned. "And when was that?"

"Over twenty-something years ago. He raised his kids as a single father," said Pam.

Reggie nodded, immediately admiring the man for taking on such a task. He was blessed to have both of his parents still living and still married to each other. He couldn't imagine otherwise. He had heard his siblings and cousins talk about the hard work that went into parenting, so he admired any person who did it solo.

"As you know, Orin Jeffries is a corporate attorney at Nettleton Industries. He's worked for them for over thirty years. And he's almost twenty-five years older than you. He'll likely flaunt the age difference and his greater experience," Brent added.

Reggie smiled. "I'm sure that he will."

"Do you need me to look over your speech for tomorrow?" Brent asked.

Reggie met his friend's gaze. "I haven't written it yet." Concern touched Brent's features, and not for the first time, Reggie thought his best friend worried too much.

"But I thought you were going to do it last night, right after you came home from the Firemen's Masquerade Ball," Brent said.

Reggie sighed. There was no way he was going to mention that he hadn't made it home from the ball until this morning, because he had made a pit stop at the Saxon Hotel. Actually, it had been more than a pit stop. The word *quickie* in no way described what he and Wonder Woman had done practically all through the night. They had refused to be rushed.

Before Brent could chew him out, Reggie said, "I'll do it as soon as the two of you leave. If you want to drop by later and look it over, then feel free to do so."

A stern look appeared on Brent's face. "And don't think that I won't."

Reggie rolled his eyes. "Just don't return before six this evening."

Brent raised a brow. "Why?"

"Because I need to take a nap."

Brent chuckled. "You never take naps."

Determined not to explain anything, Reggie said, "I know, but today I definitely need one."

As soon as Pam and Brent left, Reggie called and checked in with his parents. Usually on Sunday he would drop by for dinner, and he didn't want his mother to worry when he didn't make an appearance.

After convincing Sarah Westmoreland that he was not coming down with a flu bug and that he just needed to rest, he was ready to end the call, but she kept him on the phone longer than he'd planned to give him a soup recipe…like he would actually take the time to make it. Not that she figured he would. She was just hoping he had a lady friend available to do his bidding.

He couldn't help but smile as he climbed the stairs to his bedroom. His mother's one wish in life was to live to see her six sons all married and herself and his father surrounded by grandchildren. A bout with breast cancer a few years ago had made her even more determined to see each one of her sons happily married.

Her dream had come true—almost. Jared's recent announcement that he and his wife, Dana, would become parents in the fall meant that all of James and Sarah Westmoreland's sons—with the exception of him—were married and either had kids or were expecting them. Quade had blown everyone away with his triplets. But then multiple births ran in the Westmoreland family.

When he reached his bedroom, he began stripping off his clothes, remembering when he had stripped for an audience of one the night before. He had been aware that Wonder Woman's eyes had been directed on him while he'd taken off each piece…the same way his eyes had been on her.

As he slid between the covers, he promised himself that once he woke up, he would have slept off the memories and would be focused on the present again. That morning he'd thought about trying to find his mystery woman, and he still intended to do that, but he owed it to Brent and his campaign staff to stay focused and put all his time and energy into winning this election.

But still…

He thought about the lone earring he had in his dresser drawer. On the way into the office, he would stop by Jared's favorite jewelry store, Garbella Jewelers, to see if they could possibly tell him anything about the earring, like who had made it and, possibly, from which store it had been purchased. Checking on something like that shouldn't take too long and wouldn't make him lose focus.

As he felt himself drifting off to sleep, his mind was flooded with more memories. He wondered how long this fascination, this mind-reeling, gut-wrenching obsession with his mystery woman, would last.

He wasn't sure, but he intended to enjoy it while it did.

Olivia sat in the chair across the room, and her observant eye zeroed in on her father and Cathy. She tried not to chuckle when she noticed how they would look at each other when the other one wasn't watching. Boy, they had it bad, but in a way, she was glad. Sooner or later, her father would realize that Cathy was the best thing to ever happen to him. Even now, after working as his secretary for over fifteen years, their relationship was still professional. She knew in time that would change, and she would do her part to help it along.

"Dad?"

Orin looked up from his seat behind his desk and glanced over at her. Cathy was standing next to his chair. They'd had their heads together while Cathy critiqued his speech. "Yes, sweetheart?"

"Why did you send for me to be your escort for

all these fund-raising events when you had Cathy right here?"

As if on cue, Cathy blushed, and her father's jaw dropped as if he was surprised she would ask something like that. Before he could pick up his jaw to respond, Cathy spoke, stammering through her explanation.

"T-there's no way Orin can do something like that. I'm his secretary."

Olivia smiled. "Oh." What she was tempted to say was that secretary or no secretary, Cathy was also the woman her father couldn't keep his eyes off. She couldn't wait until she talked to Duan and Terrence.

And then, as if by luck or fate, since it also seemed to be on cue, her cell phone rang, and when she stood and pulled it out of her back jeans pocket, she saw the call was from Terrence.

Knowing it was best to take the call privately, she said, "Excuse me a moment while I take this." She quickly walked out of the room and closed the office door behind her.

"Yes, Terrence?"

"What the hell is going on with you, Libby? Why did you text me from an unknown number and then call this morning and ask that the text be deleted?"

Olivia nervously licked her lips. One thing about Terrence was that he would ask questions, but if she gave him a reason that sounded remotely plausible, he would let it go, whereas Duan would continue to ask questions.

"Last night I went to this charity party in Dad's place and met a guy. He asked me to follow him to a nightclub in Stone Mountain, and I did, but I felt I should take precautions."

"That was a good idea. Smart girl. So how was the club?"

"Umm, nice, but it didn't compare to Club Hurricane," she said, knowing he would like to hear that she thought the nightclub he owned in the Keys was at the top of the list.

"You're even smarter than I thought. So how's Dad? He hasn't dropped out of this Senate race yet?"

Olivia smiled. Terrence and Duan were taking bets that sooner or later, when Orin Jeffries got a taste of what real politics were like, he would call it quits. At first she had agreed with them, but now she wasn't so sure. "I don't know, Terrence. I think he's going all the way with this one."

"Umm, that's interesting. I still think Reed pushed Dad into running for his own benefit. I'm going to give Duan a call. We might need to talk to Dad about this."

"You might be too late. The first forum is tomorrow, and he's giving a speech. He's been working on it for two days. The only good thing coming out of all this is that he and Cathy are working together," she said.

"Libby, they always work closely together. She's his secretary."

"Yes, but they are working closely together in a different way, on issues other than Nettleton Industries business. In fact, she's over here now."

She could hear her brother chuckle. "Still determined to play Cupid, are you?"

"I might as well while I'm here, since I have nothing else to do." She thought of Jack Sprat. She had been tempted earlier to pull out her art pad and do some sketches to pass the time. She had thought about drawing her mystery man with the mask and then playing around to see if she could draw sketches of how she imagined he might look without the mask. She had eventually talked herself out of it.

"Well, I'll be coming home in a couple of weeks, so stay out of trouble until then, sport."

She laughed. "I can't make you any promises, but I'll try."

Four

Brent had given his speech a thumbs-up, so Reggie felt confident it would go over well. He walked around the luncheon reception, greeting all those who had arrived to attend the forum. This would be the first of several gatherings designed to give voters a chance to learn each candidate's agenda. He had met Orin Jeffries when he'd first arrived and thought the older man was a likable guy.

A number of his family members were present and a number of his friends as well. These were people who believed in him, supported him and were counting on him to make changes to some of the present policies.

A career in politics had been the last thing on his mind and had never been his heart's desire, until recently. He'd become outraged at the present senators' refusal to recognize the state's need for an additional college. More and more young people were making the decision to acquire higher learning, and the lower tuition costs of state universities compared to private universities were a key factor in the process. It was hard enough for students to get the funds they needed to go to college, but when they were refused entrance into schools because of campus overcrowding, that was unacceptable. Anyone who wanted a college education should be able to get one. Georgia needed another state-run college, and he was willing to fight for it.

The University of Georgia was the oldest public university in the state and had been established by an act of the Georgia General Assembly over two centuries ago. Just as there had been a need for greater educational opportunities then, there was a need now. In fact, land had been donated for that very purpose ten years ago. Now some lawmakers were trying to use a loophole in the land grant to appropriate the land to build a recreation area—a park that would be largely composed of a golf course.

Reggie was aware that getting elected would only be the first hurdle. Once he got in the Senate, he would then have the job of convincing his fellow lawmakers of the need for an additional state university as well.

He glanced at his watch. In less than ten minutes, lunch would be served, and then halfway through lunch, each person seeking office would get an opportunity to speak. There were about eight candidates in attendance.

Deciding he needed to switch his focus for a moment, he thought about his visit to Garbella Jewelers that morning. Mr. Garbella's assessment of the earring was that it was a fine piece of craftsmanship. The diamonds were real and of good quality. He doubted the piece had been purchased in this country. He thought the way the diamonds were set was indicative of European jewelry making. Mr. Garbella had gone on to say that the pair had cost a lot of money. After visiting with the jeweler, Reggie was more determined than ever to find his Wonder Woman and return the missing earring to her.

Quade and his cousin Cole, who'd both recently retired—Quade from a top security job with the government and Cole from the Texas Rangers— had joined forces to start a network of security companies, some of which would include private investigation. He wondered if they would be interested in taking him on as their first client.

He looked at his watch again before glancing

across the room and meeting Brent's eye. He had less than ten minutes to mingle, and then everyone would be seated for lunch. He hated admitting it, but he felt in his element. Maybe a political career was his calling, after all.

Olivia waited until just moments before the luncheon was to begin to make an entrance and join her father. According to his campaign manager, Marc Norris, her entrance was part of a coordinated strategy. He wanted her to ease into the room and work one side of it while her father worked the other. Subtle yet thorough.

When he had mentioned his strategy that morning while joining Olivia and her father for breakfast, she had gotten annoyed that the man assumed she didn't have any common sense. Evidently, Norris doubted she could hold her own during any discussion. But not to cause any problems, she had decided to keep her opinions to herself.

She saw noticeable interest in her from the moment she stepped into the room. Most people knew that Orin Jeffries had a daughter, but a number of them had forgotten or shoved the fact to the back of their mind in the wake of his two well-known sons. Practically everybody in the country knew of the Holy Terror, whether they were football enthusiasts or not. Since retiring from football, Terrence had been known for his work in a number of high-profile charities. He also commentated on a popular radio talk show, *Sports Talk,* in South Florida, which might go into syndication the next year. Duan had made the national headlines a few years before, when his undercover work as a detective had resulted in the exposure of a couple of unsavory individuals who'd been intent on bringing organized crime to Georgia.

But it didn't bother her in the least that her brothers' good deeds had somehow made people forget about her. Besides, she hadn't lived in this country in four years, returning only on occasion to visit, mainly around the holidays.

She began mingling, introducing herself as Orin Jeffries's daughter, and actually got a kick out of seeing first surprise and then acknowledgment on many faces. One such incident was taking place now.

"Why, Olivia, how good it is to see you again. It's been a while since you've been back home. But I do remember you now. You must be extremely proud of your father and brothers."

"Yes, I am, Mrs. Hancock, and how is Beau? I understand he's doing extremely well. You must be proud of him."

She watched the older woman's eyes light up as she went into a spiel about her son. She was a proud mother. Olivia knew Beau from school. Unless he had changed over the years, Beau Hancock was an irrefutable jerk. He'd thought he was the gift to every girl at Collinshill High School.

She glanced down at her watch. She had ten minutes left before everyone would take their seats for lunch. She had called the Saxon Hotel on the off chance that someone from housekeeping had come across her diamond earring and turned it in. That hadn't been the case. A part of her was disappointed that it had not been.

There was still one section of the room she needed to cover. Mrs. Hancock, in singing Beau's praises, had taken up quite a bit of her time. Now she was again making her way through the crowds, speaking to everyone, as Norris had suggested.

"You're doing a marvelous job working the room," Senator Reed whispered. The older man had suddenly appeared by her side.

She forced a smile. For some reason, she'd never cared for him. "Thanks."

She had already met several of the candidates since entering the room, but she had yet to meet the man who would be her father's real competition, Reggie Westmoreland.

As she continued mingling and heading to the area where Reggie Westmoreland was supposedly rubbing elbows with the crowd, her curiosity about the man who opposed her father couldn't help but be piqued. She started to ask Senator Reed about him but changed her mind. The senator's opinion wouldn't be the most valuable.

"You look nice, Olivia."

She glanced up at the senator, who seemed determined to remain by her side. He was a few years older than her father, and for some reason, he had always made her feel uncomfortable.

"Thanks, Senator." She refrained from saying that he also looked nice, which he did. Like her father, he was a good-looking man for his age, but Senator Reed always had an air of snobbery about him, like he was born with too low expectations of others.

"It was my suggestion that your father send for you." When she stopped walking and glanced at him, with a raised brow, he added, "He was in a dilemma, and I thought bringing you home to be his escort was the perfect answer."

She bit back a retort, that bringing her home had not been the perfect answer. Being in that dilemma might have prompted her dad to ask Cathy to attend some of those functions with him. No telling how things would have taken off from there if the senator hadn't butted in.

She was about to open her mouth, to tell Senator Reed that her father was old enough to think for himself, when, all of a sudden, for no reason at all, she pulled in a quick breath. She glanced up ahead, and no more than four feet in front of her, there stood a man with his back to her.

The first thing she noticed about him was his height. He was taller then the men he was talking to. And there was something about his particular height, and the way his head tilted at an angle as he listened to what one of the men was saying, that held her spellbound.

He was dressed in a suit, and she could only admire how it fit him. The broadness of his shoulders and the tapering of his waist sent a feeling of familiarity through her. She stopped walking momentarily and composed herself, not understanding what was happening to her.

"Is anything wrong, Olivia?"

She glanced up at Senator Reed and saw concern in his eyes. She knew she couldn't tell him what she was thinking. There was no way she could voice her suspicions to anyone.

She needed to go somewhere to pull herself together, to consider the strong possibility that the man standing not far away was her Jack Sprat. Or could it be that she was so wrapped up in the memories of that night that she was quick to assume that any man of a tall stature who possessed broad shoulders had to be her mystery man?

"Olivia?"

Instead of saying anything, she shifted her gaze from the senator to look again at the man, whose back was still to her. It was at that precise moment that he slowly turned around, and his gaze settled on her. In a quick second, she pulled in a sharp breath as she scanned his face, and her gaze settled on a firm jaw that had an angular plane. Her artist's eye also picked up other things, and they were things others would probably not notice—the stark symmetry of his face, which was clear with or without a mask, the shape of his head and the alignment of his ears from his cheeks. These were things she recognized.

Things she remembered.

And she knew, without a doubt, that she was staring into the face of the man whom she had spent the night with on Saturday. The man whose body had given her hours upon hours of immeasurable pleasure. And impossible as it seemed—because they'd kept their masks in place the entire time—she had a feeling from the way he was staring back at her just as intently as she was staring at him that he had recognized her, too.

"Olivia?"

She broke eye contact with the stranger to gaze up at the senator. The man was becoming annoying, but at the moment, he was the one person who could tell her exactly what she needed to know. "Senator Reed, that guy up there, the one who turned around to look at me. Who is he?"

The senator followed her gaze and frowned deeply. "The two of you had to meet eventually. That man, young lady, is the enemy."

She swallowed deeply before saying, "The enemy?"

"Yes, the enemy. He's the man that's opposing your father in his bid for the Senate."

Olivia's head began spinning before the senator could speak his next words.

"That, my dear," the senator went on to say, "is Reggie Westmoreland."

It was her.

Reggie knew it with every breath he took. Her lips were giving her away. And he wasn't sure what part of him was recognizable to her, but he knew just as sure as they were standing there, staring at each other, that they were as intimately familiar to each other as any two people could be.

It was strange. He'd been standing here with Brent, his brother Jared, his cousins Dare and Thorn, and Thorn's wife, Tara. They'd all been listening to Thorn, a nationally known motorcycle builder and racer, who was telling them about an order he'd received to build a bike for actor Matt Damon. Then, all of a sudden, he'd felt a strange sensation, followed by a stirring in the lower part of his gut.

He had turned around, and he'd looked straight into her face. His Wonder Woman.

He couldn't lay claim to recognizing any of her other facial features, but her lips were a dead giveaway. Blatantly sensual, he had kissed them, tongued them, licked them and tasted them to his heart's content. He knew the shape of them in his sleep, knew their texture, knew what part of them was so sensitive that when he'd touched her there, she had moaned.

She looked totally stunning in the stylish skirt and blouse she was wearing. The outfit complemented her figure. Even if he hadn't met her before, he would be trying his best to do so now. Out of his peripheral vision, he noted a number of men looking at her, and he understood why. She was gorgeous.

He lost control, and his feet began moving toward her.

"Reggie, where are you going?" Brent asked.

He didn't respond, because he truly didn't know what he could say. He continued walking until he came to a stop directly in front of the senator and the woman. The senator, he noted, was frowning. The woman's gaze hadn't left his. She seemed as entranced as he was.

He found his voice to say, "Good afternoon, Senator Reed. It's good seeing you again."

It was a lie, and he realized the senator knew it, but he didn't care. Approaching him would force the man to make introductions, and if it took a lie, then so be it.

"Westmoreland, I see you've decided to go through with it," replied the senator.

Reggie gave the man a smile that didn't quite

reach his eyes. "Of course." He then shifted his gaze back to the woman. The senator would be outright rude not to make an introduction, and one thing Reggie did know about the senator was that he believed in following proper decorum.

"And let me introduce you to Olivia Jeffries. Olivia, this is Reggie Westmoreland," the senator said.

At the mention of her name, Reggie's mind went into a tailspin. "Jeffries?" he replied.

"Yes," the senator said as a huge, smug smile touched his lips. "Jeffries. She's Orin Jeffries's daughter, who is visiting from Paris and will remain here during the duration of the campaign."

Reggie nodded as his eyes once again settled on Olivia. He then reached out his hand. "Olivia, it's nice meeting you. I'm sure your father is excited about having you home."

"Thank you," replied Olivia.

They both felt it the moment their hands touched, and they both knew it. It was those same feelings that had driven them to leave the party on Saturday night and to go somewhere to be alone, with the sole purpose of getting intimately connected. Reggie opened his mouth to say something, and then a voice from the microphone stopped him.

"Everyone is asked to take a seat so lunch can be served. Your table number is located on your ticket."

"It was nice meeting you, Mr. Westmoreland," Olivia said, not sure what else to say at the moment.

She honestly had thought she would not see him again, not this soon, not ever. And now that he knew their predicament—that she was the daughter of the man who was his opponent in this political race—she hoped that he would accept the inevitable. Nothing had changed. Even with their identities exposed, there could never be anything between them beyond what had happened Saturday night.

"It was nice meeting you as well, Ms. Jeffries," said Reggie. And then he did something that was common among Frenchmen but rare with Americans. Bending slightly, he lifted her hand to his lips and kissed it before turning and walking away.

Five

Olivia found that every time she lifted her fork to her mouth, her gaze would automatically drift to the next table, the one where Reggie Westmoreland was sitting. And each time, unerringly, their gazes would meet.

After their introduction, she had excused herself to the senator, smiling and saying she needed to go to the ladies' room. Once there she had taken a deep breath. It was a wonder she hadn't passed out. With his mask in place, Reggie Westmoreland had been handsome. Without his mask, he took her breath away. While standing in front of him, she'd had to tamp down her emotions and the sensations flowing through her.

His eyes were very dark, almost chocolate, and their shape, which she had been denied seeing on Saturday night, was almond, beneath thick brows. It had taken everything in her power to force her muscles to relax. And when he had taken her hand and kissed the back of it before walking off, she'd thought she would swoon right then and there.

"Libby, are you okay? You've barely touched your meal," her father said, interrupting her thoughts.

She glanced over to him and smiled. "Yes, Daddy, I'm fine."

"Westmoreland is the cause of it," said Senator Reed, jumping in. "She met him right before we took our seats. He probably gave her an upset stomach."

Her father frowned. "Was he rude to you, sweetheart?" he asked, with deep concern tinged with anger.

She was opening her mouth to assure her father that Reggie hadn't been rude when Senator Reed said, "He was quite taken with her, Orin."

She ignored the senator's comment, thinking that he didn't know the half of it. Instead, she answered her father. "No, he wasn't rude, Dad. In fact, although we spoke only briefly, I thought he was rather nice." She smiled. "Quite the charmer."

"The enemy is never nice or charming, Olivia. Remember that," the senator said, speaking to her like she was a child. "I strongly suggest that during this campaign, you stay away from him."

She was opening her mouth to tell the senator that she truly didn't give a royal damn about what he would strongly suggest when her father spoke.

"You don't have to worry about Libby, Al. She's a smart girl. She would never get mixed up with the likes of Westmoreland."

The likes of Westmoreland? Was there something about Reggie that her father and the senator knew but that she didn't? she wondered. Granted, that might be true, since she had arrived in the country on Friday. But still, she heard intense dislike in her father's voice and pondered the reason for it. Did it have to do only with the campaign, or was there more? Marc Norris was the only other person at their table, and he wasn't saying anything. But then Norris didn't look like the type to gossip. She didn't know him well. In fact, she had just met him on Friday evening.

"Well, if I didn't know better, I'd think Olivia and Westmoreland had met before," replied Senator Reed.

The senator's words almost made her drop her fork. She had to tighten her grip on it. She thought about Reggie. Had their reaction to each other been that obvious?

There was a lag in the conversation at the table, and she knew from the brief moment of silence that the men were waiting for her to respond one way or the other. So she did. "Then it's a good thing that you know better, Senator, isn't it?"

She said the words so sweetly, there was no way that he or anyone else could tell if she was being sincere or smart-alecky. Before any further conversation could take place, one of the sponsors of the event got up and went to the podium to announce that the speeches were about to begin.

"Okay, Reggie. What's going on with you and that woman at the other table? The one you can't seem to keep your eyes off," Brent said in a whisper as he leaned close to Reggie.

Reggie lifted a brow. "What makes you think something is going on?"

Brent chuckled. "I have eyes. I can see. You do know she's Jeffries's daughter."

Reggie leaned back in his chair. He couldn't eat another mouthful, although he hadn't eaten much. He was still trying to recover from the fact that he and his mystery woman had officially met. "Yes, the senator introduced us. And grudgingly, I might add. He didn't seem too happy to do so," Reggie said.

"Figures. He probably wants her for himself." At Reggie's surprised look, Brent went on to explain. "Reed is into young women big-time. I once dated someone who worked at his office. He tried coming on to her several times, and she ended up quitting when the old man wouldn't give up no matter how many times she tried turning him off. The man takes sexual harassment to a whole new level."

Reggie's jaw tightened. The thought that the senator could be interested in Olivia, even remotely, made his blood boil. "But he's friends with her father."

"And that's supposed to mean something?" Brent countered, trying to keep his voice low. "I guess it would mean something to honorable men, but Reed is not honorable. We don't have a term-limit law here, so it makes you wonder why he isn't seeking another term. Rumor has it that he was given a choice to either step down or have his business—namely, his affairs with women half his age—spread across the front pages of the newspapers. I guess since he's still married and his wife is wealthier than he is, although she's bedridden, he didn't want that."

Reggie shook his head. "Well, he shouldn't concern himself with Olivia Jeffries."

"And why is that?"

Reggie didn't say anything for fear of saying too much. In the end, he didn't have to respond, because it was his turn to speak.

"You gave a nice speech, Dad. You did a wonderful job," Olivia said once she and her father got home.

"Yes, but so did Westmoreland," Orin said, heading for the kitchen. "He tried to make me look like someone who doesn't support higher education."

"But only because you are against any legislation to build another state university," she reminded him.

"We have enough colleges, Libby."

She decided to back away from the conversation because she didn't agree with her father on this issue. The last thing she wanted was to get into an argument with him about Reggie Westmoreland and his speech. If nothing else, she had reached the conclusion at dinner that neither her father nor the senator wanted her to get involved in any way with the competition.

She glanced at her watch. "I think I'm going to change and then go to the park and paint for a while."

"Yes, you should do that while you still have good sunlight left. And feel free to take my car, since I won't need it anymore today. That rental car of yours is too small," Orin said, already pulling off his tie as he headed up the stairs.

She could tell he was somewhat upset about how the luncheon had gone. Evidently, he had assumed, or had been led to believe, that winning the Senate seat would be a piece of cake. It probably would have been if Reggie Westmoreland hadn't decided to throw his hat into the ring at the eleventh hour.

And she had to admit that although her father's

speech had been good, Reggie's speech had been better. Instead of making generalities, he had hammered down specifics, and he had delivered the speech eloquently. And it had seemed that as his gaze moved around the room while he was speaking, his eyes would seek her out. Each time they'd done so and she'd gazed into them, she'd felt she could actually see barely concealed desire in their dark depths. She had sat there with the hardened nipples of her breasts pressed tightly against her blouse the entire time.

And all she'd had to do was to study his lips to recall how those same lips had left marks all over her body, how they, along with his tongue, had moved over these same breasts, licking, sucking and nibbling on them.

After the luncheon was over, instead of dallying about, she had rushed her father out, needing to leave to avoid any attempts Reggie might have made to approach her again. She would not have been able to handle it if he had done so, and it would only have raised Senator Reed's suspicions. For some reason, the older man was making her every move his business.

Olivia had changed clothes and was gathering her art bag to sling over her shoulders when her cell phone rang. Not recognizing the local number, she answered the call.

"Hello?"

"Meet me someplace."

She got weak in the knees at the sound of the deep, husky voice. She really didn't have to ask, but she did so anyway. "Who is this?"

"This is Reggie Westmoreland, Wonder Woman."

Olivia pulled into the parking lot of Chase's Place, wondering for the umpteenth time how she had let Reggie Westmoreland talk her into meeting him there. The restaurant, he'd said, was closed on Mondays, but since he knew the owner, there would not be a problem with them meeting there for privacy.

When she'd indicated she did not want to be seen meeting with him, he'd told her to park in the rear of the building. She hated the idea of everything being so secretive, but she knew it was for the best.

Of all the never-in-a-million-years coincidences, why did she have to have an affair—one night or otherwise—with the one man her father could not stand at the moment?

Doing as Reggie had advised, she drove around to the rear and parked beside a very nice silver-gray Mercedes, the same one she'd seen Reggie driving Saturday night. After getting out and checking her watch for the time, she walked up to the back door of the restaurant and knocked. It opened immediately. A man who was almost as tall as Reggie and just as handsome opened the door and smiled at her before stepping aside to let her in.

"Olivia?" he asked, continuing to smile, as he closed the door behind her.

She was so busy studying his face, noting the similarities between him and Reggie, that she almost jumped when he uttered her name. Like Reggie, he was extremely handsome, but she didn't miss the gold band on his finger. "Yes?" she said finally.

"I'm Chase Westmoreland," he said, extending his hand. "Reggie is already here and is in one of the smaller offices, waiting for you. I'll take you to him."

"Thanks." And then, because curiosity got the best of her, she asked, "Are you one of Reggie's brothers?"

The man's chuckle floated through the air as he led her down a hallway. "No, Reggie has five brothers, but I'm not one of them. I'm his cousin."

"Oh. The two of you favor one another," she pointed out.

"Yes, all we Westmorelands look alike."

After walking down a long hallway, they stopped in front of a closed door. "Reggie is in here," Chase said, grinning. "It was nice meeting you."

Olivia smiled. "And it was nice meeting you as well, Chase." And then he was gone. She turned toward the closed door and took a deep breath before turning the handle.

Reggie stood the moment he heard voices on the other side of the door. This was the only place he could think of where he and Olivia could meet without fear of a reporter of some sort invading their privacy. The political campaign had begun officially today, and already all the sides were trying to dig up something on the others.

He'd told Brent that he wanted a campaign that focused strictly on the issues. He wasn't into dirty political games. He felt the voters should get to know the candidates, learn their stance on the issues and then decide which offered more of what they were looking for. If they wanted something different, then he was their man, and if they were used to the do-nothing agenda that Reed had implemented over the past four years, then they needed to go with Jeffries, since it was a sure bet that he was Reed's clone.

As soon as the door opened, his heart began hammering wildly in his chest, and the moment Olivia walked into the room and their gazes met, it took everything he possessed not to cross the floor and pull her into his arms and taste those lips he'd enjoyed so much a couple of nights ago.

Instead of coming farther into the room, she closed the door behind her and then leaned back on it, watching him. Waiting. His hands balled into fists at his sides. He smiled and said, "Wonder Woman." It wasn't a question; it was a statement. He knew who she was.

The butterflies in Olivia's stomach intensified

as they flew off in every direction. As she looked across the room at the extremely handsome man, she couldn't help but pose the one question that had been on her mind since they'd met earlier, at the luncheon. "How did you recognize me?" she asked in a soft-spoken voice.

He smiled, and she actually felt her heart stop. She felt her body begin to get hot all over. "Your lips gave you away. I recognized them. I would know your lips anywhere," he said. His voice was deep and throaty.

Olivia frowned, finding that strange. But it must have made some sense, at least to him, because he *had* been able to recognize her.

"What about you? You recognized me also. How?" he asked.

"I'm an artist, at least I am in my spare time. I study faces. I analyze every symmetrical detail. Although you were wearing a mask, and I couldn't see the upper part of your face, I zeroed in on the parts I could see." She decided not to tell him that there was more to it than his face. It had been his height that had first drawn her attention, and the way he'd tilted his head and his broad shoulders. If she could find the words to describe him, they would be, in addition to handsome—tall, dark...Westmoreland.

"I guess both of us can see things others might miss," he said.

"Yes, I guess we can," she agreed.

The room got silent, and she could feel it. That same sexual chemistry that had overtaken them that night, that had destroyed their senses to the point where they hadn't wanted to do anything else but go somewhere and be alone together, was still potent.

"Please come join me. I promise not to bite."

His words broke into her thoughts, and she couldn't help but smile. It was on the tip of her tongue to say, yes, he did bite and that she'd had numerous passion marks on her body to prove it. However, she had a feeling from the glint in his eyes that he'd realized the slipup the moment she had. His eyes darkened, and she felt heat settling everywhere his gaze touched.

She breathed in a deep breath before moving away from the door. She glanced around. The room was apparently a little game room. It had a love seat, a card table, a refrigerator and a television.

"This is where my cousins and brothers get together to play cards on occasion," said Reggie, breaking into her thoughts. "They used to rotate at each other's homes, but after they married and started having kids, they couldn't express themselves like they wanted whenever they were losing. So we decided to find someplace to go where we could be as loud and as colorful as we wanted to be."

She nodded and remembered how things were when her brothers used to have their friends over for poker. Some of their choice words would burn her ears. She then crossed the room to sit on the love seat.

He remained standing and was staring at her, making her feel uncomfortable. She cleared her throat. "You wanted to meet with me," she said, reminding him of why they were there.

He smiled. "Yes, and do you know why?"

"Yes," she said, holding his gaze. "It wouldn't take much to figure out that now that you know my father is one of the men you'll be running against in a few months, you want to establish an understanding between us. You want us to pretend that Saturday night never happened and that we've never met."

He continued to stare at her intently. "Is that what you think?"

She blinked. "Yes, of course. Under these circumstances, there's no way we can be seen together or even let anyone in on the fact that we know each other."

"I don't see why not. I'm running against your father, not you, so it shouldn't matter," he said.

Olivia felt her heart pounding hard in her chest. "But it does matter. Orin Jeffries is my father, and he and his campaign staff consider you the enemy," she said truthfully, although she hadn't meant to do so.

Reggie shook his head. "It's unfortunate they feel that way. I'm not his enemy. I'm his opponent in a Senate race. It's nothing personal, and I was hoping no one would make it such."

Olivia didn't know what to say. She knew Senator Reed, who seemed to be calling the shots as to how her father ran his campaign, could be ruthless at times. She had overheard the whispered conversations that took place at her table during lunch. She knew that the man had no intentions of letting this be a clean campaign, and that bothered her because it was so unlike her father to get involved in something so manipulative and underhanded.

"I'm sorry, but it will be personal. I don't agree, but politics is politics," she heard herself saying, knowing it wasn't an acceptable excuse. "If I became involved with you in any way, it would be equal to treason in my father's eyes. Things are too complicated."

"Only if we let them be. I still say us meeting and going out on occasion don't involve your father, just me and you."

She shook her head as she stood. It was time to go. She really should not have come. "I need to go."

"But you just got here," he said softly in that sexy voice that did things to her nervous system.

"I know, but coming here was a mistake," she said.

"Then why did you?" he asked softly.

She met his gaze and knew she would tell him the truth. "I felt that I should. Saturday night was a first of its kind for me. I've never left a party with someone I truly didn't know, and I've never had a one-night stand. But I did with you because I felt the chemistry. One of the reasons I came today was that I needed to see if the chemistry between us was real or a figment of my imagination."

"And what's your verdict?" he asked, holding her gaze.

She didn't hesitate in responding. "It's real."

"Does that frighten you?"

"It does not so much frighten me as confuse me. Like I said, I've never responded to a man this way before."

"And what was the other reason you came tonight?"

"We never took our masks off, and I needed to know how you were able to recognize me today. I got the answers to both of my questions, so I should leave now."

"But what about me? Aren't you interested in knowing why I wanted to see you again? Why I asked for us to meet?" He was staring intently at her, and his gaze seemed to touch her all over.

"Why did you want to see me?" she asked.

He slowly moved across the room to stand in front of her, and her pulse began beating rapidly, and heat began to settle between her thighs from his closeness. "Your lips were one reason."

"My lips?" she asked, raising a brow. He seemed to be searching her face, but she could tell his main focus was her lips.

"I claimed them as mine that night," he said in a husky whisper. "I just needed to know if they still are."

And before she could catch her next breath, he pulled her into his arms and captured her mouth with his.

They were still his.

This was what he needed to know. This was the very reason he had kept breathing since Saturday, Reggie thought as he hungrily mated with Olivia's mouth. The memories that had consumed him over the past forty-eight hours had nothing on the real thing. And she was responding to his kiss, feasting on his mouth as greedily as he was feasting on hers. Their masks were gone but not their passion.

He hadn't expected the fires to ignite so quickly, but already they were practically burning out of control. Her body was pressed fully against his, and he could feel every heated inch of her, just like he was certain she could feel every inch of him. Hard. Aroused. He knew he needed to pull back from her mouth to take a much-needed breath, but he couldn't. He had thought of kissing her, dreamed of kissing her, every since the morning they'd parted. His tongue was tangling with hers, and it seemed he couldn't get enough.

Instantly, he knew the moment she began withdrawing, and he pulled back, but not before tracing the outline of her lips with the tip of his tongue while tamping down on the stimulating effect the kiss had had on him.

"I really do need to leave." Her words lacked conviction, and he couldn't help but notice that she had wrapped her arms around his neck and hadn't yet released him. He also took note that her mouth was mere inches from his, and she hadn't pulled back.

Making a quick decision for both of them, he said, "Please stay and let's talk. Will you stay a while longer if I promise not to kiss you again? There's so much I want to know about you. I won't ask you anything about your father and his campaign, just about you."

"What good would it do, Reggie?" she asked, saying his name for the first time. The sound of it off her lips produced flutters in the pit of his stomach.

"I think it will appease our curiosity and maybe help us make some sense as to why we became attracted to each other so quickly and so deeply," he responded. "Why the chemistry between us is so strong."

Olivia pulled her arms from around his neck, thinking that what he was suggesting wasn't a good idea, but neither was kissing. But then she really didn't want to leave, and she had to admit that she'd wondered why they had hit it off so quickly and easily. But it didn't take a rocket scientist to figure out some of the reasons. He was an extremely handsome man, something she had recognized even with the mask. And his approach that night had not been egotistical or arrogant. She had somehow known he was someone she could have fun with and whose company she could enjoy.

And those things had been verified in the most intimate way.

"And we'll just talk?" she asked, making sure they understood each other.

"Yes, and about no one but us. That way you can't feel disloyal to your father."

She inhaled deeply. "But I still do," she admitted openly.

He didn't say anything for a moment. "Let me ask you something." At her nod, he asked, "If we would have met at any other time and if I was not your father's political opponent, would he have a problem with you dating me?"

She knew the answer to that, since her father had never been the kind of dad who cross-examined his children's dates. He had always accepted her judgment in that area. Now, her brothers had been another matter, especially Duan. "No, I think he wouldn't have a problem with it," she said truthfully.

"That's good to know, and that's why we should move forward on the premise that the campaign should not affect our relationship." His voice and smile conveyed that he truly believed what he was saying.

"But how can it not?" she asked, wishing things were that simple.

"Because we won't let it," he responded. "First of all, we need to acknowledge that we are in a relationship, Olivia."

She shook her head. "I can't do that, because we really don't have a relationship. We just slept together that night."

"No, it was more than that. It might have been a one-night stand, but I never intended *not* to find you after you left the Saxon on Sunday morning. In fact, I took this to a jewelry store this morning to see if I could trace where it was originally purchased," he said, pulling her diamond earring from his pocket. "It might have taken me a while, but eventually, I would have found you, even if I had to tear this town up doing so," he said, handing the earring to her.

She took it and studied it, remembering just when she had purchased the pair. It had been when she'd gotten her first position at the Louvre Museum. These diamonds had cost more than the amount of her first paycheck. But it had been a way for her to celebrate.

"Thank you for returning it." She slipped the earring into her pants pocket and then looked back at him. "So, what do you want to talk about?"

"I want to know everything about you. Over dinner. In here. Just the two of us."

She licked her lips and noticed immediately how his gaze had been drawn to the gesture. "And you promise no kissing, right?"

He chuckled. "Not unless you initiate it. If you do, then I won't turn you down."

She couldn't help but smile at that. "You mentioned dinner, but the restaurant isn't open today."

"No, it isn't, but Chase will make an exception for us. Will you join me here for dinner so we can talk and get to know each other?"

She was very much aware that if her father knew she was here, spending time with Reggie, he would think she was being disloyal, but she knew she truly wasn't. If at any time Reggie shifted the conversation to her father, as if pumping her for information about him, she would leave. But for now, she owed it to herself to do something that made her happy for a change, as long as she was not hurting anyone. If Duan or Terrence had been caught up in a similar situation, there was no way her father would have asked them to stop seeing that person. She should not be made the exception.

Olivia knew Reggie was waiting for her answer. "And our time here together will be kept confidential?"

He smiled. "Yes. Like I said, this is about you

and me, and not the campaign. As far as I'm concerned, one has nothing to do with the other."

"Then, yes, I'll join you here for dinner," she said after taking a long, deep breath.

Six

"I know your favorite color is lavender, but tell me something else about Olivia Jeffries, and before you ask, I want to know everything," Reggie said as he sat in the chair at the table while Olivia sat across from him, on the love seat, with her feet curled beneath her. They were both sipping wine and trying to rekindle that comfort zone between them.

Chase had been kind enough to take their food order and had indicated that he would be serving dinner to them shortly. He had given them a bottle of wine, two wineglasses, a tablecloth and eating utensils. Together, the two of them had set the table.

Reggie wondered if being here with him reminded her of how intimate things had been between them on Saturday night. They had shared dinner then, but only after spending hours making love, to the point where they were famished.

"I'm the baby in the family," she said, smiling. "I have two older brothers."

"And I know the Holy Terror is one of them," Reggie said, grinning. "He went to school with a couple of my cousins and two of my brothers. In fact, my brother Quade was on his football team in high school. I understand the Holy Terror has mellowed over the years."

Olivia chuckled. "It depends on what you mean by 'mellowed.' Both of my brothers tend to be overprotective at times, but Duan is worse than Terrence, since he's the oldest. Duan is thirty-six, and Terrence is thirty-four."

"And you are?" he asked, knowing a lot of women didn't like sharing their age.

"I'm twenty-seven. What about you?"

"Thirty-two."

Reggie took a sip of his wine and then asked, "Is Duan the one you sent the text message to on Saturday night?"

"Are you kidding?" she said, chuckling. "Duan would have been on the first flight back home, and he would not have erased your number. He would have had you thoroughly checked out. He has a lot of friends in law enforcement. He used to be a police detective. Now he owns a private investigation company. I sent the text message to Terrence. I can handle him a lot easier than I can Duan."

Reggie nodded. "So why is a beautiful girl like you living so far away from home, in Paris?"

She smiled. "Working. I've always wanted to work at the Louvre Museum in Paris, and I was hired right out of grad school as a tour guide. I had to start at the bottom, but I didn't mind if that's what it would take to work my way up the ladder to be an art curator. It took me almost four years, but I finally made it. I've been a curator for almost a year."

"Congratulations," he said and meant it.

"Thanks."

"So do you plan to make Paris your permanent home?" he asked, watching her sip her wine. He liked the way her lips curved around her glass. He had noticed this detail about her on Saturday night, and it had been a total turn-on…just like it was now.

"I love living over there. I miss being home sometimes, but I've managed to return for the holidays. My brothers and I make it a point to be home for Christmas. But my dream is to return home in a few years, when I've saved up enough money to establish an art gallery." She smiled wistfully.

He nodded. "So over the years, you've come home only during the holidays?"

"Yes."

He wondered if that had anything to do with the fact that her mother had walked out on them a couple of days before Christmas, according to Brent. Reggie could only imagine how disruptive that particular Christmas had to have been for them. "And how long do you plan to stay this time?"

She didn't say anything at first, just stared into her wineglass for a while. Finally, she said, "Until the election is over."

She glanced up and met his gaze, and he breathed in deeply and said, "We won't let that matter now, remember?" he reminded her gently.

"Yes," she said softly. "I remember." She shifted positions in her seat. "So, now, tell me about Reggie Westmoreland."

He took another sip of his wine and then leaned forward in his chair, resting his arms on his thighs. "I'm the youngest son of my parents. Multiple births run in my family. My father is a fraternal twin. My uncle John and my aunt Evelyn have five sons and one daughter."

"Chase is one of their sons?" she interrupted.

He smiled. "Yes, and Chase is a twin. His twin, Storm, is a fireman. So in their birth order, my cousins are Dare, who is the sheriff of College Park, Thorn, who races and builds motorcycles, Stone, who is a writer and writes adventure novels as Rock Mason, the twins Chase and Storm, and

Delaney, the only girl. Delaney and I are the same age and are very close."

"I've heard about Thorn, and, of course, I've read a few Rock Mason novels. And I remember reading years ago about your cousin Delaney and how she married a sheikh. That's awesome."

"Yeah, we all think it is, although I have to say, her brothers weren't too happy about it at first, especially with her leaving the country to live in the Middle East. But her husband, Jamal, is a real nice guy, and everyone looks forward to her trips home. All my cousins are married with children."

"What about your siblings? I understand there are quite a few. Are there twins on your side, too?" she asked.

"Yes. My oldest brother is Jared, and he is a divorce attorney here in the city. Spencer lives in California and is the financial adviser in the family. Durango lives in Montana and is a park ranger. He's thinking about retiring to play a bigger role in his horse-breeding business. And then there are the twins—Ian and Quade. Ian owns a resort on Lake Tahoe, and Quade used to work for the government, but now he owns a number of security firms around the country. Quade and his wife are the parents of triplets, and they live in Carolina, although they have another home in Jamaica."

"Wow! You weren't kidding when you said

multiple births run in your family. Are your brothers married?"

"Yes, and happily so. I'm the only single Westmoreland living in Atlanta. My father has a brother, Uncle Corey, who lives in Montana. He also has triplets, Casey, Clint and Cole, and they are all married."

At that moment, there was a knock on the door, and seconds later Chase entered with their food. "Everything smells delicious," Olivia said, getting to her feet to help place the plates on the table.

Chase smiled. "I hope the two of you enjoy it," he said, then left them alone again.

Once they were seated at the table, Reggie glanced over at her and smiled. "I'm glad you decided to stay."

Olivia returned his smile.

During dinner Olivia was so tuned in to Reggie that she could only stare at him and listen to everything he was saying. He told her about the other family of Westmorelands, the ones living in Colorado, whom his father had discovered when he decided to research the family history a year ago. A family reunion was being held later this month in Texas, where both the Atlanta-based Westmorelands and the Denver-based Westmorelands would be getting together and officially meeting for the first time. It sounded exciting, especially to someone whose family was limited to two brothers and a father. Both of her sets of grandparents were deceased, and both of her parents had been only children.

"Would you like some more dessert?" he asked.

Reggie's question reclaimed her thoughts, and she smiled over at him. He had kept his word, and although the attraction they shared was there, flowing blatantly between them, they had been able to harness it while sharing information about each other. A part of Olivia wasn't sure why they had decided to spend time together when nothing would ever come of it, but they had. Once again, the desire to be together, if only to breathe the same air and share conversation, had driven them to defy what others around them felt they should do.

"No, thanks. I do have to leave. I told my father I was going to the park to paint."

"I'm glad you agreed to meet with me and I'm sorry if I placed you in an awkward position."

"You didn't," she said. "I mentioned to Dad that I was going to the park before you called. I just didn't tell him of my change of plans, because he was resting."

"Would you have done otherwise?" he asked her.

She knew she would be honest and said, "No, he would have forbidden it. And that's the reason why, as much as I enjoyed sharing dinner and conversation with you, Reggie, we can't do it again. I hope you understand."

He met her eyes. "No, I don't understand, because like I said earlier, Olivia, the campaign doesn't concern our relationship."

"The press won't see it that way, and they would have a field day with the story of you and I being involved. I refuse to sneak around to see you." She stood. "I need to go."

Reggie stood as well. He knew he couldn't detain her any longer, but he was more determined than ever to see her again and spend time with her. And he didn't want them to sneak around, either. There had to be a way, and he was determined to find it. "I enjoyed our time together, Olivia."

She held out her hand to him. "So did I. Thank you."

Reggie took the hand she offered, felt the heat the moment he touched it and knew she felt the heat as well. His fingers tightened on hers, and they both were aware of the sensations flowing between them. This wasn't the first time such a thing had happened. It always did when they came in contact with each other.

It was she who tugged her hand away first. "And thanks again for returning my earring."

"You're welcome."

And then Olivia turned and moved toward the door. Before she opened it, she glanced back over her shoulder, saw his unwavering stare, deciphered the intense desire in his eyes. She still felt the heat of his touch on her hand.

She wanted to go back to him, wrap her arms around his neck, but she knew she could not. She would not regret the time she'd spent with him on Saturday night or today. But she was realistic enough to know that as long as Reggie Westmoreland was her father's opponent in the Senate race, her father would never accept her dating a Westmoreland. So from this day forward, she would have fond memories of their times together, but they would have to sustain her throughout the campaign and later, when she returned to Paris.

"Olivia?"

She had already opened the door to leave when she heard him call her name. Swallowing deeply, she stopped and turned around. "Yes?"

"No matter what, you will forever be my Wonder Woman."

She felt the tightness in her throat and fought the tears that had begun clouding her eyes. And you, Reggie Westmoreland, will forever be the man that I wished I'd had the opportunity to get to know better, she thought.

Their gazes held for the longest time, and then she turned and walked out the door and closed it behind her.

* * *

Olivia was surprised to find her father had already gone to bed by the time she returned home. At some point, he had come downstairs and fixed a pot of vegetable soup, which he'd left warming on the stove for her. A part of her felt awful about her deceit. She'd been served a delicious full-course meal at Chase's Place, while her father had been home, eating alone.

She quickly realized that he'd not eaten alone when she noticed two of everything in the sink and the lipstick on the rim of one of the coffee cups. She smiled. The lipstick was the shade Cathy usually wore, which meant there was a good possibility that her father's secretary had joined him for dinner.

She went upstairs and was about to undress for her shower when her cell phone rang. "Hello."

"Hey, Libby, I heard you were home."

"Duan! Where are you? How have you been?"

She heard her brother's deep laugh. "Still asking a thousand questions, are you? I've been fine. How are things there?"

"Umm, so-so. Dad gave his first speech today, and I thought it was great, but he feels his opponent did better."

"Well, did his opponent do better, Libby?"

His question threw her. Why would Duan ask her something like that? "Let's just say that they both did well, but Westmoreland made a direct hit on all the issues, whereas Dad just skated across the surface, like Senator Reed used to do."

"Politics as usual," Duan said. "I told Dad that I don't know squat about politics, but I'd think the people would want some fresh and innovative ideas. With Senator Reed tagging along, there's no way Dad can represent change."

Olivia nodded. She was glad she wasn't the only person in the family who thought that.

Duan went on. "And it's a shame that he's running against Reggie Westmoreland. I heard he's a nice guy. His cousin Dare is the sheriff of College Park. I've worked with Dare before, and I like him. Most of the Westmorelands that I know are good people."

"Dad thinks he's the enemy," Olivia said.

"I'm sorry that Dad feels that way. I was hoping this would be a clean campaign. I bet it's Senator Reed who's trying to make it dirty."

She could hear the dislike in her brother's voice. "So you will make it home for the barbecue next Saturday?" she asked him. In two weeks there would be a massive outdoor cookout in Atlanta-Fulton County Stadium for people to come out and meet all the candidates. Their father had asked her and her brothers to be there for the event so that the Jeffries family could show a united front.

"Yes, I'm in Detroit, but I hope to have everything wrapped up by then."

"Good." She looked forward to seeing both of her brothers. "Be safe, Duan."

"I will."

After leaving Chase's Place, Reggie decided to stop by and visit with his parents. He'd always admired his parents and the strength of their marriage. Everyone in the family knew the story of how James and Sarah Westmoreland had met and how it had been love at first sight. He couldn't help but chuckle when he thought about it now.

His mother and his aunt Evelyn had been the best of friends since childhood and had both been born and raised in Birmingham, Alabama. After graduating from high school, Evelyn had come to Atlanta to visit her aunt for the summer. During her first week in the city, she'd gone on a church picnic and met John Westmoreland. It had been love at first sight, and deciding not to waste any time, John and Evelyn had eloped the following week.

Evelyn had called Sarah to tell her the news, and being the levelheaded person that his mother was, Sarah could not believe or accept that someone could meet and fall in love at first glance. So Sarah had gone to Atlanta to talk some sense into Evelyn, only to meet John's twin brother, James, and fall in love with him at first sight as well. Two weeks later Sarah and James had married.

That had been nearly forty years ago, and his

parents' marriage was still going strong. There had been his mom's cancer scare a few years back, when she'd been diagnosed with breast cancer. But thankfully, she was now doing fine, although she made sure never to miss her annual checkups. His mother was a strong and determined woman who had the love and admiration of her family.

Although Reggie knew it was his mother's desire to see her last son happily wedded, he was in no hurry. He had a good career as an accountant, with a very prestigious client list, and in a couple of months, he would know if his future would include politics.

His thoughts then shifted to Olivia Jeffries. He had enjoyed the time they had spent together tonight. In bed or out, she was someone he liked being with, and it bothered him that she had refused to see him again because of her father. The last thing they needed was to let anyone or anything get in the way of what could be a promising relationship. He understood that she would be leaving the country to return to Paris once the election was over, but Saturday night and today had proven that they were good together. He had actually enjoyed sitting in the coziness of that room at Chase's Place with her while they did little more than engage in conversation with each other.

He had enjoyed studying her while she talked, watching her lips move with each and every word she enunciated. And she had been wearing the same perfume she'd had on Saturday night. It had been hard sitting there across from her, knowing that he had tasted every inch of her skin, had been inside her body and had brought her pleasure.

By the time he pulled into his parents' driveway, he knew there was no way he could willingly walk away from Olivia Jeffries. He didn't like the thought of the two of them sneaking around to see each other so her father wouldn't find out, but at the moment he didn't care. The bottom line was that he wanted to see her again and would do anything and everything in his power—even black-mail—to make it happen.

If Olivia thought she had seen or heard the last of him, she was sorely mistaken.

Seven

"I see you had a guest for dinner last night, Dad."

Olivia watched her father actually blush across the breakfast table and thought it was kind of cute that he seemed a little embarrassed.

"Ahh, yes, Cathy stopped by, and I invited her to stay for dinner."

"Oh, and why did she come by? Are the two of you working on another speech?"

"No, no," her father was quick to say. "She thought I wasn't in a good mood after yesterday's luncheon and wanted to cheer me up. She stopped by the bakery and brought me my favorite Danish. I thought that was kind of her."

"I think so, too, but then Cathy is a kind person. I like her."

Her father lifted a brow. "Do you really?"

Olivia looked over at him. She could tell her response was important to him. "Yes, and I always have. Over the years I thought she was not only a good secretary to you but a nice person, too. When I was younger and was dealing with a lot of girl stuff, I would often call Cathy."

Her father looked surprised. "You did?"

"Yes. Come on, Dad. You have to have known it was hard for me being the only girl in the house, and I couldn't talk to you, Duan and Terrence about *everything*."

"No, I guess not. I'm glad she was there for you then," her father said.

"Yes, and I'm glad she's here for you now, Dad."

Olivia watched as Orin's blush deepened. "Everything between me and Cathy is strictly business."

She was forced to hide her smile behind the rim of the coffee cup she'd brought to her lips. "Of course, Dad. I wasn't insinuating anything."

Half an hour later, after her father had left for work, Olivia decided to get dressed and go to the park and paint like she had planned to do the day before. She was about to head downstairs when her cell phone rang. For some reason, she knew who the caller was without looking. Her heart skipped several beats before she clicked the phone on. "Hello."

"Please meet with me again, Olivia."

She closed her eyes and breathed in deeply as the sensuous sound of his voice floated through her. "Reggie, I thought we decided that we wouldn't see each other again."

"I thought so, too, but I couldn't sleep last night. Thoughts of you kept invading my mind. I want to see you, Olivia. I want to be with you. Meet me today at noon. The Saxon Hotel. The same room number."

Her mind was suddenly flooded with memories of everything that had taken place in that room. And he wasn't the only one who'd been unable to sleep last night. Her body had been restless. Hot. She had dreamed of him several times, and at one point she had sat on the edge of the bed for what seemed like hours, recovering from the pleasurable memories that had swept through her, interrupting her night and filling her with a need she had never felt...until meeting Reggie.

"Will you come, Olivia? Please."

His voice was deep, quiet, yet persuasive. The sound of it poured over her skin like warm cream, and she couldn't fight it, because deep inside she wanted to be with him as much as he wanted to be with her.

She needed to see him again, to know, to understand and to explore the pull between them. Was it just sexual, or was it something else? Despite her decision not to become involved with him, she knew that she had to be with him at least one more time. These memories she was collecting would have to be enough to sustain her for the rest of her life.

"Yes," she said finally. "I'll meet you at noon."

Reggie paced the hotel room, glancing at his watch every so often. It was a few minutes before noon. He had had a news conference at nine but hadn't counted on a slew of reporters bombarding him after the news conference was over. Nor had he counted on the rumor that had quickly spread that his accounting firm, which employed over a hundred people, was facing possible bankruptcy and definite layoffs.

It was a lie that could easily be proven false, but not before mass pandemonium erupted at his business, and he'd spent part of the morning calming his employees' fears. He didn't have to think twice about where the lie had been generated, which made him angrier than hell. He'd never suspected that Orin Jeffries would allow his campaign staff to stoop so low.

For a moment he'd thought he would have to cancel this meeting with Olivia, but a part of him had refused to do it. She had consented to meet with him, and he would have moved heaven and hell to be here. Now he couldn't help wondering if she would show up. What if she had changed her mind? What if—

At that moment the door opened and Olivia walked in and his entire body went completely still. It seemed as if his heart picked that exact moment to stop beating. He was very much aware of how good she looked dressed in a pair of black tailored slacks and a light blue linen blouse.

She closed the door behind her and leaned against it, saying nothing but holding his gaze as intently as he was holding hers. He could now admit that although he had been drawn to her lips, the total package was what had captured his interest. She had the kind of presence that demanded attention, and just like at the Firemen's Masquerade Ball and yesterday, she was getting his again today. In droves.

In addition to checking her out, he was trying to get a read on her but couldn't. The sexual chemistry had hit the airwaves the moment she had walked through the door. With them, it couldn't be helped. But what about her attitude? he wondered. She had said yesterday that she didn't want them to become involved. Yet when he had defied her wishes and had called and asked her to meet with him here, she had accepted.

What was she expecting from him? What was he expecting from her?

He definitely knew what he wanted, but wanting and expecting were two different things. For the moment he was just glad to have her here, in this hotel room, alone with him. Had she come to spend time with him or to chew him out for having the audacity to call and ask her to meet with him? He was certain he was about to find out.

"Hello, Olivia."

"Reggie." And then, with her gaze still locked firmly with his, she moved away from the door and walked toward him.

His heart somehow began beating again, and it was only when she came to a stop directly in front of him that he allowed his gaze to shift and took note of the cut of her blouse. The low, square cut showed the nice swell of her breasts. They were breasts he had tasted before and was dying to taste again. Not surprisingly, something primal stirred inside him. His heart rate increased, and he breathed in deeply as a way to slow it down.

He cleared his throat. "I ordered lunch," he heard himself say and watched as she glanced behind him to see the table that had been set for two. "I'll call them to deliver the food when we're ready to eat," he said and drew a somewhat shaky breath.

She reached out and smoothed her hand along the back of his neck. "Are you hungry now, Reggie?" she asked, her voice an octave lower than he remembered.

He swallowed thickly. The feel of her fingers on his skin was pure torture. "It's up to you, since you're my guest."

A smile touched her lips at the corners. "In that case, we can wait. I'd rather do this now." And then she leaned up on tiptoe and connected her mouth to his.

At that moment whatever control he had been holding on to broke, and he instantly swept her into his arms without disconnecting their mouths. He wanted to head directly for the bedroom, but at that moment the only thing he could do was stand there with her in his arms and savor her this way, not sure when or if he would be granted the opportunity to do so again. He intended to make this their day, just like Saturday had been their night.

On the way to the hotel, Brent had tried to pin him down as to where he was going. He had told his friend that he was to be disturbed only if there was an emergency. He could tell Brent had wanted more information, but none had been forthcoming. What he did on his personal time was his business, and this lunch was on his personal time. And he was feasting on what he enjoyed most. Olivia's mouth.

He wasn't sure what had changed her mind since yesterday, when she had been adamant about not getting involved with him, but he was just glad she had. There was only so much a man could take.

He finally pulled back from her mouth. It was then that she nuzzled against his ear. The tip of her tongue trailed a path beneath it, and then she whispered. "I want to make love with you again—"

Before she could finish her words, he headed in the direction of the bedroom, sidestepping the table set for two. She laughed when he gently tossed her on the bed, then captured her laughter with his mouth when he quickly joined her there. And then it was back on. The heat was blazing. They didn't have a moment to waste, and they both knew it. As they lay fully clothed in bed, with their mouths joined in the most intimate way, their tongues dueled, tangled and mated. She refused to stay still. She was moving all over the place, and he eventually placed a thigh over hers. She had become wild, so bold and wanton. And he loved it.

She pulled her mouth back and met his gaze, their hearts pounding loudly in the room. "Make love to me, Reggie. Now," she said.

She didn't have to say the words twice. He moved off the bed and quickly undressed, trying not to rip the buttons off his shirt in his haste. And then, when he was completely naked, except for the condom he had taken the time to put on, he went for her, pulled her toward him to remove her blouse and bra before tackling her shoes, slacks and panties.

When he had pulled the latter two down her hips to reveal the lushness of her feminine mound, he knew he had to taste her right then. He tossed the items of clothing aside and held down her hips at the same time that his mouth lowered to her, kissing her intimately, with a hunger and greed that made her tremble and moan incoherently. But he didn't let up. His tongue was desperate to reacquaint itself with the taste it had relished on Saturday, and he intended to get his fill. And her body responded, generating the sweetness he wanted, and he mercilessly savored her.

He felt her hands lock around his head as if to hold his mouth in place, but that wasn't needed. He wasn't going anyplace until he got enough, and that wouldn't be anytime soon. He proved his point by plunging his tongue deeper inside of her, absorbing the wetness of her sensuality, which was being produced in abundance just for him.

Reggie finally pulled back and licked his lips, while his eyes traveled down her entire body, taking in every inch and every curve, the texture of her skin and the fullness of her breasts, which seemed to be begging for his mouth.

Leaning upward, he brushed his lips against a taut nipple, liking the sound of the quick breath that got caught in her throat. He proceeded to sample her nipples, finding both tantalizingly hot.

"Come inside me, please."

Olivia's tortured moan had Reggie moving his body over hers. When his heated shaft was at the opening of her feminine mound, he met her gaze, and then, with a hungry growl, he pushed deep inside of her.

Olivia closed her eyes as pleasure washed through her. What was there about being joined to Reggie that made her feel such joy, such mind-blowing pleasure and such spellbinding ecstasy? She felt him lift her legs, and she wrapped them around his waist while he thrust inside of her with whipcord speed and precision. Everything about him was affecting her in an elemental way, and she could barely stifle her moans as she was consumed by a tide of red-hot passion. It was only with him that she could feel not only taken but possessed. Only with him could she be not only driven but also contained. And he was making love to her without any restraint and with a voracious need, which was fueling her own. And every time the hard muscles of his stomach pressed against hers, pinning her beneath him, she trembled from the inside out.

And then an orgasm rammed through her. Never before had she felt anything so profound. She cried out his name. And he used his tongue, lips and mouth to absorb her cries of pleasure, her moans of passion. Instead of letting up, he pressed on and thrust deeper.

The flames ignited, flared and then burned in the very center of her, and when an explosion ripped through her a second time, he was there, and she felt his shaft expand before exploding in his release. And as passion tumbled her over into the depths of turbulent, sensual waters, she cried his name once more before she felt herself drowning in a sea of ecstasy.

Propped up on his elbow, Reggie stared down at Olivia. In the middle of the day, she had actually drifted off to sleep. He smiled, understanding why. He had shown her no mercy in taking them both through waves and waves of pure pleasure. Somewhere in the back of his mind, he heard the sound of his cell, but at that moment he chose to ignore it. His main focus, his total concentration, was on the most beautiful creature he had ever laid eyes on.

He glanced over at the clock on the nightstand. They had been in the room for two hours already—two hours of nonstop lovemaking in which he would get hard again before even coming out of her. They would start another bout of lovemaking right on the tail end of the previous one. Nothing like this had ever happened to him before. He felt totally obsessed with this woman.

He could vividly recall the first moment he had seen her at the Firemen's Masquerade Ball. He had known then, just like he knew now, that she was the one that he would make his. At the time he just hadn't known the depth to which he would do so. Now he did.

And he also understood why his brothers and cousins seemed so happy these days, so blissfully content. They had been able to find that one person who they knew was their soul mate. The question of the hour was, how was he going to convince Olivia that she was his? Especially considering the fact that they were sneaking around just to be together.

He wanted to introduce her to his family. He especially wanted her to get to know his mother and his brothers' and cousins' wives. He wanted to take her to the Westmoreland family reunion, which would be held in Texas at the end of the month. He wanted to take her to one of Thorn's motorcycle races later this year. There were so many things he wanted to share with her. But the most important thing of all was his life.

There was no need to tell her that he loved her, because she wouldn't understand that one thing about being a Westmoreland was recognizing your mate when you saw her or him. Although, he thought, with a smile, he would have to admit some of his cousins and brothers had refused to accept their fate at first. But in the end it hadn't done any good. Love had zapped their senses just the same. And it had done the same thing to him. It had hit him like a ton of bricks on Saturday night, and like his parents, he had fallen in love at first sight.

She had her defenses down now, but he wouldn't be surprised if they were back up before she left the hotel today. It didn't matter. He was not going to let her deny them what was rightfully theirs to have. She didn't know it yet, but in time she would. No matter what the situation was between him and her father regarding the campaign, it had no bearing on the two of them.

He noticed her eyes fluttering before they fully opened, and then she was staring up at him. She had to be hungry now. He would feed her, and then he would make love to her again.

Or so he thought. Suddenly she lifted her body and pushed him back onto the covers to straddle him, placing her knees on the sides of his hips to seemingly hold him immobile. She tilted her head back and looked down at him. And smiled. He felt the effects of that smile like a punch to his gut, and his shaft suddenly got hard, totally erect.

"I thought you would be hungry," he said, reaching out and placing the palm of his hand at the back of her neck.

"I am," she whispered, holding his eyes with her own. "For you."

He drew her head down to brush his lips against hers. "And I for you."

When he released her mouth, she glanced at him with a confused look in her eyes. "What are you doing to me, Reggie Westmoreland? How do you have the ability to make me feel wild and reckless? Make me want to yield to temptation?"

A hot rush of desire sent shivers through his

body. "I should be asking you the same thing, Olivia Jeffries."

And then she lowered herself on him, and he knew it was a good thing he'd already donned a new condom, because there was no way he could have said stop when she embedded him inside of herself to the hilt. The look on her face told him that she was proud of her accomplishment. She had wanted, so she had taken.

And then she began moving, slowly at first and then with a desperation that sent fire surging through his loins and made it feel as if the head of his shaft was about to explode. But she kept moving, dangling her twin globes in front of his face with every downward motion.

He reached out and grabbed hold of one, brought it to his mouth, and she threw her head back as she continued to ride him in a way he had never been ridden before. The woman had power in her thighs, in her hips and in her inner muscles, and she was using them to make shivers race all through him.

In retaliation, he covered her breasts with his kisses, using his lips and tongue to push her over the same edge that he was close to falling from. And when an explosion hit, he bucked until they were almost off the bed, but then her thighs nearly held him immobile. His body was locked so tightly with hers, he wondered if they would be able to separate when the time came. And at that moment he really didn't care if they couldn't. He would love to stay inside of her forever, in the place where he would one day plant his seed for their child.

That thought triggered another explosion inside of him, and he groped hard for sanity when Olivia came apart on top of him. Her inner muscles clamped him tightly, and she drew every single thing she could out of him. His lungs felt like they were about to collapse in his throat when he tried to keep from hollering out. Burying his face in her chest, he found a safe haven right between her breasts. He knew from this day forward that whatever it took, one day he would make her totally, completely and irrevocably his.

"We never ate lunch, did we?" Olivia asked as she slid back into her slacks.

"No, and I owe you an apology for that," Reggie said, pulling up his pants. He stopped what he was doing and stared at her, watched how she was struggling with the buttons on her blouse.

"Come here, Olivia."

She glanced over at him and smiled before crossing the room to him. "I don't know why I wore this thing when it has so many buttons. It's not like I didn't know that you would be taking it off me."

He didn't say anything as he took over buttoning her blouse. She was right. It did have a lot of buttons. That wouldn't have been so bad if his attention hadn't been drawn to her flesh-toned bra. "Your bra is my favorite color," he said, smiling down at her.

"I figured as much when I put it on," she said, grinning. "You were right. Flesh tone is a color."

"If you're hungry, we can still—"

"No. I noticed your cell phone went off a few times. You need to get back to work."

He chuckled. "Have you noticed the time, Olivia? The day is practically over. We've been here for five hours. It's past five o'clock." And he really wasn't bothered by it. "There. All done," he said, dropping his hands to his sides before he was tempted to do something, like pull her into his arms and kiss her.

"Thanks. Now I definitely need to know something," she said, looking up at him.

"What?"

"Do you have stock in this place?"

Another smile touched his lips. "Wish I did, but no."

"Then what kind of connections do you have?" she asked, with an expression on her face that said she was determined to know.

"My connection is my brother Quade. Dominic Saxon is his brother-in-law. Both recently became fathers. Quade has triplets—a son and two daughters and Dominic's wife, Taylor, gave birth to a son a few months ago."

"Oh. Proud fathers, I gather."

Reggie smiled. "Yes, they are."

He slipped into his shirt while he watched her stand before the dresser's mirror to redo her makeup. Although he knew he would probably get some resistance, he decided to go ahead and have his say. "I got the room again for this Saturday night, Olivia."

Olivia met his gaze in the mirror before slowly turning around to stare at him. He had just issued an open invitation, and it was one he wanted her to accept. She continued to stare into his dark eyes, and then she shifted her gaze to study his face. There was something, something she couldn't decipher, in his eyes and on his face.

"Coming here today was risky, Reggie," she finally said softly.

"I know," was his response. "But I had to see you."

"And I had to be with you," she said honestly.

Too late she wondered why she would admit such a thing to him, but deep down she knew the reason. She wanted him to know that she had wanted to be here and that she thought their time together was special.

Reggie crossed the room to her, and without giving him the chance to make the first move, she reached up and drew his mouth down to hers. And he kissed her with a gentleness that he had to fight to maintain.

When she released his mouth, he gazed down at her. "Sure you had enough?"

She licked her lips. "For now." She then smiled. "I'll get the rest on Saturday."

He lifted a hopeful brow. "You will come?"

She smiled. "Yes, I will come."

Although he knew they needed to finish getting dressed and be on their way, he reached out, caught her around the waist and pulled her gently into his arms, immediately reveling in the way her body seemed to cling to his, perfectly and in sync. And then he lowered his mouth to hers for a kiss that would keep him going strong until Saturday night, when they would come together once again.

Eight

"Cathy will be calling you later today, Libby."

Olivia lifted her gaze from her cereal bowl to glance over at her father, with a questioning look on her face. "For what reason?"

"To schedule all those fund-raisers that you and I will need to attend over the next couple of weeks, beginning this Saturday."

Panic shot through Olivia. "Not this Saturday night, I hope."

Her father quirked a thick brow. "No, it's Saturday midday at the home of Darwin Walker and his wife."

She nodded. Darwin and Terrence used to play

together for the Miami Dolphins. Last year Darwin, who, like Terrence, had retired from the NFL, moved to Atlanta after accepting a coaching position with the Falcons.

"And why are you concerned about Saturday night? Do you have plans or something?" Orin asked.

Olivia swallowed. She hated lying to her father, but there was no way she could tell him the truth. Running for political office had made him somewhat unreasonable, especially when it came to Reggie. She was convinced that the only reason he didn't like Reggie was that he was the main person standing in the way of him becoming a senator. However, she intended to do as Reggie had suggested and believe that the election had no bearing on what was developing between them.

She met her father's gaze. "Yes, I have plans. I ran into a friend at the party Saturday night, and we're getting together again this weekend." At least what she'd said wasn't a total lie.

Her father's features softened. "That's good. I've been feeling badly about asking you to put your life in Paris on hold to come here and be my escort for all these campaign events. I'm glad you've managed to squeeze in some fun time."

If only you knew just how much fun I've had thanks to Reggie, she thought.

Both she and her father resumed eating, and the

kitchen became quiet. There was something she needed to ask him, something she truly needed to know. The issue had been bothering her since she'd heard about it yesterday.

She glanced across the table at her father. He had resumed reading the paper and was flipping through the pages. She hated interrupting, but she had to. "Dad, can I ask you something?"

"Sure, sweetheart," Orin said, looking up to meet her gaze and placing the newspaper aside. "What is it?"

"Reggie Westmoreland," she said and watched her father's jaw flex.

"What about him, Libby?"

"Did you authorize any of your staff members to put out that false statement about his company facing bankruptcy and layoffs?"

Her father frowned. "Of course not. Why would I or my staff do something like that?"

"To discredit him."

His features tightened. "And you believe I would do something like that or give my staff permission to do so?"

"I don't want to believe that, but I'm not naive. I know how dirty politics can be, Dad."

Orin leaned back in his chair. "Are you taking up for Reggie Westmoreland?" he asked, studying her features.

She sighed deeply. "No, Dad, I'm not taking up

for anyone. Such tactics can backfire, so my concern is actually for you."

What she didn't say was that she was sure Reggie was aware of the rumor, which had circulated yesterday, but he hadn't mentioned it to her. Although he had to have been upset about it, Reggie had given her his full concentration and had kept his word not to mix his competition with her father and his relationship with her.

Now it was her turn to study her father's features, and she could see that what she'd said had him thinking. Was he so disjointed from his campaign staff that he truly didn't know what was going on? Did he not know what they were capable of?

"I'm having a meeting with my campaign staff this morning, and if I discover that someone on my staff is connected to yesterday's story in any way, they will be dismissed."

She came close to asking if that included Senator Reed. She had a feeling he was behind the rumor. "Thanks, Dad. I think it will be in your best interest in the long run."

"Where were you yesterday, Reggie? I tried reaching you all afternoon," Brent said, looking across the breakfast table at his friend. They were sitting in Chase's Place, where they had met for breakfast.

Reggie shrugged. "I was busy. Did anything come up that you couldn't handle?"

"Of course not." Brent set his coffee cup down, and his blue eyes studied Reggie intently. "But it would have been nice if I'd been able to contact you. Someone from *Newsweek* called to do an article on you. We're not talking about a local magazine, Reg. We're talking about *Newsweek*. You know how long I've been trying to get you national coverage."

Yes, Reggie did know, and he felt badly about it. But at the time all he could think about was that he wanted to spend uninterrupted time with Olivia. "I'm sorry about that, Brent."

"You're seeing her, aren't you?"

Reggie lifted a brow and met Brent's stare. "It depends on who you're referring to."

"Orin Jeffries's daughter."

Reggie leaned back in his chair. He and Brent had been friends for a long time, since grade school, actually. After attending college at Yale, Brent had worked for a number of years in Boston before moving back to Atlanta a few years ago to care for his elderly parents. A couple of months ago, Reggie had been the best man at Brent's wedding.

As far as Reggie was concerned, other than his brothers and cousins, there wasn't a man he trusted more. He met his best friend's eyes. "Yes, I'm seeing her."

Brent let out a deep sigh. "Do you think that's smart?"

Reggie chuckled. "Considering the fact that I plan to marry her sometime after the election, yes, I would have to say it's smart."

Brent's jaw dropped. "Marry!" And then he quickly glanced around, hoping no one had heard his outburst. After turning back around, he nervously brushed back a strand of blond hair that had fallen onto his face. "Reggie, you just met the woman on Monday at that luncheon."

"No," Reggie said, smiling, as he absently swirled the coffee around in his cup. "Actually, we met before then."

Brent lifted a brow. "When?"

"Saturday night, at the Firemen's Masquerade Ball."

"Saturday night?"

"Yes," replied Reggie.

"That wasn't even a week ago. Are you telling me you decided once you saw her at a party that you were going to marry her?"

"Something like that. And at the time I didn't know who she was. I found out her true identity on Monday, at that luncheon, the same time she found out mine." Reggie could only smile. Brent was staring at him like he had totally lost his mind. "Trust me, my friend, I haven't lost my mind. Just my heart."

Brent took a sip of his orange juice. His expression implied that he wished the juice was laced with vodka. "Do the two of you understand the implications of what you're doing? Hello," he said, putting emphasis on that single word. "Her father is your opponent in a Senate race."

"We're aware of that. However, we've decided that has nothing to do with what's going on between us," Reggie said.

"And you love her?" Brent asked incredulously.

"With all my heart and then some," Reggie answered truthfully.

He had thought about it a lot last night. To be honest, he hadn't been able to think about anything else. As crazy as it might seem to some people, yes, he had fallen in love with her. He had never been totally against marriage, especially since his family over the past seven years—starting with Delaney—seemed to be falling like flies into matrimony. He just knew he wouldn't ever settle down until the right woman came along. Because of his career and his decision to get into politics, he hadn't expected that to happen anytime soon. He thought he would at least be in his late thirties when he tied the knot, although he knew his mother wished otherwise.

"And she feels the same way?"

Brent's question invaded Reggie's thoughts. "Not sure. I've never asked her. In fact, I haven't even shared my feelings with her yet. It will be best to wait until after the campaign."

Brent took another gulp of his orange juice. "I swear, Reggie, you're going to give me heart failure."

Reggie smiled. "Don't mean to. I'm sure you remember when you met Melody. What did you tell me? You claimed you had fallen in love with her instantly."

"I did. But her father wasn't my political opponent," Brent countered.

"Shouldn't matter, and we intend not to let it affect our relationship, either. So wish us luck."

Brent couldn't help but smile. "Hey, man, what you need are prayers, and I'll be the first to send one up for you."

Olivia stepped off the elevator and glanced around. Over the years, not much in her father's office had changed. The placement of the furniture was still the same. She remembered coming here as a child after school and sitting on the sofa and watching television—but only after she had completed her homework. Duan and Terrence had been into after-school sports, so instead of letting her go home to an empty house, her father had hired a private car to pick her up from school and bring her here.

"Libby, it's good to see you. You didn't need to come in to meet with me."

Olivia couldn't help but return Cathy's warm smile. "I didn't mind. I wanted to get out of the house, anyway."

That much was true. She had tried to paint, but the only subject that had readily come to mind was Reggie, and she couldn't risk her father finding sketches of him all over the place. She slid into the chair next to Cathy's desk.

"If you wanted to see your dad you're too late. He stepped out. I think he went over to his campaign headquarters," Cathy was saying, with a concerned expression on her face. "He was on the phone earlier with his campaign staff, and he wasn't a happy camper. He suspects someone released that false information on Westmoreland yesterday. Now it says in this morning's paper that your father's campaign is turning to dirty politics."

Olivia sighed. She'd been afraid that would happen. "Well, I'm glad Dad is addressing it. Otherwise, it could backfire even more if whoever is responsible keeps it up."

"I agree."

Olivia liked Cathy. She was attractive, responsible, and Olivia knew the woman had her father's interests at heart. At least her father was beginning to notice Cathy as a woman, although he was moving way too slowly to suit Olivia. "Well, as you can see, I brought my planner," she said to Cathy. "Dad wants me to pencil in all those important dates of those campaign events. I still don't understand why he just didn't ask you to go with him."

Cathy blushed. "Your father would never do that. I'm his secretary."

Olivia rolled her eyes. "You're not just his secretary, Cathy. You're his right hand in more ways than one, and I'm sure he knows it. Frankly, I'm concerned about him and the election. Sometimes I think he wants to become a senator, and other times I'm not sure. What's your take on it?"

Cathy hesitated in responding, and Olivia knew it was because she thought that to say anything negative about Orin or the campaign might be construed as disloyalty. "I think that if it had been left up to your father, he would not have run," Cathy said hesitantly.

"Then why did he?"

"Because Senator Reed talked him into it."

Olivia shook her head, still not understanding. "My father is a grown man who can make decisions on his own. Why would he let Senator Reed talk him into doing anything? That doesn't make sense. It's not like they have a history or have been friends for a terribly long time. It's my understanding that they met playing golf just a few years ago."

Cathy shook her head. "No, their relationship goes back further than that."

Olivia blinked, surprised. She had a feeling Cathy knew a lot more than she was telling. Definitely a lot more than Olivia or her brothers knew. "So, what's the relationship?"

Cathy, Olivia noted, was nervously biting her lips. "I'm not sure it's my place to say, Libby," she said.

Olivia knew that if she didn't get the information from Cathy, then she would never get it. Deciding to go for broke, she said in a low and soft voice, "I know you love Dad, Cathy." At the woman's surprised look, Olivia lowered her voice even more. "And I'm hoping Dad realizes, and very soon, what a jewel he has in you, not only as an employee, but, more importantly, as a woman who, I know, has his back. But I'm honestly worried that something is going on that my brothers and I wouldn't agree with, and if that's the case, then we need to know what it is."

Cathy stared at her for a long moment. "Your father feels indebted to the senator."

Olivia raised a brow. "And why would he feel that way?"

Cathy didn't say anything for a long while. "Because of your mother," the older woman said.

Olivia's head began spinning. "How does my mother have anything to do with this? My brothers and I haven't heard from her in over twenty-something years. Are you saying that my father has? That he and my mother are in contact with each other?"

"No, that's not what I'm saying."

With a desperate look in her eyes, Olivia took hold of the woman's hand. "Tell me, Cathy. You need to tell me what's going on and what my mother has to do with it."

"Years ago, your mother ran off with another man, a married man," Cathy said.

Olivia nodded. She knew all that. Although she had been only three then, years later she had overheard one of her grandparents talking about her mother in whispers. "And?"

"The man's wife had a child."

"Yes, I know that as well," Olivia said. "I also know the woman was so torn up about what happened that eventually she and her child moved away."

"Yes, but what you probably don't know is that eventually, a couple of years later, that woman committed suicide. She could never get over losing her husband."

Olivia gasped. Cathy was right. She hadn't known that. "How awful."

Cathy nodded sadly in agreement. "Yes, it was. And what's even worse, when she decided to stall her car on the train tracks and just sit there waiting for the train to come, she had her child in the car with her. They were both killed."

Tears she couldn't hold back sprang into Olivia's eyes. It was bad enough that her mother's actions had broken up a family, but they had also caused a woman to end her own life and that of her child.

"I didn't want to tell you," Cathy said softly, handing Olivia a tissue.

Olivia dabbed at her eyes. "I'm glad you did. But what does all that have to do with Senator Reed?"

Now it was Cathy who reached out to hold Olivia's hand. "The woman who committed suicide was his sister, Libby, and your father feels responsible for what eventually happened to her and her little girl because of what your mother did."

The first thing Olivia did when she got home was to pull out her sketch pad and water colors, determined to go to the park. Painting always soothed her mind, and she needed it today more than ever.

She had come home soon after her conversation with Cathy; otherwise, she would have gone looking for her father just to cry in his arms. It just wasn't fair that he felt responsible for the choices his wife had made over twenty years before, choices that had ultimately led to a sad tragedy. And if Senator Reed was intentionally playing with her father's conscience, he would have to stop.

Once at the park, she found several scenes she could concentrate on and tried her hand at doing a few sketches, but her concentration wavered. A part of her wanted to call her brothers and tell them what she'd found out, but she resisted doing so. They would be in town next weekend, and she would tell them then. They would know how to handle the situation. She loved her father and if he really wanted to enter politics and become a senator, then he had her support. But if he was being railroaded into doing something out of misplaced guilt, then she definitely had a problem with that.

For the first time in years, she thought about the woman who had given birth to her. The woman had walked out of her, her father's and her brothers' lives without looking back. When Duan had gotten old enough, he had tried contacting her, to satisfy his need to know why Susan Jeffries's maternal instincts had never driven her to stay in contact with the three kids she had left behind. Instead of finding a woman who regretted what she had done, he had found a selfish individual who had been married four times and had never given birth to another child. Instead, she had been living life in the fast lane and was the mistress of a race-car driver, apparently working on hubby number five. That had been six years ago. There was no telling what number she was on now.

The more Olivia thought about her mother, the more depressed she became, and she found that even painting couldn't soothe her troubled mind. It was strange that the happiest of her days were those she'd spent with Reggie. Not just sharing a bed with him, but sharing a bit of herself like she'd never shared with a man before. They would talk in between their lovemaking. Pillow talk. She felt so good around him.

A child's laughter caught her attention, and she glanced across the pond to see a mother interacting with a child that appeared to be about three, the same age she'd been when her mother left. The woman seemed to be having fun, and the exuberance on the face of the little girl left no doubt that she, too, was having the time of her life. That's what real mothers did. They put smiles on their children's faces, not sad frowns that lasted a lifetime.

Aware that she had begun thinking of her poor excuse for a mother again, she shifted her thoughts back to Reggie. She would love to see him now, be held by him and kissed by him. It was hard to believe that they had met less than a week ago, but since then they had shared so much.

Half an hour later she was still sitting on the park bench, thinking about Reggie. They had spent most of yesterday together. Would he want to see her today? Would he meet her somewhere if she were to call, just to hold her in his arms and do nothing more?

Olivia swallowed. There was only one way to find out. She took her cell phone out of her bag and dialed his number.

"Hello. This is Reggie Westmoreland."

The sound of his sexy voice oozed all over her. "Hi. This is Olivia. I didn't want to call you, but I didn't have anyone else to call."

"Olivia, what's wrong?"

She swiped at a tear. "Nothing really. I just need to be held."

"Where are you?"

"At a park. I came here to paint and—"

"What's the name of the park?"

"Cypress Park."

"I know where it's located. I'm on my way."

"No, it's out in the open. Is there a place near here where we can meet?" she asked.

There was a pause, and then he said, "Yes, in fact, there is. My cousin Delaney and her husband, Jamal, own a town house a few blocks away. It's on Commonwealth Boulevard. Delaney's Square."

"A town house just for her?" Olivia asked.

"Jamal was the first tenant and decided to buy out the others so he, Delaney and the kids could have their privacy whenever they came to town. I have a key to check on things when they're not here. Go there now, sweetheart. I'll be waiting."

Olivia recognized Reggie's car parked in front of a massive group of elegant buildings, all town-homes, around ten of them, on a beautiful land-scaped property.

She strolled up the walkway to the center build-ing; her pulse rate increased with every step she took. When she reached the front door, she glanced around. She lifted her hand to knock on the door, but before her knuckles could make contact, the door opened and Reggie was there. He captured her hand in his and gently pulled her inside and closed the door behind her.

Olivia looked up at him, and he gently pulled her into his arms. He wrapped his arms around her waist and pressed her face to his chest.

She inhaled deeply. He smelled of man, a nice, robust scent that sent shivers down her spine. This was what she needed. To be held in his arms. Riding over here, she kept thinking about how it would feel to be in his arms again. Her life was in turmoil, and right now he was a solid force in her mixed-up world.

Suddenly, she felt herself being lifted in his arms, and she linked her arms around his neck. "Where are you taking me?" she asked when he began walking.

"Over here, to the sofa, so I can hold you the way I want to, and so you can tell me what's bothering you."

Olivia pressed her lips together, not sure she could do that without implicating her father, and that wouldn't be good. He didn't need to know that her father had felt compelled to enter the Senate race because Senator Reed, a man he felt indebted to, had encouraged him to do so, and that her father's heart might not be in it.

Reggie adjusted her in his arms when he sat down on the sofa and angled her body so that she could look up at him. "What happened, Olivia? What happened to make you call me?"

She hesitated and then decided to tell him some of what was bothering her, but not all of it. "I was at the park and saw this mother and child. The little girl was about the age I was when my mother walked out on my dad, my brothers and me. Seeing them made me realize how easy it was for my mother to walk away without looking back."

"And she's never tried contacting you?" Reggie asked, softly stroking the side of her face with the pad of his thumb.

Oliver shook her head. "No, she never has."

Reggie tightened his hold on Olivia, and she clung to his warmth. She wasn't sure how much time passed before she lifted her head to look at him. He looked at her, studied her face. "Are you okay?" he asked softly.

She nodded. "I am now. But I have to go. Dad will worry because it's getting late."

He stood with her in his arms and let her slide down his body until her feet touched the floor. For a long moment, she stood there and stared at him, realizing that he hadn't kissed her yet. He must have read her mind, because he lowered his mouth to her. She craned her neck to meet him halfway and let out a deep sigh when their lips met.

His tongue was in her mouth in a flash, moving around in a circular motion before winding around hers, taking it in total possession. She wrapped her arms around his neck and groaned out loud when he deepened the kiss. Sensations throbbed within her, and she felt a shiver pass through her body.

Moments later, she pulled back from the kiss, gasping for breath. Nobody could kiss like Reggie Westmoreland. She was totally convinced of that. They had to stand there a moment to catch their breaths. In a way, it did her heart good to know he had been just as affected by the kiss.

"Do you want me to show you around before you go?" Reggie asked her in a ragged voice, taking her hand in his.

Olivia glanced around. The place was absolutely beautiful, with its sprawling living room that was lavishly decorated in peach and cream, its bigger-than-life dining room and kitchen and its spiral staircase. Fit for a king. And from what she'd read, Sheikh Jamal Ari Yasir would one day inherit that title.

"Yes, I'd love to see the rest of it."

Reggie showed her around, and she was in total awe of the lavishly decorated bedrooms and baths, and when they toured one of the beautifully decorated guest rooms, with a huge four-poster bed, he didn't try to get her in it. Instead, he looked at her. "Saturday night will be ours. Today you just needed me to hold you," he whispered.

His words went a long way to calm her, soothed

her troubled mind and actually made her feel special, mainly because she had called and he had come. "Thank you for coming, Reggie."

He looked down at her and pulled her closer to him. "I will always come when you call, Olivia."

She met his gaze, thinking that was a strange thing to say. They didn't have a future together. At the end of two months, she would be returning to Paris.

"Come on. Let me walk you to your car," Reggie said huskily as he placed his arms around her shoulders.

Olivia regretted that her time with Reggie was about to end and appreciated that he had been there for her when she had needed him. That meant a lot.

Nine

The following week Olivia kept busy by attending several functions with her father. She had decided not to discuss her conversation with Cathy with him. Instead, she would meet with her brothers and get their take on the matter when they came to town later that week.

She had to catch her breath whenever she thought of the times she and Reggie had spent together, especially on Saturday night. On Wednesday he had called and asked her to have a midday snack with him at Chase's Place. It was then that she had met Chase's wife, Jessica, who was expecting the couple's first child. Jessica, who liked to bake, had treated her to a batch of brownies, which had been delicious. Olivia wondered what Reggie had told Chase and Jessica about their relationship, and if they knew that she was the daughter of his opponent in the Senate race.

Olivia couldn't help but note over the past few days that her father seemed excited about this weekend. He would have his three children home to attend the huge barbecue that was being planned for all the candidates on Saturday evening.

Tonight she would attend yet another political function with her father. All the candidates would be there. She and Reggie would have to pretend they barely knew each other. They had talked about it on Wednesday, and she knew he wasn't overjoyed at the thought of that, but he had promised to abide by her wishes. She wasn't crazy about them sneaking around to see each other, either, but under the circumstances, it was something they had to do.

She smiled as she continued to get dressed, thinking that sneaking around did have its benefits. It made them appreciate the time they were together, and they always found ways to put it to good use. It would be hard tonight to see him and not go over to him and claim him as hers. And a part of her felt that he was hers. Whenever they were together, he would use his mouth to stamp his brand all over her, and she would do likewise with him.

She tried not to think about the day when the campaign would finally be over and she would have to return to Paris. She was even thinking about calling the Louvre to see if she could extend her leave for a couple more weeks. She wanted to be able to be with him in the open after the election. She didn't want to think about how he and her father would feel about each other then, depending on which one of them was victorious.

She glanced at her watch. She needed to hurry, because the last thing she wanted was to make her father late to a campaign event. Besides, although she had just seen Reggie yesterday, she was eager to see him again.

Reggie clung to his patience when he glanced at the entrance to the ballroom. He had thought about Olivia most of the day and couldn't wait to see her. Last night he had begun missing her and wished he could have called her to ask her to meet him somewhere. This sneaking around was unpleasant, and his patience was wearing thin. He wasn't sure he would be able to hold out for another month. Because her brothers would be arriving in town this weekend, she'd said it wouldn't be wise for her to try to get away for a tryst at the Saxon on Saturday night, after the barbecue. The fact that Duan and Terrence Jeffries would be in town until next Wednesday meant his and Olivia's time together would basically be non-existent.

"And how are you doing this evening, West-moreland?"

Reggie turned to look at Senator Reed. The one man he really didn't care to see. "I'm fine, Senator. And yourself?" he asked, more out of politeness than a sense a caring.

"I'm doing great. I think, for you and Jeffries, it will be a close election."

Reggie wanted to say that this view was not reflected in the most recent poll, which indicated that he had a substantial lead, but he refrained from doing so. "You think so?" he said.

"Yes, but what it all will eventually boil down to is experience."

Reggie smiled.

"And the candidate I endorse," the senator added.

What the senator didn't add, Reggie quickly noted, was that he was not endorsing him. That was no surprise. The man had already endorsed Orin Jeffries and was working with Jeffries's campaign. "Sorry you think that, Senator, since I'm equally sure that I don't need or want your endorsement."

"And I'm equally sorry you feel that way, because I intend to prove you wrong. I will take great pleasure when you lose." The older man then walked away.

"What was that about?" Brent asked when he walked up moments later.

"The good senator tried convincing me of the importance of his endorsement."

Brent snorted. "Did you tell him just where he could put his endorsement?"

Reggie chuckled. "Not in so many words, but I think he got the picture."

Brent glanced to where the senator was now standing and talking to a wealthy industrialist. "There's something about that man that really irks me."

"I feel the same way," Reggie said. He was about to tilt his glass to his lips when he glanced at the ballroom entrance at the exact moment that Olivia and her father walked in. He immediately caught her gaze, and the rush of desire that sped through his body made him want to say the hell with discretion, cross the room and pull her into his arms. But he knew he couldn't do that.

Brent, who was standing beside Reggie, followed his gaze. "Do I need to caution you about being careful? You never know who might be watching you two. I don't trust Reed. Although he's backing Jeffries, I wouldn't put anything past him."

Reggie's gaze remained on Olivia's face for a minute longer, until she looked away.

Senator Albert Reed frowned as he watched the interaction between Olivia and Reggie. He had a strong feeling that something was going on between them, but he didn't have any proof. And that didn't sit well with him. He had suggested to Orin that he send for his daughter under the pretense that she could be an asset. But the truth was that he really wanted Olivia for himself.

He had discovered that women her age enjoyed the company of older men, especially if those men were willing to spend money on them. With his wife bedridden, he had needs that only a younger woman could fulfill.

When he had seen all those pictures of Olivia that Orin had on the wall in his study, he had made the decision that he wanted her as his next mistress. Getting her into his bed would be the perfect ending to his quest for revenge against the Jeffries family for what Orin's slut of a wife had done. Orin felt guilty, and as far as Senator Reed was concerned, his guilt was warranted. He should have been able to control his unfaithful wife.

He took a sip of his drink as he continued to watch Olivia and Reggie looking at each other. Umm, interesting. It was time to take action. Immediately.

"I'm sure England is just beautiful this time of the year."

Olivia nodded as Marie Patterson rattled on and on to the group of four women about her dream to one day spend a month in England. Then Olivia took a sip of her drink and glanced around the room, her gaze searching for one man in particular. When she found him, their gazes met and held.

She knew that look. If they had been alone, she would have crossed the room to him and wrapped her arms around his neck while he wrapped his around her waist. He would have brought her close to him and pressed his hard, muscular body against hers to the point where she would cradle his big, hard erection at the junction of her thighs.

"So, what about Paris, Ms. Jeffries? I understand you've been living there for a while. Is the weather there nice?"

Olivia swung her attention back to Mrs. Patterson when the woman said her name. She took a quick sip of her wine to cool off her hot insides before answering. "Yes, the weather in Paris is nice."

When the conversation shifted from her to the latest in women's fashion, Olivia's gaze went back to Reggie. He was talking to a group of men. Because the men had that distinguished Westmoreland look, she could only assume that they were relatives of his—brothers or cousins.

She was about to turn her attention back to the group of women around her when Senator Reed, who was standing across the room, caught her eye. He was staring at her. For some reason, the way he was looking at her made her feel uncomfortable, and she quickly broke eye contact with him.

* * *

Reggie had endured the party as long as he could and was glad when Brent indicated he could leave. He headed for the door, but not before finding Olivia. He smiled at her and nodded. He knew she would interpret the message.

He had been in his car for about five minutes when she called. "Where are you, sweetheart?" he immediately asked her.

"The ladies' room. I'm alone, but someone might walk in at any minute. You wanted me to call you?"

"Yes," he said hoarsely. "I want you."

The depths of his words almost made Olivia groan. She turned to make sure she was still alone in the ladies' room. "And I want you, too," she whispered into her cell phone.

There was a pause. And then he said, "Meet me. Tonight. Our place."

Olivia inhaled deeply. Meeting him later wouldn't be a problem, because her father was a sound sleeper. She knew it would be their last time together for a while. Her brothers would be arriving sometime tomorrow. She could pull something over on her dad, but fooling her brothers was a totally different matter. "Okay, I'll be there. Later."

She then clicked off her cell phone.

"Did you enjoy yourself tonight, Libby?"

Olivia glanced over at her father as they walked

up the stairs together. "Yes, I had a good time, and the food was excellent."

Orin couldn't help but chuckle. "Yes, it was good, and I was glad to see you eat for a change, instead of nibbling."

When they reached the landing, he placed a kiss on her forehead. "Good night, sweetheart. I'm feeling tired, so I'm going on to bed. What about you?"

"Umm, I may stay up a while and paint. Good night, Dad. Sleep tight."

He chuckled. "I will."

As soon as Olivia walked into her room and closed the door behind her, she began stripping out of her clothes, eager to get to the Saxon Hotel and meet Reggie. Going to her closet, she selected a dress. She felt like going braless tonight. Within minutes she was slipping her feet into a pair of sandals and grabbing her purse. Opening the door, she eased out of her room, and within seconds she was down the stairs and out of the house.

She couldn't wait until she was with Reggie.

Reggie stood when the door to the hotel room opened and Olivia walked in. Without saying anything, she tossed her purse on the sofa and then crossed the room to him. The moment she was within reach, he pulled her into his arms and swept her off her feet.

On other nights he had stamped his ownership all over her body, but tonight he wanted to claim her mouth, lips and tongue and locked all three to his. At the party she had been so close, yet so far, and he had wanted her with a force that had him quaking.

He pulled his mouth back. He was moving toward the bedroom when she began wiggling in his arms. "No. Here. Let's make love in here."

The moment he placed her on her feet, she went for his clothes, pushing the shirt off his shoulders and greedily kissing his chest. He was tempted to tell her to slow down, to assure her that they had all night, but he knew that they didn't. She would need to leave before daybreak.

Her hands went to the buckle of his pants, and he watched as she slid down the zipper before easing her hand inside to cup him. He threw his head back and released a guttural moan as sensations spiraled through him, almost bringing him to his knees. And when she began stroking him, he sucked in a deep breath.

"I want this, Reggie," she said as she firmly held his shaft.

"And I want to give it to you," he managed to say, slowly backing her up to the wall.

When they couldn't go any farther, he reached out and pulled down the straps of her dress and smiled when he saw she wasn't wearing a bra. Her breasts were bared before his eyes. He licked his lips. "Are you wearing anything at all under this dress?" he asked when his mouth went straight to her breasts.

"No."

"Good."

He lifted up the hem of her dress and planted his hand firmly on her feminine mound. "And I want this."

Taking a step back, he tugged her dress the rest of the way down, and the garment drifted to the floor. His gaze raked up and down her naked body. "Nice."

He then removed his clothes, and, taking a condom out of his wallet, he put it on. Then he reached out and lifted her by the waist. "Wrap your legs around me, Olivia. I'm about to lock us together tightly, to give you what you want and to get what I need."

As soon as her legs were settled around his waist and his shaft was pointing straight for the intended target, he tilted her hips at an angle to bury himself deep inside of her and then drove into her. She arched her back off the wall, and his body went still. Locked in. A perfect fit. Silence surrounded them, and they both refused to move.

Flames roared to life within him, and he felt himself burning out of control, but he refused to move. Instead, he held her gaze, wanting her to see what was there in his eyes. It was something he couldn't hold in any longer, but first he wanted to see if she could read it in his gaze.

Olivia stared back at Reggie. She saw desire, heat and longing. She felt him planted deep inside of her. But it was his gaze that held her immobile. In a trance. And she knew at that moment why she kept coming back, kept wanting to be with him when she knew that she shouldn't.

She loved him.

The result of that admission was felt instantly: her body shivered. In response, Reggie, she noted, never wavered in his relentless stare, and then he spoke in a deep, husky voice. "I love you."

She immediately stifled a deep sigh before reaching up and placing her arms around his neck and saying, "And I love you."

Reggie's lips curved into a smile before he leaned down and sank his mouth onto hers as his body began moving, slowly, then fast, in and out of her with powerful thrusts, stirring passion, fanning the fire and then whirling them through an abyss of breathless ecstasy. Over and over again, he made love to the woman he loved and captured her moans of pleasure in his mouth. And when she shattered in his arms and he followed her over the edge, he knew he wasn't through with her yet.

They had just begun.

He tightened his hold on her, and on weak legs,

he moved toward the bedroom. For them, time was limited tonight. Their passion was raging out of control. But moments ago they had let go and claimed love, and when they tumbled onto the bed together, he knew that tonight was just the beginning for them.

"Wake up, sweetheart. It's time to go."

Olivia lifted her eyes and gazed up at Reggie. He was standing beside the bed, fully dressed. "What time is it?" she asked sleepily, forcing herself to sit up.

"Almost four in the morning, and I got to get you home," he said.

She nodded. Although they had driven separate cars, it was the norm for him to follow behind her and see her safely inside her house. Excusing herself, she quickly went to the bathroom, and when she returned moments later, he was sitting on the edge of the bed.

He reached out his hand to her. "Come here, baby."

And she did. She went to him, and he pulled her down onto his lap and kissed her so deeply and thoroughly, she could only curl up in his warmth and enjoy. When he finally lifted his mouth from hers, he gazed down at her lips.

"You have beautiful lips," he whispered softly.

"Thank you."

His gaze then moved to her eyes. "And I meant what I said earlier tonight, Olivia. I love you."

She nodded. "And I meant what I said earlier, too. I love you." She didn't say anything else for a minute, and then she added, "Crazy, isn't it?"

"Not really. My dad met my mom, and they were married within two weeks. Same thing with my aunt and uncle. Westmorelands believe in love at first sight." He paused for a second. "This changes everything."

She lifted a brow. "What do you mean?"

"No sneaking around."

She wondered why he thought that. "No, Reggie. It changes nothing." She eased out of his arms and began getting dressed.

"Olivia?"

She turned to him. "My father is still running against you, and the election is not until the end of next month and—"

"You would want us to sneak around until then?" he asked incredulously. When she didn't answer, he said, "I want you to meet my family. I want you to attend my family reunion with me in Texas in a few weeks. I want you by my side and—"

"I have to think about my father. He would not want us to be together," she said.

"And I told you in the beginning, this doesn't involve your father. You are a consenting adult. You shouldn't need your father's permission to see me."

"It's not about his permission. It's about me being there for him, Reggie. I owe my father a lot, and I refuse to flaunt our affair in front of him," she persisted.

"And I refuse to sneak around to see you any longer. That's asking a lot of me, Olivia. I love you, and I want us to be together."

"But we are together, Reggie."

He was silent for a moment, and then he said, "Yes, behind closed doors. But I want more than that. I want to take you out to dinner. I want to be seen with you. I want to do all those things that a couple does together when they are in love."

Olivia sighed. "Then you will have to wait until after the election."

They stared at each other for the longest time. Then Reggie said quietly, "When you're ready to let nothing get in the way of our relationship, our love, let me know, Olivia."

Then he turned and walked out of the hotel room. As soon as the door closed behind him, Olivia threw herself on the bed and gave in to her tears.

Olivia slowly walked out of the Saxon Hotel, with a heavy heart. She'd told a man that she loved him, and then she'd lost him in the same day. She had stayed in the hotel room and cried her eyes out, and now she felt worse than ever.

Crossing the parking lot, she stopped walking

when she glanced ahead and saw Reggie leaning against her car. She stared at him, studied his features, not wanting to get her hopes up. Inhaling deeply, she moved one foot in front of the other and came to a stop in front of him.

They stood, staring at each other for a long moment, and then he reached out and pulled her into his arms and kissed her.

Moments later he pulled back slightly and placed his forehead against hers. "I love you, and I want you with me, out in the open, not sneaking around, Olivia. But if that's the only way I can have you right now, then that's what I'll take."

Olivia felt a huge weight being lifted off her shoulders, but she knew it was at Reggie's expense. He deserved to have a woman by his side, one that he could take to dinner, take home to meet Mom and invite to his home.

Leaning closer, she snuggled into his arms, close to his warmth and his heart. She knew that this was the man that would have her heart forever.

Ten

"You've been rather quiet, Libby. Aren't you glad to see us?"

Olivia glanced over at Duan and forced a smile. "Yes. I missed you guys."

"And we missed you," Terrence said, coming to join them at the breakfast table. "So why haven't you been your usual chipper self the past couple of days?"

She sighed, thinking there was no way she could tell her brothers what was really bothering her. But she could tell them what Cathy had shared with her. "I'm fine. I'm just in a funky mood right now. It will pass soon," she said.

Her brothers had flown in yesterday for the barbecue to be held that afternoon. It was an event she wasn't looking forward to, because she knew that Reggie would be there. It would be hard to see him and not want to be with him.

"There is something I need to talk to you two about while Dad is at campaign headquarters. It's something that Cathy told me, and it might explain why Dad decided to run for the Senate."

Duan raised a brow. "What?"

She then told her brothers everything that Cathy had shared with her. She saw Duan's jaw flex several times.

"I knew there was a reason I didn't like Senator Reed," Duan said.

"Same here," Terrence said. His eyes had taken on a dark look, and she now understood why the sportscasters had dubbed him the Holy Terror when he played professional football.

"I think we should talk to Dad to make sure he's entered politics for the right reason," Duan said. "If he did then he has our blessings. If he didn't, then I think he should reconsider everything before going any further."

Olivia nodded. "I agree."

"And what do the three of you agree on?"

Olivia, Duan and Terrence glanced up. Their father had walked into the kitchen, and he had Senator Reed with him. Olivia looked at her brothers. "It's nothing that we can't talk about later, Dad," she said quickly. She then glanced at Senator Reed, who was looking at her oddly. "Good morning, Senator."

The man had a smug look on his face when he responded. "Good morning, Olivia." He then slid his gaze to her brothers. "Duan. Terrence."

They merely nodded their greeting.

Her father studied her and her brothers and then reached into his pocket and pulled out an envelope. "Can you explain this, Olivia?" he asked, tossing several photographs on the table.

Olivia picked them up and studied them. They were photographs taken of her in Reggie's arms two nights ago in the parking lot of the Saxon Hotel. Several were of them kissing. "Who took these?" she asked, glancing at her father.

It was Senator Reed who spoke. "We have reason to believe Westmoreland himself is responsible. It seems you put more stock in the affair than he did. I was able to get these before the newspapers printed them."

Olivia glanced back at the photographs, and when Duan held out his hand for them, she handed them over to him. The room got quiet while Duan looked at the pictures before passing them on to Terrence.

"Were you having an affair with Westmoreland, Libby? Knowing he is my opponent in the Senate race?" Orin asked his daughter, as if he was insulted by such a possibility.

Refusing to lie, Olivia lifted her chin. "Yes. Reggie and I met at the firemen's ball two weeks ago. It was a masquerade party, so we didn't know each other's identity."

"But what happened once you found out?" her father asked quietly.

She sighed deeply. "Once we found out, it didn't matter. Our involvement had no bearing on your campaign," she said.

Senator Reed chuckled. "And I'm sure he convinced you of that. It's obvious he wanted to make a spectacle of you and your father. It's a good thing I stepped in when I did."

Olivia glared at the man. "You would like my father and brothers to believe the worst of Reggie, wouldn't you?" she said in a biting tone. "Well, it truly doesn't matter, because it's what I don't believe that does."

"And what don't you believe, Libby?" Duan asked, standing next to her.

She glanced up at her oldest brother. "What I don't believe, Duan, is that Reggie had anything to do with this." She turned back to her father. "And knowing that only makes me wonder who does."

At that moment the doorbell rang. "I'll get it," Terrence said, walking away, but not before gently squeezing his sister's elbow, giving her a sign that she had his support.

"So if you don't believe Westmoreland sent out these photos, Libby, then who did?" Orin asked his daughter.

"That's what I'd like to know," said a male voice behind them.

Olivia swung around. Terrence had escorted Reggie into the kitchen.

Orin frowned. "Westmoreland, what are you doing here?"

Reggie looked at Orin. "Someone thought it was important that a courier deliver these to me before eight in the morning," he said, throwing copies of the same pictures Olivia had just seen on the kitchen table. "I figured someone was trying to play me and Olivia against each other, and I wasn't having it."

Reggie then turned to Olivia. "I had nothing to do with those photos, Olivia."

"I know you didn't," she said softly.

"Well, the rest of us aren't so gullible," Senator Reed snapped.

Duan stepped forward. "Excuse me, Senator, but why are you here? What goes on in this family really doesn't concern you."

The man seemed taken aback by Duan's words. "If it wasn't for me, those pictures would have been on the front page of today's paper. I saved your father the embarrassment of this entire town knowing that his daughter is having an affair."

Terrence's smile didn't quite reach his eyes as he came to stand beside Duan. "You do mean his *grown* daughter, don't you?"

"She is having an affair with *him,*" Senator Reed said, almost at the top of his voice, pointing at Reggie.

"And what business is it of yours?" Olivia snapped.

"It is my business because I had your father bring you home for *me,*" Senator Reed snapped back. The entire room got quiet, and the senator realized what he'd said. Five pairs of eyes were staring at him. "What I meant was that I—"

"We know exactly what you meant, Al," Orin said in a disgusted voice, seeing things clearly now. "And just to set the record straight, I didn't ask my daughter to come home for you. The only reason I summoned Olivia home was to be here with me for the campaign."

Seeing he had lost his footing with Orin, Senator Reed said, "Aw, come on, Orin. You know how I spout off at the mouth sometimes. Besides, why are you getting mad at me? She is the one who is sneaking around with your opponent behind your back. She reminds you of your ex-wife, don't you think?"

Before anyone could blink, Orin struck the

senator and practically knocked him to his knees. "Get up and get out, and don't ever come back. You're no longer welcome in my home, Al," Orin said, barely holding back his rage.

The senator staggered to his feet. "Fine, and you can forget my endorsement," he said heatedly, limping toward the door.

"I don't need it," Orin shot back. "I plan to pull out of the race."

When the door slammed shut, Olivia quickly moved over to her father. "Dad, are you going to pull out because of what I did?" she asked softly.

Orin pushed a strand of hair out of her face. "No, sweetheart. Your old man realizes that he's not cut out to be a politician. Al had convinced me that running for office was what I needed to do, but it was not truly what I wanted to do. I never really had my heart in it."

He glanced down at the pictures on his kitchen table and then over at Reggie. "I hope for your sake that you care for my daughter, Westmoreland."

Reggie smiled as he came to stand beside Olivia. "I do. I'm in love with her, sir," he said.

Orin's features eased into a satisfied smile. "And the way she defended you a few moments ago, I can only assume that she's in love with you, too."

"I *am* in love with him," Olivia affirmed.

"Good." Orin then looked at his two sons. "It

seems our family will be increasing soon. What do you think?"

Duan chuckled. "He loves her. She loves him. It's all good to me."

Terrence smiled. "As long as they don't decide to marry before today's barbecue. I was looking forward to checking out the single ladies there today."

Orin rolled his eyes and shook his head. He then offered Reggie his hand. "Welcome to the family, son," he said.

The barbecue was truly special. Orin made the announcement that he was pulling out of the Senate race, and he gave his endorsement to Reggie. In the next breath, Orin announced that there would be a Jeffries-Westmoreland wedding in the very near future.

With Olivia by his side, Reggie introduced her to all the many Westmorelands in attendance.

"Just how many cousins do you have?" she asked him a short time later.

He smiled. "Quite a number. Just wait until you meet the Denver Westmorelands at the family reunion in a few weeks."

"Have you met them all?" she asked curiously.

"No, but I'm looking forward to doing so."

Olivia nodded. So was she. She and Reggie had discussed her move back to the States, and a wedding was planned for next month after the election. She was truly happy.

Reggie held her hand as they walked around the grounds, greeting everyone. She smiled, thinking she was beginning to like the idea of becoming a politician's wife.

"You know what I think?" Reggie whispered to her when they claimed a few moments to be alone.

She glanced up at him. "No, what do you think?"

He smiled. "I think we should go to the Saxon Hotel tonight and celebrate. What do you think?"

She chuckled. "I think, Reggie Westmoreland, that you are a true romantic."

He pulled her into his arms. "If I am, it's because I've got a good teacher." And then he sealed his words with a kiss.

Epilogue

The following month, in a church full of family and friends, newly elected senator Reginald Westmoreland and Olivia Marie Jeffries exchanged vows to become man and wife. Reggie thought Olivia was the most beautiful bride he had ever seen. His mother was crying. The last Atlanta-based Westmoreland was now married.

At the reception, when they made their rounds to speak with everyone, Reggie got to spend time again with his new cousins, the Westmorelands of Denver. Everyone had met and gotten acquainted at the family reunion. Talk about a good time. And it was great knowing there were more Westmorelands out there. Everyone on both sides was looking forward to spending time together, getting to know each other and having family reunions each year.

"I can't believe how the men in the Westmoreland family favor each other," Olivia said, glancing across the room at five of Reggie's cousins from Denver—Jason, Zane, Dillon and the twins, Adrian and Aidan. They were just five of the tons of cousins from Colorado, and she had liked all of them immediately, including the women her age.

Olivia had enjoyed the family reunion and getting to know Reggie's family. And they had accepted her with open arms. She felt blessed to be a part of the Westmoreland clan.

Later that night Reggie presented his wife with her wedding gift. They had flown to the Caribbean right after the wedding reception to spend a week at the Saxon Hotel that had recently been built in St. Thomas.

"This, sweetheart, is for you," Reggie said, handing her a sealed envelope. They had just enjoyed dinner in the privacy of their room.

"Thank you," Olivia said, opening up the envelope. It contained a key. And then she glanced at the card. She suddenly caught her breath and then stared over at Reggie as tears sprang into her eyes. "I don't believe it."

"Believe it, darling. You once told me what you wanted, and as your husband, I want to make it happen for you. Years ago I bought the building and when my first partner and I dissolved our business partnership, I kept the building. I think it would be perfect for your art gallery. It's in a good location."

She got out of her seat and went around the table to thank Reggie properly. He pulled her into his lap and kissed her with the passion she had gotten used to receiving from him.

"Thank you," she said through her tears. "I love you."

"And I love you, my Wonder Woman."

Reggie gathered her into his arms, and when she leaned up and caught his mouth with hers, he shivered as a profound need rushed through him. This was their wedding night. They were in a Saxon Hotel. And they were in each other's arms.

Life was wonderful.

* * * * *

THE MORETTI SEDUCTION

BY
KATHERINE GARBERA

Dear Reader,

The idea for this book came from an article I read in *Newsweek* about the most expensive luxury car in the world: the Bugatti Veyron. This car is not only superfast and overpriced, it is also very hard to obtain. They make only a limited number, so having one is for an exclusive few.

When I started researching the reason the car was called the Veyron, I found that it was named after an F1 driver, and the story for Antonio, Marco and Dominic fell out of that. Once I started thinking about a car company whose focus was driven by drivers, I knew what I wanted to write.

In *The Moretti Seduction*, Antonio has to try to get the rights back to one of the famous Moretti F1 drivers, Pierre-Henri Vallerio, a man who was once Lorenzo Moretti's best friend. But when Lorenzo married and then divorced Pierre-Henri's daughter, Anna, the two men became enemies. And Pierre-Henri took back the rights to his name being used on the Morettis' number one production car, the Vallerio Roadster.

Antonio is the second Moretti brother to choose between love and the curse that he's grown up under. For Antonio, a playboy and a man used to winning, falling in love doesn't sound threatening. But once he meets and starts to fall for Nathalie Vallerio, all bets are off.

Happy reading!

Katherine

Katherine Garbera is a strong believer in happily ever after. She's written more than thirty-five books and has been nominated for *Romantic Times BOOKreviews'* career achievement Awards in Series Fantasy and Series Adventure. Her books have appeared on bestseller lists for series romance and on the *USA TODAY* extended bestsellers list. Visit Katherine on the web at www.katherinegarbera.com.

To my daughter...awesomeness in human form.
I am always amazed at the woman you are becoming.
You are smart, funny, pretty and I love you very much.

One

The corporate offices of Moretti Motors were lush and exquisite, combining the best of Italian architecture with the cutting edge of modern design. No expense was spared in the five-story office building in Milan or in the state-of-the-art factory next door where the fastest and priciest production car in the world would soon start rolling off the line.

The only problem was a little sticking point with the name of the car. The Moretti Motors engineering team had reenvisioned the classic and most-talked-about model they had ever made—a 1969 sport roadster that had taken the sports car world by storm and made Lorenzo Moretti a billionaire. Now forty years later they were reintroducing the world to the Vallerio—the car named after the second Formula 1 driver to race for Moretti Motors.

The rights to the name were in question, something that Dominic, Antonio and Marco—the current generation of Morettis—hadn't realized until they had sent out a press release announcing their new car and gotten a cease-and-desist order from Vallerio Inc.

Pierre-Henri Vallerio had started the company after leaving Moretti Motors. Pierre-Henri had been a genius with engine design, and Vallerio Inc. was still at the forefront of that industry today. So it seemed to Antonio that they should be excited to have their name on the tongues of car aficionados everywhere.

The only problem was, as with everything that Antonio's grandfather Lorenzo touched, he'd somehow managed to piss off the Vallerio family.

"Do you ever wonder if *Nono* just had no mojo when it came to women?" Antonio asked his older brother, Dominic.

Dominic was the head of Moretti Motors operations. His title was CEO but he'd always been bossy even when they had been kids.

"The thought has crossed my mind a time or two.

Regardless of what his problem was, he left us a mess to inherit, didn't he?"

"You like the challenge of unraveling his messes," Antonio said. Dom was one of those men who lived for work. Bringing Moretti Motors back to the forefront of the auto world wasn't an easy thing to do. But a challenge like this latest wrinkle with the Vallerio family wouldn't ruffle his older brother. Nor him.

"We need the Vallerio family on board—yesterday."

"I know. It would have been much easier to handle it if we had realized that the rights to the name reverted to them. I mean, who would have signed a contract that said after twenty years of no production car we lost those rights?" Antonio asked.

"Papa," Dominic said.

Their father was a wonderful man and the best father in the world, but when it came to business, Giovanni Moretti just didn't care. Which was why he and his brothers had grown up the poorer relations of the Moretti family.

"Well, I have a meeting scheduled with the attorney." Antonio closed the file folder. The family's attorney was the older daughter, Nathalie Vallerio. From her corporate photo he'd sensed a keen intelligence, as well as an innate beauty that reflected her family's French heritage.

"Good," Dom said. "With Marco falling for Virginia, I'm afraid that our luck may be changing. I don't want to let anything compromise the new production car."

Antonio didn't know if his brother's falling in love with the granddaughter of the woman who'd originally cursed the family was going to change their luck or not. Antonio had never put much stock in luck.

The curse had been put on their grandfather by his onetime lover Cassia Festa. Lorenzo had spurned her love and Cassia, being a Strega—an Italian witch—had gone home and spent days getting angrier and angrier at Lorenzo. When Lorenzo decided to marry Pierre-Henri Vallerio's sister, Cassia had come back to Milan and put a curse on Lorenzo. The words of the curse had been written in her diary, and Virginia, Cassia's granddaughter, had figured out a way to break the curse. Antonio recalled the curse. No Moretti male would ever be lucky in business *and* lucky in love.

Antonio's father had no head for business—hence this mess with Vallerio Inc. But Gio had fallen in love with Philomena and those two had found a deep love and happiness in their life.

He and his brothers had grown up realizing they could be either wealthy or happy in love. Being practical boys, they had taken an oath long ago not to mess things up the way their grandfather had. That meant that they would be lucky in business and not risk falling in love and losing everything they worked to build.

Antonio had found that determination and drive covered what luck didn't. That and his refusal to accept defeat. His entire life he'd never lost at anything once he put his mind to it. And he certainly wasn't about to let Nathalie Vallerio win this battle.

"No problem. The Vallerio family will sign our agreement and I'll bring you back the contract."

Dom rubbed the back of his neck. "I don't need to tell you this, but I won't feel right unless I say it."

Dom rarely worried about the effect of his words, so Antonio raised one eyebrow at him in question. Whatever was on his brother's mind must be something outside the bounds of morality or business ethics. Though at times they'd considered doing things that were in that shadowy gray area, they never had.

Antonio believed that with his determination, Marco's racing talent and Dom's drive, the Moretti brothers didn't need to do anything shady.

"Are you still worried about the corporate espionage?" he asked his brother. They had first realized there was a leak of proprietary information last year at the start of the Grand Prix season. Somehow their main rivals, ESP Motors, had announced an engine intake that was exactly the same as the one that Moretti Motors had been working on for the previous six months.

"I think we can find our leak without doing anything illegal," Antonio said.

"Tony! I'm not going to ask you to do anything illegal. I have got a lead on our corporate spy."

"Then what were you going to ask me?"

Dom leaned over his desk, both arms resting on the dark walnut finish. "Use any means necessary, Tony. If you have to seduce her, then do it. Women like romance."

"Comments like that are the reason why you are single."

Dom made a rude hand gesture, but Tony just laughed. His brother was a great businessman and a natural leader, but when it came to women, Dom didn't trust them and he treated them like disposable commodities. Tony knew that was because of Liza, the woman whom Dom had loved and lost.

There was a knock on the door and Dom bade the person to enter. It was his secretary, Angelina de Luca.

"Sorry to interrupt, Signore Moretti, but the Vallerio family is here for Signore Antonio."

"*Grazie,* Angelina. Please direct them to the conference room and get them some refreshments."

Angelina nodded and left the room. Dom watched his secretary leave and Tony wondered to himself if his big brother wasn't as immune to women as he appeared to be.

"You know, with Marco's engagement to Virginia, it might not be a change in our business luck, only our love luck."

Dom shook his head. "For you maybe but not me. I think I have *Nono*'s bad woman mojo."

Tony laughed and stood, clapping his brother on the back.

"I don't have that mojo. And Ms. Nathalie Vallerio," Tony said, looking back down at her photo in the folder, "isn't going to know what hit her."

"Buon!"

Nathalie Vallerio had heard all about the Moretti family. Her earliest memories were of her grandfather and father plotting to bring down Lorenzo Moretti. The man was a legendary race car driver who was one of only four drivers to win the Grand Prix championship numerous times. The only person to win more championships was another Moretti. Marco.

And now she was sitting in the lion's den. Back in the one place her grandfather had vowed that no Vallerio would ever stand again. For being her personal hell, the boardroom was quite comfortable.

There was a trophy case at the end of the room with all the Formula 1 racing trophies won by the Moretti drivers, including the ones her grandfather had earned.

On another wall hung photos of the Moretti drivers and of their production cars. They were all good-looking men who had an air about them that seemed to say life was one big adventure. Her grandfather, Pierre-Henri, had always taken great pride that the bestselling production car had borne his name. And of course when Lorenzo broke Nathalie's great-aunt's heart and caused her to die early of heartbreak, Pierre-Henri had done everything in his power to see that Lorenzo no longer had use of the Vallerio name.

Lorenzo's son Giovanni had let the rights to the name lapse in the late '80s and since then Moretti Motors had floundered. But recently under the helm of Dominic, Antonio and Marco the company had resurged and was once again on the verge of taking the car world by storm.

Something that Nathalie was here to make certain they did without involving her family or their name.

She paced around the room, well aware that Antonio was keeping her waiting. Their appointment was supposed to have begun five minutes ago.

One of her pet peeves was tardiness. Disrespect

was the only reason Antonio was keeping her waiting and she would make sure he understood that she wasn't someone to toy with.

"*Ciao,* Signorina Vallerio. I am sorry to have kept you waiting."

She turned to see Antonio Moretti striding toward her. With dark curly hair and classic Roman features, he was quite striking. But that wasn't what held her attention. It was the intelligence and humor she saw in his obsidian eyes. This was a man who made her catch her breath—and that wasn't like her.

She lifted her hand to shake his and then realized that she'd been doing business with Americans for too long. She'd forgotten that Italians always greeted with a kiss on the cheek.

Antonio took her hand and pulled her close. The woodsy scent of his aftershave was intoxicating as he dropped a brief, warm kiss on her cheek. She stood transfixed feeling as if it were her first time in a boardroom.

All because of a handsome face, she thought, disgusted with herself and so very glad that her sister Genevieve wasn't here to see this.

In Antonio's eyes she saw a hint that he knew how he'd rattled her. She forced herself to kiss his cheek and totally ignored the fact that the five o'clock shadow on his jaw made her lips tingle.

She stepped back and retrieved her hand. "I only have twenty minutes to talk to you, Signore Moretti."

"Then I had better talk fast," he said with a grin.

She fought to keep her face stoic. She could see that he was charming. He wasn't trying hard; he just seemed unflappable.

She was too. She had spent her entire life being the reliable sister. The one that her father and grandfather could count on. She wasn't going to be a disappointment to them the way her great-aunt Anna had been when she'd lost Lorenzo's attention and the family name.

"I don't really see the point to this meeting. As you know, Moretti Motors has resigned all rights to the Vallerio name when you let that contract lapse. At this time we aren't inclined to license it to you again."

"You have not even heard what we are offering."

"I don't need to. You have nothing we want," Nathalie said. But she was interested in hearing what they were offering. Even her father thought that the Morettis must realize that they couldn't come to the bargaining table without offering substantial compensation. Her father wanted a half share in Moretti Motors. To be honest, Nathalie was confident they'd never go for that and she thought this entire exercise was one big time waster.

But she was here because her father had asked her to try to get this deal on the table. That was the problem with family feuds, she thought. There were never really any winners. No matter what deal she and Antonio negotiated.

"Are you sure about that? Everyone wants something they can't have," Antonio said.

"Well, if they can't have it, then they are just asking for frustration," Nathalie said.

"*Touché.* But I'm offering you whatever you want."

"Anything, Signore Moretti?"

"*Sì,* Nathalie. But you are going to have to do something before we can go any further with these negotiations."

Nathalie liked the way he said her name. The Americans she was used to dealing with didn't know the right emphasis to place on it the way Antonio did. "What is that?"

"You must stop calling me Signore Moretti. I am Antonio to my business associates and Tony to my intimates."

"Very well, Antonio."

He laughed and she found herself smiling. She liked this man and she hadn't expected to. From reputation she knew he usually won most of his corporate encounters, but then so did she and she'd expected him to be like other men.

She was pleasantly surprised to see that he wasn't. She had to remember that he was being charming for only one reason. He wanted something from her and he wasn't planning on taking no for an answer.

Antonio seldom met a woman he couldn't easily charm, but then he seldom met a woman who blinded him with only her smile. It didn't matter that there was something about Nathalie that said she saw through him. He tried to keep his eyes on business, but all he could think of was how soft her skin had felt when he'd shaken her hand and kissed her cheek.

He wanted to kiss her lips, to feel that full lush mouth under his. Every time she spoke he felt a little jab as she no doubt intended him to. He'd known from the moment he set up this meeting that negotiations between the Vallerio family and the Moretti family weren't going to be easy.

All of the research he'd done on Nathalie had helped him form the opinion that this was a woman who wasn't going to be easily swayed by charm.

Seduction, as Dom had suggested, wouldn't work either. She was too smart and she watched him carefully, adjusting her plan of action to fit his.

"Have a seat, Nathalie. And we will see if I can't find something the Vallerio family will take in exchange for letting us use the name that your grandfather made famous."

Nathalie brushed past him, her scent clean and re-
freshing, and sat down at the head of the table. He
bit the inside of his cheek to keep from smiling. It
was obvious to him that she was used to being in
charge.

He was the type of man who didn't like to let
anyone take the lead. But he knew sitting at the head
of the table didn't give one power. Power came from
the person who wielded it.

Nathalie too knew that, he suspected. She'd
learned it from her grandfather. Pierre-Henri Vallerio
was a proud French F1 driver who loved racing, de-
signing cars and, at the end of his life, anything that
would upset Lorenzo Moretti—the man who had
once been his best friend and his teammate on the F1
circuit for Team Moretti.

"Antonio, we do want something from Moretti
Motors," she said.

"Of course you do," he said. "I'm here to make
sure we both get what we want."

"*Bien*. Vallerio Incorporated wants half share in
all of the profits from Moretti Motors and seventy
percent of the profit from the Vallerio production
model. We also want the right to change the styling
of the Vallerio trademark."

Antonio shook his head. "I said we'd negotiate,
not give away everything my brothers and I have

worked to rebuild. What we are offering is a share in the profits from the Vallerio model and a seat on the board for the head of Vallerio Incorporated."

"Êtes-vous fou?"

"No, I'm not crazy. We think this offer is very generous."

She shook her head. "Of course you do. You are used to holding all the cards, but in this case, you must realize that you do not. Without the Vallerio name, you cannot release your new production car."

"Of course we can, Nathalie. We'd just have to rename it, which we are prepared to do if need be," Antonio said. He wasn't lying. It was a car that everyone talked about.

And they wanted to recapture the magic that *Nono* had first discovered with Moretti Motors.

"Then I suggest you start redesigning your car. As you know you can't use the name or any likeness to the original Vallerio Roadster."

She pushed to her feet and reached for her designer leather briefcase and he knew that this woman wasn't going to be an easy opponent. And damn if that didn't excite the hell out of him.

"Nathalie, we are just starting our talks. There is no need to get up from the table yet."

She shook her head, that beautiful red hair swinging gently around the shoulders of her conservative black Chanel suit that accented her curves. "Are you willing to meet our terms?"

"No, I am not. We can talk about a small share of profits for your company, but it won't be fifty percent."

"I'm afraid that our terms aren't really negotiable," Nathalie said.

"Then why are you here? You know that we won't agree to give you that kind of money."

"You asked for this meeting, Antonio. No one on the board at Vallerio Incorporated cares much for Moretti Motors. They would rather have Grandfather's name drop into obscurity than license its use to your family."

Antonio leaned back in the leather chair and thought about Nathalie. He couldn't keep just turning on the charm and hoping that would crack her composure.

She was smart and willing to stand her ground, so that meant he was going to have to reevaluate how he dealt with her.

"Why are you staring at me like that?" she asked. She rubbed her fingers over her lips and then tucked a strand of hair behind her ear.

"Am I staring?"

She tipped her head to the side. "You know you are."

"Indeed I am. I am looking for a chink in your

armor. Trying to figure out what makes you tick," he said, knowing that honesty was a very powerful tool in the boardroom because so many of his opponents often felt the virtue overrated.

She nibbled on her lower lip. "I don't have any chinks."

He threw his head back and laughed at her bravado. Damn, but he liked this woman. If she wasn't a Vallerio he'd even ask her out, but he knew that his family and hers had bad karma between them. And despite what he'd said to Dom earlier, he didn't want to take the chance that *Nono*'s bad woman mojo might touch him.

"I like the way you laugh," she said.

"Really? Why is that?"

"It makes you seem human."

He wanted to laugh again. "I am human, Nathalie. Do not ever doubt that."

"Well, your reputation would say otherwise."

"What does my reputation say about me?"

She leaned forward, bracing her arms on the table. The movement caused her blouse to hang away from her skin and he saw the briefest hint of the curve of her breast. He wondered if he should follow Dom's advice and seduce Nathalie—not to win the negotiation but because he wanted her.

"Well, the gossip about is that you are cold-blooded when it comes to business."

"I've heard the same thing about you," he said. And he had. She was known as the Ice Queen, and men that had dealt with Vallerio Incorporated spoke of her in unkind terms, often using words like *bitch*.

"That simply isn't true," she said.

"Then what is the truth about you?" he asked.

"I just believe that all is fair in love and war," she said.

"Me too."

"Well, then we are evenly matched and I'd say let the war begin."

Two

Nathalie knew exactly how she'd come to be sitting at Cracco Peck on Via Victor Hugo in the City Centre of Milan later that evening. She'd never met a man who was uniquely suited to her. But Antonio was.

He was smart, savvy and sexy as hell and she knew that no matter what the outcome, she was going to enjoy her negotiations with him. She liked being with him because unlike the previous lawyers she had dealt with, he didn't seem to resent that she was a strong woman.

He was several yards away talking to the chef-owner, Carlo Cracco, which allowed her to study him unabashedly. He had an easy way about him, and she realized the charm that she'd first noticed in the Moretti conference room was a part of him, not something he turned on strictly for women.

"Nathalie?"

She smiled as she stood up to greet an old family friend, Fredrico Marchessi.

"*Buona sera,* Fredrico," she said, kissing him warmly on the cheek. He had been at the university with her father. "Is Maria with you?"

"I'm afraid not. This is a business trip for me."

"For me as well," she said.

"With the Moretti family?"

"*Oui,* Fredrico."

"Your father is worried about this," Fredrico said.

Nathalie got annoyed at the way Fredrico talked to her as if she were still twelve. She'd been successfully handling the Vallerio family business for a number of years now.

"Papa knows he can trust me to do what is right by our family."

"*Bien,* Nathalie. We must have dinner when you are back in Paris."

"*Bien sur.* I will call your office."

Fredrico left and she felt a hand on her back as she started to sit back down. Antonio was back at their table.

"Nathalie, allow me to introduce you to Carlo Cracco."

They exchanged pleasantries and then the chef left and she was alone with Antonio at the intimate table for two.

"I am sorry for leaving you alone."

"It's okay," she said. "I'm not your date."

"And if you were?"

"Well, then I'd expect you to not leave me alone. A woman deserves to be the center of her man's attention."

"What does a man deserve?"

"The same thing."

"Are you a romantic?" he asked.

She shook her head. "No. I just don't believe in wasting my personal time with someone who's not worth it."

He gave her that crooked grin, revealing his straight white teeth. "Another point we agree on."

She shrugged one shoulder, trying not to acknowledge that Antonio was the kind of man she didn't believe existed. Someone who could be her equal in the boardroom and out of it. "What did your chef friend recommend for dinner?"

"I've never been disappointed with anything I've ordered here. My favorite dish is salt-crusted sole and dark chocolate crochettes with caviar."

She pretended to study the menu. This meeting was supposed to be about the Vallerio family. She had to concentrate and keep reminding herself that her family had been waiting for this moment for a long time. No matter how much she enjoyed the novelty of Antonio Moretti.

He was just that. A novelty. This was nothing more than a chance for her grandfather to even the score with Lorenzo Moretti, even though the latter was long gone from this world. Her grandfather wouldn't have a moment's peace until he knew that he'd been able to retrieve the honor that Lorenzo had swindled him out of.

"You look very serious, *mia cara*. Would it be so bad to let me recommend a dish for you?" He named two selections.

She looked up at him. "I see you are the type of man who will exploit any sign of weakness in your opponent."

"I thought we were beyond pointless shows of power."

Was that what he thought this was? She was always aware that she was a woman in a man's world and that she couldn't for a minute appear weak. She never cried, she didn't chat or laugh with the other women in the office and she certainly didn't let a man order for her at a business dinner. That was too fem-

inine, too girly, and she knew a man's man like Antonio Moretti would see it as a sign of weakness.

"Thanks for the recommendations. I'll consider
them."

He laughed. "You do that."

The wine steward arrived and Nathalie again felt
the pressure of their roles. The steward automatically talked to Antonio about the wine selection, and
even though he selected the exact vintage she would
have chosen, she spoke up and picked something different.

Meals and drinks ordered, she sat back at the table
and took control of this evening. "Tell me more about
the Moretti Motors plans for the Vallerio model."

"I can only share so much information with you
before we hammer out an arrangement. As I am sure
you can understand, it's privileged."

"Of course. Tell me why we should even consider doing business with the Moretti family again.
The last time we did my beloved great-aunt Anna
was destroyed by her dealings with your grandfather and my own grandfather was swindled out of
his share of the profits."

The feud between their families had at its heart the
emotions of a young bride. Decades ago her *tante*
Anna had married her brother's best friend—Lorenzo Moretti—and then found herself ignored and

very unhappy. Lorenzo was a womanizer and Anna spent three miserable years married to him before she left him, something that Lorenzo didn't even realize for another six months. It was that treatment of Anna that had started the feud. When Anna divorced Lorenzo, something that left her ostracized from her devoutly Catholic community in Paris, Lorenzo had terminated production of the Vallerio Roadster, saying that he wouldn't share profits with a family that had betrayed him.

He felt Anna should have sucked up her hurt feelings and stayed with him.

"You make us sound like the Machiavellis. I assure you we aren't."

"Assurances are okay, Antonio, but I'd rather have some facts that I can take back to my board of directors."

"How about the fact that Vallerio Incorporated hasn't had a new innovation in the car world in over twenty years?"

"We know what our history is," she said. "We aren't in the automobile world anymore."

"Which is why you are here with me. The Vallerio-Moretti collaboration went all wrong last time. Our generation will be the ones to put both of our family names back into the limelight and give them the place in history they deserve."

* * *

Milan was vibrant and alive on this cool spring night and Antonio took a deep breath as he led Nathalie through the center of town to the Piazza del Duomo.

He knew the key to getting the Vallerio team to sign the deal was to break down the monster that his *nono* had become to them. And this square was the very place to do that.

"Why did you bring me here?" Nathalie asked. She seemed a little tired and a little leery.

He hoped to use that to his advantage. "I wanted you to understand why history is so important to us at Moretti Motors.

"I know that the Vallerio family harbors some bad feelings toward the Moretti family, but I believe that that stems simply from misunderstanding the man that my grandfather was."

Nathalie tipped her head to the side. Her red-gold hair swung against her shoulder and distracted him, made him want to touch the cool silky waves.

"Your grandfather may have had another side, but I doubt he showed it to anyone outside of the Moretti clan."

"Then let me tell you about him now."

Nathalie sighed. "Do you really believe this will make a difference?"

Antonio looked at her standing there in the moon-light and knew that even if it didn't he wanted to tell her about his family. He wanted to change the image she had in her head of the Morettis as the big bad guys. "When I was a boy I'd come to Milan to visit my *nono,* he'd bring me here to church every morn-ing. He never missed a day."

"My *grandpere* was the same way. He said it was because God had blessed him on the racetrack," Nathalie said.

Antonio smiled to himself. *Nono* had told him how Pierre-Henri had been a devout man. It was one of the few positive things that *Nono* had ever men-tioned about Pierre-Henri. Lorenzo Moretti had known from an early age that the Lord watched over him each time he got in his race car and attempted things no other man had ever done.

"See? We already have something in common."

She arched one eyebrow at him. "Really? That's the connection you are going to make?"

"In this battle, with the stakes being what they are, I'll start as small as I have to."

"Why do you want this so bad? As you said, Moretti Motors can rename the car."

"Because Moretti Motors' Vallerio Roadster is revered by car collectors all over the world. The demand for this model, the styling and racing lines that Lorenzo designed along with Pierre-Henri's engine design are legendary."

"So you do need us?" she asked.

"Maybe."

Antonio took Nathalie's hand and drew her closer to the cathedral. "Did you know that Duomo here has never really been completed?"

She shook her head. "I don't know that much about this church."

"I won't tell you the history, only that she is constantly being updated and added to. The church itself is never going to be finished because there is always some way to improve on its beauty, to improve on its function.

"It is the same for Moretti Motors. We are not content to sit around and think that we have accomplished one thing and that is enough. We must constantly change, constantly drive forward into the future. What we are offering you, Nathalie, and the entire Vallerio family and its investors is a chance to be a part of our drive to the future."

Nathalie drew her hand free of his. "You are a smooth talker, you know that, right?"

"*Sì*," he said with a smile. "I think you like that about me."

"I like a lot about you, Antonio. But that doesn't

mean that I think doing business with your company would be in our best interests."

"Why not?" he asked.

She walked around the entrance to the cathedral. The statues that guarded it looked down upon them. This cathedral was one of the most famous in the world, the second largest to St. Peter's Basilica in Rome itself. Every Catholic in Milan was proud that this was their house of worship, and Antonio offered a quick prayer that God would make this moment a turning point for him and Moretti Motors.

"*Grandpere* used to say that Lorenzo was a smooth-tongued devil who had a way of seducing even the staunchest rival," she said. "And I can see now what he meant. I think you inherited Lorenzo's charm."

"You should meet my father."

"I guess all of the Moretti men have that gift. Do you know what we Vallerios have?"

"A gift for speed and a quest for knowledge," he said. The legacy of Pierre-Henri wasn't one that he took lightly. That was one of the main reasons why he, Marco and Dominic had decided to go this route. They could have taken an easier path with relaunching their production car, but the only car they wanted to relaunch was the Vallerio.

"We also have a way of seeing through the smoke and mirrors to the truth behind them," she said.

"Keep looking, Nathalie. There is nothing but truth and sincerity here. At Moretti Motors we want both of our companies to grow and prosper. We want both of our names to be remembered by history."

"You paint a pretty picture, Antonio, almost as pretty as this Gothic cathedral you've brought me to see, but I know that inside the walls of this place and behind the beauty of your offer lie more secrets."

"In the church perhaps, but I have laid all my cards on the boardroom table."

"Somehow I doubt that. It would leave you with nothing new to negotiate with."

He laughed at that. "Well, maybe I've kept one or two back."

"I have too. I'm not going to change my position tonight. To be honest I doubt we will ever be able to reach an agreement. There is too much bad blood between our families."

"But not between us. That was two stubborn old men who liked to argue. We are two young, vibrant people who know that there is more to life than fighting," Antonio said.

"Do we?"

"Yes, Nathalie, we do," he said, and drew her into his arms. "The night is young and so are we. Let's make the most of it."

* * *

At the end of the evening Antonio walked her back to her hotel. She was tired but pleasantly so. She had enjoyed the evening with him and she understood now what real charm was.

Her *grandpere* had been a brusque man by the time she'd gotten to know him, and a part of her was saddened by that. And she knew that the Moretti family—especially Lorenzo Moretti—was responsible for his bitterness.

But right now, as Antonio walked her to her room, that didn't seem to matter.

She knew starting an affair with Antonio Moretti was about the dumbest thing she could do. But she was so tempted.

They stood right outside her suite and though she had the feeling it would be unwise, she wanted to invite him in for a nightcap.

Antonio broke into her thoughts. "You are looking at me like I have something you want."

"You do."

"Name it and it is yours."

She tipped her head to the side. "Did you mean it when you said that all's fair in love and war?"

"Yes, I did."

"You aren't going to renege on that?"

"No, I'm not. Are you?"

"No. But I've found that men get mad when they don't win, regardless of what they've said before everything got going."

"I think you are trying to ask me if I'm going to act like a baby if I don't get my way. You should know that I am a man…not a boy."

She smiled at the way he said it. She knew Antonio was trying to seduce her. He wanted her to get to know the man behind the corporation and it was in her interest to do the same. Let him get to know the woman she was. Without that she'd never get the advantage over him.

"So, *bella mia,* are you going to tell me what you want?"

"Maybe."

"Maybe?"

"I think being mysterious has some benefits," she said.

"Indeed it does in a woman as beautiful as you."

She suspected that comment was at least seventy-five percent bullshit, but… "It's hard to resist such charm."

He laughed again, his deep, melodious tones wrapping around her in a dangerous way. She knew she needed to get rid of Antonio. She wasn't going to invite him in tonight, not after an evening of a full moon shining down over the city as she listened to

KATHERINE GARBERA 37

him weave his tales of the past in that deeply erotic voice of his. Tonight she wasn't up to sparring with him.

Her plan was to let him think *he* seduced *her* and she wasn't sure yet if she could sleep with this man and keep her emotions at bay.

To be honest she'd never been able to do that.

"Good night, Antonio."

"I will see you first thing in the morning for a tour of the Moretti Motors facility."

"I'm not sure—"

"You already agreed to it," he said. "It will do you good to meet the people who have worked on the design of the Vallerio model. I think you should see the pride that our workers take in being part of that legendary car."

"I think you should stop referring to the car as the Vallerio."

"Of course. It's just that I feel that once you see this car you will change your mind."

His passion for the car and for the company was obvious and it made her realize she'd made the right choice in not inviting him into her room. She had to understand that with Antonio the company was always going to come first.

And Nathalie had a personal vow about men who were workaholics. She'd never get mixed up with one. Her father, uncles and grandfather all had been workaholics—and had been absent in the lives of their children and wives, something that Nathalie didn't want for her own life.

Not that she was thinking of having kids with Antonio. It was just that getting involved with a man when you knew you were destined to be second in his life was not a smart thing to do.

And she was a smart woman.

She met Antonio's gaze and nodded. "I like your confidence. Tomorrow we will see if you are simply bragging or if you have the goods."

He arched one eyebrow at her. "*Cara mia,* do I look like a man who doesn't have the goods?"

She shook her head. "I refuse to answer that on the grounds that no matter what answer I give you, you will take it as a positive."

Antonio shrugged his big shoulders. "I'm used to making everything into a positive. That is why Moretti Motors is where it is today."

"I'd heard that about you. That you never take no for an answer. Much like Lorenzo Moretti when he ran right over Anna Vallerio."

"That is very true about my not taking no for an answer. But I promise you, Nathalie, I'm not going to run over you or your family. This generation of Moretti Motors is committed to doing business differently."

KATHERINE GARBERA   39

He walked away on that note and she watched him leave. She wanted to believe his words, but at the end of the day Antonio was still a Moretti. And he was going to put those interests before her or her family.

Three

Antonio's mobile phone rang as soon as he pulled out of the parking lot of Nathalie's hotel. He glanced at the caller ID. Damn. His brother was very well connected in Milan—hell, they all were— but if Dom was seriously following his moves that closely, then there was more at stake than just the Vallerio car model.

"*Buona sera,* Dom."

"How'd the meeting with Ms. Vallerio go?"

Dom wasn't one of those guys who wasted time on small talk. There had been a leak in their office over the last year and though they had gotten closer to the snitch, they still hadn't found him. Something that Antonio knew annoyed Dom to no end.

"Fine."

"I'd say better than fine. Genaro said that you were upstairs with her for more than thirty minutes."

"Gee, Dom, I hope that you don't think I seduced her in thirty minutes."

"Well…it is a little quick, but I figured you might have your mind on other things."

"No wonder your relationships don't last longer than a tank of gas. Women want to be seduced by a man. They want a man who will linger and act interested in them."

"Which is neither here nor there. What did she say?" Dom asked.

Antonio activated the hands-free option that was built into his GPS.

"Can you hear me?"

"Yes," Dom said. "What happened?"

"We talked. The Vallerio family isn't going to be easy. Are you sure we need his name?"

"I'm going to pretend I didn't hear that," Dom said.

"I just wanted to make sure. The negotiations are going to be long and hard on this one, and right now we don't need that."

That was an understatement. Not only was the

production date breathing down their necks, but they still hadn't identified the leak in their office.

As if he read his mind, Dom said, "I am close to figuring out the leak. I have set some things in motion now that will take care of it."

"What things?" Antonio asked.

"More proprietary information given only to two people. I've almost narrowed it down. If I'm right about who it is, it's going to be someone close to us."

"Whom do you suspect?" Antonio asked, not even thinking about the Vallerio business for a minute. Corporate espionage was a big deal and the leaks they had lately were enough to seriously cripple Moretti Motors.

"I'd rather not say at this moment. I'll take care of the leak. You just do what you need to with Vallerio. So, if you didn't seduce the girl, what's your plan?"

Antonio had turned onto the street where he lived. He had a nice place with assigned parking on the street. There were times when he wished he had the space his parents did in their palatial house outside of the city limits, but he liked city living.

He switched his phone back to the handset and got out of the car. His street was quiet this late at night.

"My plan is the same as it always is. Find her weakness and then use it to our advantage," Antonio said. Though for the first time he was torn. He really did believe that all was fair in love and war, but this time he didn't know that he wanted to exploit the weaknesses he found in Nathalie. He would, he knew, but this time he might regret it.

"Her weakness or Vallerio's?" Dom asked.

"Aren't they the same?" Antonio asked.

"In most cases I'd say yes, but if you are going to seduce the girl, then I imagine your thinking could get muddled."

"I have to remember that. There is no gray area here."

"Don't let Nathalie get her hooks in you. I don't think *Nono's* legacy is going to withstand two of us falling in love."

"So you don't believe that Marco and Virginia have broken the curse?" Antonio asked. He had read the words of Cassia Festa's curse in the journal that Virginia had. He thought about the curse he'd read.

My love for you was all-encompassing and never ending and with its death I call upon the universe to bring about the death of your heart and the hearts of succeeding generations.

As long as a Moretti roams this earth, he shall have happiness in either business or love but never both. Do not disdain the power of my small body. Moretti, you may be strong, but that will no longer help you. I am strong in my will and I demand retribution for the pain you have caused me.

Virginia might have broken the curse for Marco by combining Festa and Moretti blood, but Antonio wasn't too sure.

Dom replied, "Maybe as far as Marco is concerned they have, but I have the feeling you and I aren't out of the woods yet."

"You better be careful, old man. I would never be so weak as to fall for any woman."

"That's what Marco thought."

"Our baby brother was distracted by the races. I am not about to be."

"Remember that, Tony. We are on the cusp of taking Moretti Motors to heights that it has never seen before," Dom said.

Antonio knew that better than anyone. He and his brothers had been born to a legacy of both pride and powerful determination but also to the curses that Lorenzo Moretti had left behind. This mess with the Vallerio family was only one of them. If Dom was right and Marco managed to appease the curse put on them by Cassia Festa, Lorenzo's spurned lover, then thank the stars. The fact that no generation of

Moretti men had ever been lucky in business and in love wasn't going to be easily forgotten by either himself or Dom.

"Do I have your permission to act without checking in?" Antonio asked.

"Why?"

"I might need to act quickly to get Nathalie to agree."

"Nathalie?"

"Ms. Vallerio."

"Yes, you can act without checking in with the board. I will back you. But make sure that you get the results we need, Tony."

"Have I failed you yet?"

"No. No, you haven't."

He rang off with his brother and entered his house. The town house was opulently decorated and quiet at this time of night. He had never noticed the silence of the place before, but tonight with Dom's words echoing in his head and after the evening he'd spent with Nathalie, he wondered if he, like *Nono,* was doomed to spend his life alone.

Nathalie had a restless night's sleep and woke early. She stood on the balcony of her hotel suite and looked out over the city of Milan. In the distance she saw Duomo and heard the bells of the cathedral still calling the faithful to worship. She touched the small gold cross at her neck and thought of her father.

He wanted her to succeed because it had been his aunt who had been so badly used by Lorenzo, and his father who had been duped by his onetime friend.

She took a sip of her cappuccino and leaned back in the cushioned wrought-iron chair. Her family wasn't used to failing. After their disastrous business deal with Lorenzo Moretti, the Vallerios had made it their mission to never walk away from any deal the loser.

And Nathalie followed a proud tradition of being the one to make sure that her family won.

There was a knock on her hotel door and she glanced at her watch to check the time. It was too early to be anyone from Moretti's office coming to check on her.

She walked across the room with a feeling of dread. The timing was exactly right for someone to arrive if they'd taken the early flight from Paris.

She checked the peephole and groaned out loud.

"Papa, what are you doing here?" she asked as she opened the door.

Emile Vallerio crossed the threshold and kissed her on both cheeks. "We wanted to make sure that everything was okay here in Milan."

"We?"

Like magic, her sister appeared in the doorway. "I decided to come with Papa to see if I could help out in any way," Genevieve said.

Nathalie's older sister was renowned for her beauty and charm. Nathalie had never really minded being the smart sister, but if her father had brought Genevieve he must think… "Why?"

"Let's discuss this over coffee. I see you aren't ready for your meeting."

"Papa, I've been handling these things for a long time. I don't need you and Genevieve here. I can handle it. Go back to Paris."

"We will. After we are sure you know what you are doing," Emile said.

"I love you both very much, but I don't need you to tell me how to do my job."

"I know," Genevieve said. "But the Morettis can be tricky."

"I'm not untried. I can handle Antonio," she said, wondering if the words were true. Could she handle him? Last night had tested her and she suspected each day they spent together in the boardroom was going to make resisting him more difficult.

"Antonio?" Genevieve questioned.

"How is he in person? I've heard that he's a shark," Emile said.

"He's a lot like me. I think we'll get some of the

things we want, but we're not going to be able to rake them over the coals as you might have wanted."

"At the end of the day, I just want a fair deal for our family. Lorenzo manipulated my aunt out of her share of the Moretti fortune. We don't want that for this generation. She was promised a share of Moretti Motors and in order to get Lorenzo to sign the annulment so she could marry again he made her give up her rights to those shares."

"I agree, Papa. I've told Antonio that we aren't going to take just any deal. There's nothing in this for us unless they sweeten their offer."

She glanced down at her watch. "I have to start getting ready."

"Go ahead," her father said. "We will wait here for you."

She rolled her eyes. She knew how important this was to her family. Her great-aunt had been in a bitter marriage and had died young. They had almost no contact with her son and his family. The split of the Vallerio and Moretti families was complete.

"What are you going to wear today?" her sister asked.

"I don't need fashion advice, Genie."

"I know. But this man is used to very sophisticated women."

Her sister had a point. She was used to winning

in the boardroom based on her smarts and her determination. But with Antonio, maybe she could use
clothing and feminine wiles to distract him.

She sighed. "What do you think I should wear?"

Genevieve laughed. "I took the liberty of bringing
a dress with me that I think will look super on you."

"Do you really think so?" Nathalie asked. In this
case she deferred to the pretty sister.

"Nat, you goof, of course it will. You probably
already have him dazzled. This is just going to take
away his ability to look anywhere but at your cleavage."

She shook her head. "I don't like to use my body
as a tool."

"Why not? Nature made us this way, Nat. We're
not stronger than men but we are smarter." Genevieve winked. "And sexier."

"You haven't met Antonio."

"Really?"

"Yes," she said. "He's very sexy."

"Good. Then he'll use his looks to his benefit. You
won't be taking advantage of him by bringing sex
into the boardroom."

Her sister had a point. And Antonio had agreed that
all was fair in love and war. And this most definitely
was war, she thought. Last night he'd pushed the
boundaries of the attraction between them. Normally
Nathalie wouldn't try to be some sort of femme fatale,

but in this instance and with Genevieve's help she had the feeling she couldn't lose.

The meeting went long into the afternoon. Everyone else looked tired and frustrated, but Nathalie looked more beautiful than when she'd first come to the Moretti Motors building this morning.

Her father and sister were also at the table, and Dom had joined them when he'd realized there were more Vallerios in here other than just Nathalie.

"Let's take a break," Antonio suggested. "We need to all stretch and get some air. I've asked my staff to set up some drinks in the garden."

"I don't think fresh air is going to resolve the issues on the table," Emile said.

Nathalie's father had the same sharp intelligence as his daughter but none of her charm. He was still angry with Lorenzo and because of that he was a liability at the negotiating table. He sensed Nathalie knew it, but how did one tell a family member to get lost? He knew it couldn't be done. When family and business were mixed, there was no way to win.

"I realize that, Emile. I thought a break will give us all a chance to regroup and then get back to work."

"Sounds good," Dom said. "My assistant, Angelina, will lead you to the garden."

"Where will you be?"

"In my office," Dom said. "Antonio and I need a moment and then we'll be right down."

Angelina led the Vallerio family out of the boardroom and he turned to Dom. "What did you need to discuss?"

"That Emile is an ass. I don't see the point to all of this. His only agenda seems to be to taunt us with the fact that we can't use his father's name."

"I know. Give me a few minutes to think this over."

"I already have. Screw them. We are going to use Marco's name instead. He's made a name for himself on Grand Prix. One that even Pierre-Henri didn't have."

"But he doesn't have the cachet that Pierre-Henri does, thanks to that roadster he helped design and gave his name to. No matter that Pierre-Henri drove for our team—Team Moretti. The Vallerios think they are owed more than the compensation they were given. And because of the way *Nono* treated Anna Vallerio, I guess Emile is right to feel that way."

Dom stood up and walked over to the floor-to-ceiling windows and looked down into the courtyard garden where the Vallerio family was assembled. "I'm not going to play Emile's game. Whatever *Nono* did to his aunt, we're not responsible for it. This is business, not revenge."

"I'm not ready to throw in the towel yet. I need

some time alone with Nathalie. We both are seasoned at negotiating so I'm sure we can get to something workable."

"Not if her father is in the room. And why is the sister here? She didn't add a single thing."

"I have no idea. Why don't you offer to take them on a tour of the factory and show them the mock-up of the new Vallerio? That will give me a chance to talk to Nathalie privately."

"I think I'll have Angelina take care of that."

"You can't. Emile will be offended if it's not you or I doing the tour. I think it's important that we give him his due here. What *Nono* did to the Vallerios…well, from their perspective wasn't right."

"We didn't exactly prosper from his actions either. But I understand what you're saying. I'll do my part. It's just Marco's luck that he's not here."

"He will be next week and then we can send him to deal with Emile and Genevieve."

"But not Nathalie?"

"No. I'm the one who can handle her."

"Are you sure? You seemed distracted a few times."

He had been distracted. Yesterday he'd been struck by Nathalie's brains and wit more than her looks. But today she'd pulled out all the stops and he couldn't help but remember how she'd felt in his arms the night before.

"It was nothing. I can handle Nathalie," Antonio said. "Any word on the leak?"

"No. Nothing. But the information I am using as bait is highly sensitive and I don't think we'll hear about it for a few days."

"Should we bring in an outside company?"

"I thought of that. I hired Stark Services to help."

"Good. I like Ian and he's not afraid to go for blood. He sees corporate spying as a real international crime."

"I agree. He's going to get stuff we can use in court."

"Good. Does he know about the bait?"

"Yes, it was his suggestion. He's on his way here from London. We should see him in the offices in the next day or so."

Ian Stark had been a college friend of Dom's and he'd gone into his family's business of protecting the rich and famous. Not as a bodyguard but as an intellectual properties security officer. He protected the secrets of the famous and he did a damn fine job of it.

"I'm glad Ian's working for us."

Dom shrugged. "I was hoping to handle it ourselves, but I'm not taking any chances on this."

Antonio knew that. He felt the same way. There was something about going from moving in wealthy

circles to being beholden on their wealthier relatives
that had cemented in all his brothers the belief that
success was the most important thing in life. Money
might not be able to buy happiness, but it did buy
security and that was a very important commodity.

"We've come too far to fail now," Antonio said.

Dom looked him straight in the eye and smiled.
"True enough."

"You seem relieved to hear me say that."

"Sometimes I feel like I forced my dreams on
both you and Marco."

Antonio shook his head. As teenaged boys,
Marco, Dominic and he had made a vow to never fall
in love. They had promised and sealed it with blood
that they would be the generation to be lucky in
business. "We took that blood oath together, remember? We all want this."

"Yeah, until a pretty face comes along."

"I think that little Enzo won Marco over as much
as Virginia did," Antonio said.

Dom shrugged. "If he broke that curse on our
family I'll be happy, but I'm not convinced."

"Me either. I know that Virginia thinks the mingling of their blood broke it, but I remember that she
said that they couldn't fall in love. That seems like
a mighty big oops on their behalf," Antonio said.
"Not that I've ever put much stock in the curse."

"That's because you've never been in love."

"Nor tempted to be," Antonio said. "Women are meant to be enjoyed and savored but never permanently."

Dom's mobile rang and he stepped into the hall to answer it. Antonio straightened his papers on the boardroom table and felt someone watching him. He glanced up to see Nathalie standing there.

"So women are like chocolates?" she asked.

"I never said that. Just that men and women seldom want things for the long haul."

"What about your parents?"

"They are the exception to the rule. And I'm not sure that they would have survived as a couple if my papa was interested in business."

"I'm not following," she said.

"I'm the kind of man who is all or nothing, so a woman could never compete with my business interests."

She nodded. "That's good to know."

Four

Nathalie had come back upstairs to see if she could have a minute of Antonio's time. His brother and her father were both so stubborn and not at all suited to the kind of discussions that needed to happen if they were going to come to any sort of arrangement.

Hearing him say so baldly that love and forever with a woman was the last thing on his mind didn't really surprise her. From her experience, men couldn't have both a family and a successful career. Her father was interested in her and Genevieve only because they were involved in the family business.

Before they had graduated from college he'd only

been a distant figure, leaving their upbringing to their mother. Which Genevieve hadn't minded. But Nathalie always had. She'd craved her father's attention and from her earliest memory knew that the only way to get it was through Vallerio Inc.

"Dom is going to take your father and sister on a tour of the car factory so that we can have some time to talk about what we both want. I think together we can find a solution that will work for both of our families."

"I agree."

Nathalie did agree. She wanted this over with. She needed to finish up the negotiations in Milan and make her way back to Paris where her real life was. She didn't need to stay here under Antonio's influence any longer than necessary.

"Would you like to continue working in here?"

"Yes, I think it would be for the best."

"Okay, then, please have a seat."

Nathalie took the same seat she'd had before, expecting Antonio to sit across from her. Instead he took the seat right next to her.

"At the end of the day what will please Vallerio Inc.?"

"Besides our original offer?"

"Yes. You know I won't agree to those terms."

"I'm not sure. I know we want to make sure that the new Vallerio production car represents Pierre-

Henri's legacy. Profits are something we can haggle on, but *Grandpere*'s legendary status as a racer…I'd like to see that brought forward."

Antonio leaned closer, the scent of his aftershave surrounding her. Last night after he left she'd noticed that she still could smell and feel him around her. And she realized she was going to be feeling that until this business meeting was over.

"How do you want to handle that?" Antonio asked.

"He's already in the hall of fame, but I think I'd like to see the marketing campaign focus on why the car is named for my *grandpere*. I'd like him to be the focus and not Lorenzo."

Antonio made some notes on the yellow pad in front of him. His handwriting was scrawling and masculine.

"We can't leave Lorenzo out completely, but I'll see what we can do. What else do you want?"

"We will take the seat on the board that you offered."

"Of course."

"And we want profit sharing for our investors."

Antonio shook his head. "I'll have to talk to our board. Are you offering a reciprocal arrangement for our shareholders?"

"No. Why would I?"

"I don't know that we are going to go for it. What else do you want?"

"I'm still thinking seventy percent of the profits from the Vallerio Roadster."

"Well, you go back and see if you can get a reciprocal arrangement for us and I'll see about giving you fifty percent of the profits. Dom wanted to offer you guys thirty."

Nathalie jotted down a few notes. She thought she could talk the board and more importantly her father into accepting a fifty percent profit margin from the Vallerio production model. But the reciprocal deal…that was going to be harder. No one wanted another company to be a part of Vallerio Inc. On the other hand, they wouldn't turn down the money to be made from the roadster. R & D was expensive and they could always use more money for that. Though they didn't build cars, they developed engines and Vallerio Inc. was on the cusp of launching a new biofuel engine.

That was why they weren't too concerned about coming to an agreement with Moretti Motors for the Vallerio. The company stood to make huge profits from its groundbreaking engineering patent.

"I will have to go back and discuss it with my board. Why don't we reconvene in a couple of weeks?"

"You haven't heard what else we want," Antonio said.

"What else do you want?"

"If you can get your board to go for reciprocal profit sharing, then we'd like a seat on your board. Just so we can keep track of our investments."

"Antonio, let me be straight with you. The chances of us doing a reciprocal deal are slim."

"Then your shareholders should know they'll get no stake in the Vallerio Roadster."

She knew he wasn't going to give away the shop. And he knew at the end of the day that he wasn't going to give up until he had everything he wanted.

But then she remembered his comment from yesterday. *All's fair...* Pivoting her chair to face him, she leaned forward so that she was almost touching him. He glanced away from the table and down her body.

Inside she smiled. Genevieve's dress was right on the money and the perfect tool to distract Antonio. "I think we're both too tired to discuss this anymore today. How about if I send you an e-mail with the things we want?"

She was careful to keep her shoulders back so that her breasts were thrust forward. Inside she knew her business school mentor, Professor Stanley Muchen, would have told her that this behavior was deplorable.

But as Antonio leaned forward and took her hand in his she realized that she didn't care. She wanted to flirt with Antonio, and using her "wiles" to distract him was exactly what she needed to get what she wanted.

Nathalie suspected that Antonio wasn't paying as close attention to the meeting as he normally would have. She had to wonder if it was because of her new clothes. But that seemed a bit silly to her. Antonio was a sophisicated man who was used to attractive women.

But this wasn't like her normal boardroom maneuvering, and frankly, as Antonio leaned closer to her, she knew she was out of her league. The dress was just a costume she wore. It hadn't changed who she was on the inside. To be honest he knew she had no idea how to use her body to manipulate the deal.

"What are you thinking?" he asked.

"That I've started something I can't finish."

He stood up and leaned against the table in front of her. She arched her neck back to maintain eye contact.

"What do you mean, *cara?* This?" He gestured to the two of them.

"Yes, this. My sister said… Oh, man, am I really saying this out loud?"

"What did your sister say? That you should seduce me and get me to agree to all of your terms?"

She tipped her head to the side and realized that either he had thought of the idea of seducing her or someone on his team had suggested the same thing. "Perhaps."

"We are both adults, Nathalie," he said. "We are

attracted to each other. It doesn't have anything to do with our families or the companies they own."

She wished it were that easy. That she could simply turn off the corporate lawyer part of her brain and pretend that an affair with Antonio would have no repercussions beyond the emotional ones she felt when affairs ended.

"I'm trying to decide if you really believe that or if you are just trying another tactic to get me to agree to your terms," she said.

Antonio reached down and took her hand in his. "I always believe what I say. I might not tell you all the reasoning behind it, though."

"I am not sure—"

"Don't think about this, Nathalie. We both have agreed to go back to our board of directors and to discuss the new terms. There is nothing more to be said or done this day. Why not enjoy each other's company?"

"Why not?" she asked, shaking her head. "I imagine Romeo must have said the same thing to Juliet."

He laughed. "I don't intend for either of us to die and I'm pretty sure that Dom and Emile won't draw blood while touring the car factory."

"I'm not trying to be melodramatic. It's just we aren't two people whose paths have crossed without consequences. As much as I might want to have an affair with you—"

"You want to have an affair with me?" he asked, leaning forward.

Any other man would have been crowding her, but with Antonio he couldn't get close enough. She stood up and put her hands on his shoulders.

"You're a smart man. You can figure that out."

He reached up and touched the side of her face with one long finger and she shivered under that touch.

"I already have," he said, leaning up to rub his lips over hers.

She tunneled her fingers into his thick hair and held his head still. She wasn't about to let Antonio take control of any part of their relationship, and she had realized over the last few minutes that they were going to have a relationship. There was too much spark between them for her to ignore it. That wasn't true, she thought. She would have been able to ignore it if Antonio wasn't attracted to her.

But he was.

His tongue sliding over her lips made her entire body tingle. She tipped her head to the side and opened her mouth as he deepened the kiss. She had never reacted this quickly to a man before.

He tasted so good, so right. And for once everything about a man felt as though he was made for her.

He slid his hands down her back, stroking the length of her spine and then drawing her closer to him. As he sat there, she was nestled between his legs and felt the warmth of his body heat wrapping around her.

She pushed his suit coat off his shoulders and he shrugged out of it. She put her hands on his chest, wanting to feel his pulse beating under her fingers. She sucked his lower lip into her mouth and felt his hands flex against her hips. He lifted her up and set her on the table, then nudged her legs apart to make room between them for his hips.

The skirt of the dress she wore flowed over her thighs and onto the conference room table. She looked down at their bodies knowing that the time for talking was long gone.

"Antonio…"

"Sì, la mia amore?"

She realized she didn't know what to say. She wasn't going to call a halt to their lovemaking, so instead she took his face in both of her hands and brought their mouths together again. She kissed him with all the pent-up passion she'd carried for a lifetime. She refused to think of anything but this moment. Refused to occupy anything but his arms right now.

He groaned into her mouth and she felt his hands sweep up her sides to cup her breasts. She found his hips with her hands and drew him closer to her. She felt his erection nudging her center, but it only made her hungrier for him. She wanted—

A sound in the hallway made them pull apart. Antonio looked at her, something solid and steady in his eyes. Something she'd never really seen on a man's face before.

"I'm going to lock the door."

All she could do was nod because she knew she didn't want this moment to end.

Antonio locked the door and turned back to Nathalie. He knew the boardroom wasn't the place for this kind of encounter, but he couldn't wait to have Nathalie. Filled with the demands and pressures of their families as they were, he knew their coming together like this was a complication. Yet he couldn't walk away.

She looked so tempting with the sun streaming in from the tinted windows onto her red-gold hair. Her creamy pale skin was like a beacon, guiding him back to her. Unable to resist, he loosened his tie and hurried back to her side.

She was sitting just as he'd left her, her legs parted, those impossibly high peep-toe shoes on her tiny feet, the skirt of her dress draped over her thighs. Her breasts rose up and fell with her breaths.

"Lean back on your elbows for me, *cara*," he said.

She did as he asked. She was temptation incarnate, everything a man could want, and she wasn't doing anything but sitting there, just as she had all morning. She'd cast a spell over him just as powerful as the curse that Cassia Festa had put on Lorenzo all those years ago. But this spell was enchanting and he wanted nothing more than to indulge himself in her.

And he could. He wasn't going to deny himself the pleasure of Nathalie and her body.

Her green-gold eyes were shy as he tossed his tie on the credenza and unbuttoned his shirt, but once he touched her, took a strand of that red-gold hair of hers in his hand, all that melted away.

She stayed where he'd asked her to as he leaned down to take her mouth in his. She was the first woman he'd kissed who tasted like home to him.

She smelled of spring flowers and her skin was softer than anything he'd ever touched. He ran his hands down her arms, linking their fingers together as his mouth moved over hers.

He slid his hand down her side, finding the zipper hidden in the seam, and lowered it slowly. "I want you naked, *cara mia.*"

"Me too, Antonio."

Blood rushed through his veins. Antonio knew the boardroom wasn't the sexiest place in the world, but with Nathalie that didn't matter. The fabric of her bodice gaped away from her chest and he wanted to see more.

"Arch your shoulders," he said.

"Like this?" Her shoulders moved and the loose bodice gaped further.

"What are you wearing under this?" he asked, tracing his finger along the seam where fabric met flesh.

"Why don't you find out?"

He growled deep in his throat. Leaning forward, he brushed soft kisses against her shoulder and collarbone, following the lines of her body down to where the loosened bodice was and then he took the soft fabric in his teeth and pulled it away from her skin. There was no strap from a bra there. Just the smooth skin of woman.

He pushed the fabric out of his way, letting it pool at her waist. She was exquisite, her breasts just the right size for her frame, her nipples a pretty pink accent to her creamy white skin. He hesitated to touch her, wanting to just look at her for a long moment.

"Take your shirt off," she said.

But he shook his head. "You do it."

She shifted on the table and reached between them, pushing his shirt off his shoulders. He took her wrists in his hands and drew them to his hips. He caressed the length of her arms and then slid his hands down her chest, caressing every bit of skin he touched.

"Come closer, Antonio."

"Like this?" He drew her into his arms, held her so her nipples brushed against the light dusting of hair on his chest.

"Yes."

He rotated his shoulders so that his chest rubbed against her breast. She squirmed delicately in his arms.

"I like that," she said.

Blood roared in his ears. He was so hard right now that he needed to be inside her body.

Impatient with the fabric of her dress, he shoved it up and out of his way. He caressed her creamy thighs. *Dio,* she was soft. She moaned as he neared her center and then sighed when he brushed his fingertips across the crotch of her panties.

The lace was warm and wet. He slipped one finger under the material and hesitated for a second, looking down into her eyes.

Her eyes were heavy lidded. She bit down on her lower lip and he felt the minute movements of her hips as she tried to move his touch where she needed it.

He was beyond teasing her or prolonging anything. He ripped her panties aside, plunged two fingers into her humid body. She squirmed against him.

He pulled her head down to his so he could taste

her mouth. Her mouth opened over his and he told himself to take it slow, but Nathalie was making him go naught to sixty in less than 3.5 seconds. She was pure fire. Like putting jet fuel in a car, she was sending him skyrocketing.

He nibbled on her and held her at his mercy. Her nails dug into his shoulders and she leaned up, brushing against his chest. Her nipples were hard points and he pulled away from her mouth, glancing down to see them pushing against his chest.

He caressed her back and spine, scraping his nail down the length of it. He followed the line of her back down the indentation above her backside.

She closed her eyes and held her breath as he fondled her, running his finger over her nipple. It was velvety compared to the satin smoothness of her breast. He brushed his finger back and forth until she bit her lower lip.

Her intelligence, wit and unwillingness to back down at the bargaining table had turned him on before, but seeing her today as a sexy, confident woman had been more than he could handle.

She moaned a sweet sound that he leaned up to capture in his mouth. She tipped her head to the side, allowing him access to her mouth. She held his shoulders and moved on him, rubbing her center over his erection.

He scraped his fingernail over her nipple and she shivered in his arms. He pushed her back a little bit so he could see her. Her breasts were bare, nipples distended and begging for his mouth. He lowered his head and suckled.

He held her still with a hand on the small of her back. He buried his other hand in her hair and arched her over his arm. Both of her breasts were thrust up at him. He had a lap full of woman and he knew that he wanted Nathalie more than he'd wanted any other woman in a long time.

Her eyes were closed, her hips moving subtly against him, and when he blew on her nipple he saw gooseflesh spread down her body.

He loved the way she reacted to his touch. He kept his attention on her breasts. Her nipples were so sensitive he was pretty sure he could bring her to an orgasm just from touching her there.

He suckled the inside of her left breast, needing to leave his mark on her so that later when she was away from him and surrounded by her family, she'd remember this.

He kept kissing and fondling her until her hands clenched in his hair and she rocked her hips harder against his length. He lifted his hips, thrusting up against her. As he bit down carefully on her tender, aroused nipple, she screamed his name and he hurriedly covered her mouth with his, wanting to feel every bit of her passion.

He rocked her until the storm passed and she quieted in his arms. He held her close. Her bare breasts brushed against his chest. He was so hard he thought he'd die if he didn't get inside her.

Then he remembered he had no protection with him.

Maybe this time it was better to leave things as they were, he told himself. He'd just realized that keeping his head and his heart separate were going to be harder than he'd thought.

Damn, did he say heart? He wasn't the kind of man to fall for a woman. Even one as sexy as Nathalie Vallerio.

Five

Nathalie heard the door rattle a second before Antonio moved off her. She didn't regret what had just happened. How could she when every nerve ending in her body was still pulsing? But now the thought of getting caught horrified her.

"Mon dieu," she said.

"Shh, *cara mia*," he said, helping her off the table. Her dress started to fall down her body, but Antonio caught it and drew it back up her body. "We will finish this later."

She nodded. There was no way she'd deny herself an affair with this man now. She put herself to rights and turned to see he'd done the same. His shirt was buttoned and he had his tie back on.

"Antonio—"

"Shh. Say nothing now. We will talk later," he said, shrugging into his suit jacket.

She sat down in her chair and drew her notes to her, staring down at the table as if it held some kind of answer, but all she saw was what she should be focused on. Her family and the board of directors at Vallerio Inc. were expecting her to beat Antonio Moretti at this game. They'd expected her to get him to agree to her terms.

Instead she'd just been writhing in his arms. Even now she could fall into a simpering puddle at his feet because that had been the best orgasm of her life.

"Nathalie?"

"Hmm?" she asked, looking up to see Angelina standing there.

"Your family insists we accompany them on the tour of the factory."

"Very well. We had finished our discussion anyway," Nathalie said. She gathered her folders and put them into her leather briefcase.

"I can hold that for you at my desk, Ms. Vallerio," Angelina said.

The other woman was shorter than Nathalie with an hourglass figure that she showcased in her form-fitting sweater and pencil skirt. Angelina had big brown eyes and thick curly hair and a hesitant smile as she took the case from Nathalie.

"Thank you."

"My pleasure. They are waiting for you in the lobby of the factory, Antonio."

"*Grazie,* Angelina."

They left the boardroom together and Nathalie tried to force her mind to accept that nothing had changed between the two of them, but it had. The awkward silence between them underscored that for her.

"Antonio?"

"*Sì,* Nathalie?"

"I don't want this to interfere with our negotiations."

"It won't. I'm still going to be hard on you."

She had no doubt about that. Had she meant her words more for herself? Did she really need a reminder that she had made a mistake?

Had she?

Antonio hadn't been uninvolved and unless he was more of a playboy than his reputation indicated, she had to assume he felt something for her.

Did she use that to her advantage?

He paused to put on a pair of sunglasses and she wished she'd brought hers, for the midday sun in Milan was bright on this spring morning. He put his hand at the small of her back as they walked across the courtyard and she realized he'd fallen back into the mode that she needed to.

"I will send you an offer when I get back to Paris. It will expire in a week, Antonio. After that time we will no longer need to be in contact for the sake of our companies."

"What if I accept the offer you send?"

"I'm assuming you will," she said, not thinking about defeat. She had nothing to lose. But those words didn't ring true for her anymore. She did have something very personal to lose.

"Good. Will you join me for dinner tonight?"

"Um..."

"Not to discuss anything about Vallerio Incorporated. As a date."

"I don't think it's a good idea for us to be dating."

"Too bad. I don't care what other people think and you didn't strike me as the kind of woman who'd let that stop her either."

"I'm not going to go out with you because you dared me to."

"You're not? What would it take?" he asked.

The sincerity in his voice made her stop walking and all she could was look up at him. "I guess if you promised we'd go somewhere private, then I'd say yes."

"Consider it done. I'll pick you up at the hotel—"

She shook her head. "That won't work. I know we aren't teenagers and sneaking around might not be what you want."

"I like it," he said. "Right now being seen in public isn't in our best interest, for either of us. Tell me what you had in mind."

"I'll meet you in front of Duomo and we can go wherever you have planned."

"Okay. Be there at nine," he said. "Dress casual."

"Fine," she said, taking a step away from him. But his hand on the back of her neck stopped her. It was a light touch, a casual caress, but she shivered from it.

"If our families weren't waiting behind that glass door," he said softly, "I'd take you in my arms and kiss you again."

"I might let you," she said, just to let him know she wasn't passive. She walked away, anticipating the coming night as she'd looked forward to nothing else in the last few years.

Antonio stood to the back of the group as Dom led the tour through the factory. He'd heard the stories before and seen the model of the car they were already producing a million times before. This car—the Vallerio Roadster—was the cornerstone of the Moretti plan to retake their place in the car-making world.

He was more interested in planning his total conquest of Nathalie. He knew he'd made a lot of headway this afternoon in breaking down barriers between them. Tonight he'd do the rest of what he needed to.

He felt a twinge of something that might be guilt as he thought about using her, but it was the only way he knew how to take control of his feelings for her. He had to make their relationship about the Moretti-Vallerio feud. Otherwise he'd never be able to keep himself on track.

And that was the one thing he had to do.

He wasn't about to let all of the work he, Marco and Dom had done go by the wayside because of a woman. No matter how pretty she was. Or how much he liked her smile or even sparring with her in the boardroom. He and his brothers were the Morettis that would set the world on fire.

That wasn't going to be easy to do if he was lusting after a Vallerio.

While the Vallerio family congregated around the model car and Genevieve got behind the wheel, Dom came over to him. "What were you two doing locked in the conference room?"

"Do you have a life outside of following me around?"

"No, I don't. Moretti Motors is my life."

Antonio clapped his brother on his shoulder. "It's mine too."

Dom looked him in the eye, his hard stare very reminiscent of their grandfather's. "Good. I'm not sure what the Vallerio family is up to, but Emile is sitting on something big. He sounded very smug when we talked earlier."

"Maybe it's just his French attitude."

"Or maybe he's a bastard."

"Dom. We have to work with them. *Nono* messed around with a woman in their family. How would you feel if the situation were reversed?"

"I'd be out for blood."

"Exactly my point. Having Nathalie do the negotiation was probably the best thing Emile could do. I know that we will come to some sort of arrangement that works for all of us."

"I wanted to give you more time alone, but—"

Antonio shook his head. "We will probably do the next phase of the negotiations via e-mail. I think you and I need to show them that they can't walk away from this deal. I've given in on a few things, but they want the moon."

"This car should make them want it."

"I know that and you know that, but now we need to show them why," Antonio said. Dom was a first-class salesman and if he could genuinely talk to the

Vallerio family, Antonio knew he could win them over. And that really was the first step, because until they wanted to be a part of the new roadster they weren't going to give in. They weren't going to be willing to let Nathalie truly bargain with him. Without that, the Vallerio was never going to be more than a pipe dream.

"Why is there only a V on the hood and not the signature lion's head emblem that Pierre-Henri used on his racing uniform?" Emile asked.

"We don't have rights to that," Dom said. "We wanted to use it and incorporate as much of the Vallerio legacy as we could, but we only own the rights to this new V we've created."

"Well, if we are even going to be serious about talking of using my father's name, you are going to have to use the lion's head."

"Perfect," Antonio said. "I've asked Nathalie to go back to your board and send us an e-mail of the things you want. She knows how far we are able to go on some issues."

Emile glanced at his daughter. *"Tres bien."* Then he turned back to Dom. "I'm interested in seeing the rest of the factory. No sense in not knowing everything we'd be getting involved in."

"We do have some proprietary areas that I'm afraid we can't show you," Dom said, moving to the front of the group. "But given our shared past in F1 racing, I think you'll want to see this next area."

Dom led the way into the showcase area for their F1 program. The open-wheel car that Marco had driven the last season in his final victory was on display there. On the wall were photos of his brother in Victory Circle, and Antonio felt a rush of pride as he looked at Marco. Their younger brother was really dynamite behind the wheel. When they had been younger and talking about who would do what in Moretti Motors when they grew up, they all knew that Marco would be the face of Moretti. He craved speed the way Antonio craved winning and the way that Dom craved power.

Everyone walked around the car, which was polished to perfection and looked showroom perfect. But Antonio smelled the oil and tire rubber that had been in the air in Sao Paulo, Brazil, when Marco had become the winningest driver in Grand Prix history.

"Will you be running the Vallerio Roadster in any rally races?" Emile asked.

"That is our hope. We'd like to use it at the 24 hours of Le Mans," Dom said.

Emile stepped forward and ran his hand along the edge of the racing car. Antonio wondered if the other man had ever wanted to be a driver like Pierre-Henri.

From his own perspective he knew that not everyone inherited the desire to drive at top speeds.

"This is a fine machine. Even my father could never find fault with your F1 program."

"That is at the root of our company and something vital to Moretti Motors. We will always preserve this first, which is the main reason we are reissuing the Vallerio Roadster. We want to pay tribute to those who helped build the Moretti name to the heights it once enjoyed and will enjoy again."

"We want the same thing for the Vallerio name. My father shouldn't drop into obscurity," Emile said.

"If you are reasonable," Antonio said, "I'm sure that we will be able to come to an acceptable arrangement."

Nathalie convinced her father and sister that she needed time alone that evening to think over the proposal that Antonio had outlined. In truth she'd already made notes and recommendations to the board of the directors and had an e-mail ready to send to them in the morning. Feeling very much like a teenager, she got dressed and snuck out of the hotel to meet Antonio.

She wore a pair of slim-fitting jeans and a button-down white blouse that made her feel very American. She draped one of her favorite scarves over her head and took the stairs instead of the lift to the first floor.

Instead of hailing a cab out front, she walked the short block to the Metro station and found the proper train to Duomo.

She couldn't wait to see Antonio again. To be with him away from the pressures of their families. She rubbed the spot on her breast where Antonio had left his mark.

She felt she was doing something illicit and daring. And it was out of character for the straitlaced business-focused woman she'd always been.

She walked through the Piazza del Duomo. The crowds of people were a nice buffer and helped her to feel anonymous as she walked to the cathedral. She stood on the steps where she and Antonio had been the night before. Looking up at the wedding-cake perfection of the old stone church, she had a sense of how small her slice of time was. That her lifetime, like her grandfather's, was going to be nothing more than a wrinkle in time. Legacies, especially one like this, were all that they'd have.

She realized she was going to do whatever she could to make sure that her father and the rest of the board came to an agreement with Moretti Motors. Sure, she wanted to win and it would be nice to get this deal sealed. But she also wanted her grandfather to be remembered for generations to come. She wanted the car named after him to be talked about the way the Shelby Cobra was to muscle-heads of the world.

"Are you ready?"

He'd come up behind her, startling her.

"*Oui.* I wasn't sure where to meet you. Am I dressed okay?"

Antonio took her hand in his and led the way through the crowded piazza to a stand where motorcycles were parked. "You look perfect as always."

"Flattering me won't win you any points," she said.

"Why not?"

She studied him for a moment. He wore casual jeans and a cashmere sweater. His hair was perfectly styled and his Italian leather boots were shined. The bike he stood next to was slim and sleek. "Because I don't like lies, even the social kind, and I am very aware of what I look like in the mirror."

He opened up the seat and took out a helmet, handing it to her. "You will never convince me you don't know you are a beautiful woman."

She shook her head. "Beauty is in the eye of the beholder and I know that emotions can make a man see a woman in a different light, but you don't feel anything for me, Antonio."

"What makes you so sure?"

"Do you?" she asked, because she was fairly confident he was still playing a game with her. A game he was desperate to win. After seeing the Moretti show-room and the hall of trophies, she understood why succeeding was important to him, but she still didn't know exactly how she personally figured into his plans.

He set his helmet on the seat of the bike and then took the one from her hands. "Yes, I feel something for you. Didn't this afternoon prove that?"

"Ah, lust."

He laughed. "Women always treat that emotion with disdain, but it's very important to the mating ritual."

Mating ritual. Was he thinking of his time with her as more than just an affair? Or was he simply trying to throw her off her guard?

"Stop thinking so much, *cara mia*. Let's enjoy the night and the time that we have together."

"Where are we going?"

"To Lake Como. I have my yacht waiting for us."

"Isn't that a bit far for dinner?"

"Not at all. I wanted the evening with you and I want privacy. We won't have that here in Milan."

Still, driving two hours to the deepest lake in Italy didn't sound practical. But Antonio wasn't trying for practical. This was romance, she realized, looking into his dark blue eyes. He was going to a lot of trouble to seduce her; the least she could do was enjoy it.

"Fine," she said. "I've never ridden on a motor-bike before."

"I promise you are in good hands."

She sensed that she was.

He put the helmet on her head and pulled her hair free of the back. There was a sincerity and a caring to all of Antonio's moves that made her realize that he was thinking about her. Not about the Moretti-Vallerio feud or the deal that each was fighting tooth and nail to win at the other's expense.

"Is this okay?" he asked. "We can go to my place and pick up my car. But I thought this mode of transportation was more autonomous."

"It's fine. I think. I mean I've never ridden on anything without doors before."

"You'll enjoy it, *cara mia*. Riding on the bike is a sensuous feast."

She believed him. And when he helped her onto the bike and then put his own helmet on and climbed on in front of her, she realized how intimate the ride was going to be.

"Put your arms around me," he said, but she heard it close to her ear in the helmet. His voice was strong and deep and sent a sensual shiver through her.

She scooted forward and wrapped her arms around his lean waist. He put his hand over hers for a moment and then the bike roared to life as he started it. The machine vibrated between her legs and Antonio pressed against her breasts.

This was going to be the most sensual night of her life. For once she was going to forget about being a Vallerio and just enjoy being a woman.

Six

His family had had a home on Lake Como for as long as Antonio could remember. Lake Como was a jewel-like oasis of tranquility, a magical combination of lush Mediterranean foliage and snowy alpine peaks. It was one of the most beautiful spots in Italy and Antonio always felt more at peace as soon as he came out here.

He also remembered the five long years when they had to rent it out instead of coming here in the summers because money had been tight. All of that had changed as soon as Dominic, Marco and he had taken over Moretti Motors and rebuilt the family fortune in the last five years. It was that knowledge—the fact that his family had been so close to losing all of their legacy—that really drove him and his brothers.

He liked the way Nathalie felt pressed against his back as they drove through the winding streets toward Lake Como. Feeling her against him immediately brought back his arousal from earlier that afternoon.

He wanted her. No mistake about it. And he was past debating whether that desire had anything to do with Moretti Motors. He was going to be as fair as he could be with the Vallerio family. Not because of his interest in Nathalie but because he'd seen the pain in Emile's eyes when he'd spoken of his own father.

Antonio understood where Emile had been coming from. He knew too that pride was an important commodity. At Lorenzo's knee he'd grown up learning that the Moretti name was the most important thing that he, Antonio, had inherited.

"What did you tell your family you were doing tonight?" he asked to distract himself from the feel of her hands on his body.

"I told them I needed the night alone to prepare your terms." She hesitated, then added, "I don't want you to think that lying is a habit of mine."

"I don't," he said. He had a sense that Nathalie

was the type of woman who prided herself on doing what was necessary. He knew from his own experiences in life that sometimes meant white lies.

"You're a grown woman. I doubt your sister and your father are your keepers."

She laughed, the sounds soft and melodious in his ear. He liked riding like this. It had been a gamble to take her out of Milan where the deck was definitely stacked in his favor. But he had guessed that she needed to see more of the man he was than just the Moretti Motors company man.

He certainly wanted to see more of Nathalie. He wanted to see the part of her that wasn't tied to Vallerio Inc.

"My father still thinks of us as his little girls when we are in a situation like this. And he feels so tied to the Moretti Motors issue that he can't let me handle it."

"I can understand that."

"I bet you can't. Isn't it different for men? I mean your parents don't treat you like a boy, do they?"

He thought about that for a moment. His mother always did things for him that she'd done when he was little. Silly things like making sure his favorite soft drink was stocked in the house and sending him her lasagna for dinner once a week…

"I think it's different. My brothers and I are more interested in business than our father was, but I know he worries when we travel a lot. And my mother… well, she just mothers us."

Nathalie stroked her hand down his chest, resting her hand on his thigh. "It is different. My dad thinks I'm twelve."

Antonio laughed, taking her hand in his. "You are definitely not twelve."

"Definitely."

He noticed she'd neatly turned the subject away from business, which suited him. The last thing he wanted to do was have Moretti Motors be between them tonight. He wanted them to just be Antonio and Nathalie.

Two lovers who were enjoying the romance of this beautiful spring evening in the countryside.

"What are you thinking?" she asked.

He shrugged and turned off the motorway and onto a small road that curved around the lake to where his family's summer home was.

"That I'm glad you took a chance on me tonight."

"Is that what I'm doing?"

"Aren't you?" he asked, very aware that Nathalie could be playing a game with him. Hell, she probably was. All's fair, he reminded himself.

Though he had set out to seduce her with the romance of the evening and the beauty of his home on Lake Como, he realized that he had to be careful not to be seduced himself, because there was something about Nathalie tonight. Maybe it was the way her curves pressed against his back and the way her arms wrapped around his chest as he maneuvered the bike through the curves and turns of the road, or maybe it was something more.

"Are we close to your house? I read somewhere…"

"What?"

"Something very silly."

"If you read it I doubt it is all that silly."

"Well, this is. I was going to say I heard that celebrities lived in the area."

The comment was out of character for the woman he'd come to know in the boardroom. "My brother is considered a celebrity in some circles."

"Dominic?"

"Marco. You must know drivers too, right? Vallerio Incorporated is still very involved in the racing world."

"That is true," she said. "We still have patents for engines and stuff that my grandfather designed."

"Stuff?"

"Yes. Where is your home?"

"Right up here," he said, turning off the road and onto the long winding driveway that led to the stone cottage. He pulled to a stop next to the house and turned off the bike.

He removed his helmet and took Nathalie's from her when she did the same. He hung them both off the handlebars of the motorcycle and then got off the bike.

He held his hand out to her. She took it and slowly dismounted, losing her balance when she stepped off and falling right into his arms.

He only hoped she'd fall as easily into his arms later tonight.

Nathalie tried to pretend this was nothing new to her, that being on a private yacht in the middle of the very romantic Lake Como was like every other date she'd been on, but in her heart of hearts she knew it wasn't.

It had little to do with the yacht or the setting and everything to do with the man who was with her. Antonio hadn't brought up business since they'd set foot in his home. And clearly this was his home. He pointed out the home his parents owned and the ones that were his brothers'.

But he didn't focus too much on anything that wasn't personal. "Where did your family go on holiday?"

She tried to recall. She didn't dwell in the past and she'd attended a year-round boarding school with Genevieve. "We have a flat in London and my grandparents have a house in Monte Carlo. And we had holidays in London growing up. But otherwise we didn't really go anywhere. Except I had a pen pal in Cairo when I was a girl and I visited her one time."

"What about as an adult? Where is your favorite place to go on holiday?"

"I don't take them."

"How very American of you," Antonio said.

"It's not that…. You know how earlier I said my father still thinks I'm a girl?"

"Yes."

"I still feel like I'm proving myself to him and to the board."

Antonio handed her a pomegranate martini. They were anchored in the middle of the lake, music played through the speakers and a small table had been set on the deck of the yacht. There were lights draped from the mast.

"I can understand that. I think I've been trying to prove myself for most of my career."

"To whom?" she asked. "You said your father wasn't interested in business."

"Lorenzo. Dom, Marco and I made a promise to each other that we'd be the generation to get back the promise and the fortune that Lorenzo had made."

That made sense. It also explained why they'd come to Vallerio Inc. for permission to use the Vallerio name.

"Isn't it odd that no matter how old we get we are still trying to prove something to our elders?"

"Not necessarily odd," Antonio said. "I think we are both tied so much to our families that failure is simply not an option."

She smiled at him. "Maybe that is why we are both used to winning."

"Probably. But that doesn't matter tonight. I want this evening for us."

"You've said that a couple of times. I'm not thinking about work with the moon shining down on us."

He smiled over at her. "*Buon.* Are you hungry yet?"

She shook her head. She didn't want to eat right now. She could eat any time, but this moment with Antonio wasn't going to last forever.

"Dance with me?"

"Yes." She set her martini glass down. The music was slow and bluesy. A pure American sound that sounded familiar to her but she was unable to identify the artist. She soon stopped trying when Antonio drew her into his arms.

He put one arm around her waist, drawing her as close as he could, while the music slowed its pace. His hips moved in time with the drumbeat and hers soon did the same. She wrapped her arms around his shoulders as she'd wanted to do since they'd gotten off that motorcycle of his. She had been invigorated by the ride out here, and more than ever craved his solid body pressed to hers.

The passionate encounter they'd had in the boardroom that afternoon had whet her appetite for him. And now she wanted more.

He kept his other arm in the middle of her back, stroking her spine as he danced her around the deck of the yacht. He sang softly under his breath and she thought she felt herself falling for him.

Maybe it was the magic of this night or the fact that she'd spent all day battling more with her own family than him, but at this moment she realized there was something likeable about Antonio.

His hands skirted along her sides and around to her front. "You have the sexiest body."

"Thank you," she said with a confidence that she was definitely starting to feel with this man.

"You don't give an inch, do you?"

"Do you?" she asked.

"Never."

They were perfectly suited, she thought. Perfectly suited for not only the negotiations they were brokering but also a love affair.

"Antonio?"

"*Sí?*"

"I want more than this dance with you," she said, taking the bull by the horns. Neither of them would be satisfied with anything less than this.

"Me too. I want this evening and many more, *cara mia.*"

"Am I really yours?"

He tipped his head to the side to look down at her. It was hard to see his expression in the dim light, but when he spoke she heard his confidence and the sincerity in his voice.

"You will be."

She stood on her tiptoes and met his mouth as it descended toward hers. Their lips met and she darted her tongue out to taste his, but he opened his lips and sucked her tongue deep inside his mouth. Both of his arms wrapped around her, making her feel she'd found in his arms the one place she'd always searched for.

They ate a light supper and then he drew Nathalie to the aft of the yacht where he'd had his staff arrange large soft pillows for them to lie on. The staff had followed his instructions exactly.

He left her standing by the bow to go and change the music on his iPod/Bose system.

Soon soft music filled the air. The breeze was cool but not cold, and to be honest Antonio couldn't remember the last time he'd enjoyed an evening with a woman so much. And they hadn't even had sex, he thought.

"*Merci,* Antonio."

"For what?" he asked. He loved the soft sound of her voice. But mostly he loved the feel of her in his arms. He pulled her back into his arms, dancing her around the deck.

"For this evening. I really enjoyed it."

"It's not over yet."

"Good," she said.

He caressed her back and she shifted in his arms. Blood rushed through his veins, pooling in his groin as she turned in his arms and smiled up at him. An expression of intent spread over her face.

He led her over to the pillows and drew her down to them. He lay back against them and drew her into his arms. She curled against his side, her head resting on his shoulder and her arm around his waist. He stroked her arm.

"Climb up here," he said, gesturing to his lap.

"Not yet."

He arched one eyebrow at her. "Do you have something else in mind?"

"Yes," she said. "Take off your shirt."

He arched one eyebrow at her but sat up and did as she asked. "Now you do the same."

She shook her head. "I'm going to be in charge."

He captured both of her hands and turned so that she was under him. "I don't think so."

He held both of her hands loosely in one of his and undid her white blouse with the other one. Once it was unbuttoned, he let go of her hands and drew the blouse off her body.

The bra she wore was creamy white lace and afforded only partial coverage. He could see the pink color of her nipples through the pattern on her bra.

"Now you can do as you wish," he said, trying to pretend he wasn't her slave at this moment. He might want to believe he was in charge, but he knew he wasn't.

He growled deep in his throat when she brushed kisses against his chest. Her lips were sweet and bold as she explored his torso, then nibbled their way down his body.

He watched her, loving the feel of her cool hair against his heated skin. His pants felt damned uncomfortable. When her tongue darted out and brushed against his nipple, he arched off the pillows and put his hand on the back of her head, urging her to stay where she was.

Still, she eased her way down his chest. She traced each of the muscles that ribbed his abdomen and then slowly made her way lower. He could feel his heartbeat in his erection and he knew he was going to lose it if he didn't take control.

But another part of him wanted to just sit back and let her have her way with him. When she reached the edge of his pants, she stopped and glanced up to his face.

Her hand brushed over his erection. "Did you like that?"

"Sì, cara mia," he said, pulling her to him. He lifted her slightly so that her lace-covered nipples brushed his chest.

"Let's see what you like," he said.

She suddenly diverted her gaze and nibbled her lips, and he realized she didn't want to let him see what made her vulnerable. Moments before, he had no problems with letting Nathalie know exactly how much her body and her touch turned him on.

He told her so, in softly whispered words. He buried his face against her neck and drew her body close to his until she was pressed to him, tucked tightly to him.

He skimmed his hands all over her body, up and down her back, unclasping her bra and pulling it down her arms and tossing it away.

"I like the feel of your chest against me," she said.

Blood roared in his ears. He was so hard right now that he needed to be inside her.

But he took his time making love to her. Slowly he unbuttoned her jeans and drew them down her legs. They were long and lean and so soft to his touch. He pushed the fabric aside and then sat on his heels near her feet and just looked at her.

She lay back against the multicolored pillows. Clad only in a pair of pink panties, she was exquisitely beautiful and he was glad that he was the man who would claim her tonight.

He caressed her creamy thighs. *Dio,* she was soft and so responsive. It was as if she were made to be his. They were equals in other areas of life, so he shouldn't have been surprised that they were here as well.

She moaned as he neared her center and then sighed when he brushed his fingertips across the crotch of her panties. When her long legs shifted and opened, he moved between them, keeping his eyes on her.

The cotton was warm and wet. He slipped one finger under the material and hesitated for a second, looking down into her eyes.

Her eyes were heavy lidded. She bit down on her lower lip and he felt the minute movements of her hips as she tried to move his touch where she needed it.

He wasn't done teasing her or himself with the building passion between them. He nudged her panties aside and teased her opening. Tracing with his fingers, feeling the humid warmth of her body spilling out, beckoning him to come deeper. He teased her with just the tip of his finger, and she moaned and reached down to grasp his shoulders.

"What are you feeling?" he asked in Italian, needing to know.

"I can't translate Italian now," she said breathlessly.

He laughed. She'd brought him down to the very base of the man he was. He'd forgotten to speak English, which they'd almost used exclusively in their conversations. "Pardon me. You go to my head."

"Good." She squirmed against him.

He kissed her, and her mouth opened under his, her tongue tangling with his. He was so hard right now he thought he'd come in his pants. She was pure feminine temptation and he had her in his arms.

He nibbled on her and held her at his mercy as his fingers continued to tease between her legs. Her nails dug into his shoulders and she arched into him.

He rolled over so that he was under her. He stroked her back and spine, scraping his nail down the length of it. He followed the line of her back down the indentation above her backside.

She closed her eyes and held her breath as he fondled her. A sweet sound escaped her lips before he captured them. She tipped her head to the side, allowing him access to her mouth. She held his shoulders and moved on him, rubbing her body over his erection.

He shifted her back a little bit so he could see her face and watch her expression. Her breasts were bare, nipples distended and begging for his mouth. He lowered his head and suckled.

He buried his hand in her hair and arched her over his arm. Both of her breasts were thrust up at him. He had a lap full of woman and he knew that he wanted Nathalie more than he'd wanted any woman in a long time.

He realized that he wanted to erase all other men from her memory. Whatever lovers she had in the past he wanted to ensure she never recalled again. That when she thought of sharing her body with a man, his was the only face she saw.

Her eyes were closed, her hips moving subtly against him, and when he blew on her nipple he saw gooseflesh spread down her body.

"Nathalie?"

"*Oui,* Antonio?" Her voice was husky and her words spaced out. And he loved it. Loved the way she reacted to him.

"You're mine," he said.

He kept his attention on her breasts. Her nipples were so sensitive he was pretty sure he could bring her to an orgasm just from touching her there.

The globes of her breasts were full and fleshy, more than a handful. He licked the valley between her breasts. She tasted sweet and a bit salty. And like nothing he'd tasted before.

He kept kissing and rubbing until her hands clenched in his hair and she rocked her hips harder against his length. He lifted his hips, thrusting up against her. He sucked hard on her tender, aroused nipple. "Come for me, *cara mia*."

But she braced her hands on his shoulders and pulled her body away from his. "I don't want this to just be about me."

"It won't be. I want you to come for me, Nathalie, and then we can come together."

"Promise?"

"Yes."

She lowered her body to his again and he rebuilt her passion, aroused her with all the skill he'd learned since he'd had his first woman years ago. He was glad for the knowledge gained from his past lovers because he needed to do so much more than just please Nathalie.

When he felt her hips moving against him, he caressed her feminine mound and then slowly entered her with one finger and then two. She moaned his name as he teased her. He couldn't help but smile as he continued to draw the reaction he wanted from her. He kept touching her and whispering words of sex against her, telling her what he wanted and how to give it to him.

She gasped and he felt her body tighten around his fingers as her orgasm rolled over her until she collapsed in his arms, falling down on his chest.

A moment later he set about arousing her again. He held her close, enjoying the feel of her rapid breath against his neck. The creamy moisture at the apex of her thighs told him that he'd done a good job of bringing her pleasure.

He glanced down at her and saw she was watching him. The fire in her eyes made his entire body tight with anticipation.

"I want you inside me this time, Antonio," she said, no shadows in her eyes now. "I really want you. Come to me now."

Shifting off him, she settled next to him on the pillows. She opened her arms and her legs, inviting him into her body, and he went. He took his pants off, tossing them on the deck next to her shirt and jeans. Then he lowered himself over her and caressed every part of her.

She reached between his legs and fondled his sex, cupping him in her hands, and he shuddered. He needed to be inside her now. But he had to take care of a condom first. He fumbled in his pants pocket and pulled out the condom he'd optimistically put there earlier. He sheathed himself quickly, before coming back between her legs. He shifted and lifted her thighs, wrapping her legs around his waist. Her hands fluttered between them and their eyes met.

Mine, he thought.

He held her hips steady, entered her slowly, then thrust deeply until he was fully seated. Her eyes widened with each inch he gave her. She clutched at his hips as he started thrusting, holding him to her, her eyes half closed and her head tipped back.

He leaned down and caught one of her nipples in his teeth, scraping very gently. She started to tighten around him. Her hips moved faster, demanding more, but he kept the pace slow, steady. He wanted her to come again before he did.

He suckled her nipple and rotated his hips to catch her pleasure point with each thrust and he felt her hands clench in his hair as she threw her head back and a climax ripped through her.

He varied his thrusts, finding a rhythm that would draw out the tension at the base of his spine. Something that would make his time in her body, wrapped in her silky limbs, last forever.

Leaning back on his haunches, he tipped her hips up to give him deeper access to her body. Then she scraped her nails down his back, clutched his buttocks and drew him in. His blood roared in his ears as he felt everything in his world center to this one woman.

He held her in his arms afterward, neither of them saying anything, and he feared that was because both of them knew that this had changed the stakes in their friendly little game. The family feud that had started with her great-aunt and his grandfather couldn't be continued with their generation.

Seven

Back in Paris, life seemed too hectic. Her father and sister had gone back to their lives and now that she was home Nathalie thought that Antonio and the night they'd spent together would seem less intense, but it wasn't. She had been working day and night not just on the Moretti Motors negotiations but also on the other work that crossed her desk.

Her parents had invited her to dinner tonight and she'd tried to turn them down, but Nathalie never could disappoint her mother.

It was the same with Genevieve. Maybe it was because they'd grown up closer to their mother than their father. Whatever the reason, she admitted as she drove her Peugeot on the roundabout in front of the Arc de Triomphe, she didn't care. She wanted to get through dinner as quickly as she could and then get back to work.

It was the only way she'd found to keep her mind off of Antonio. When she was at home in her luxurious condo, all she did was imagine him there with her. When she slept he haunted her dreams, making love to her and speaking to her in that beautiful Italian voice of his. When she worked out at the gym, she sometimes thought she heard his footfalls on the treadmill next to hers.

He was haunting her. Damn him.

In the office he'd sent her a very official-sounding e-mail telling her that he looked forward to hearing from her on the Vallerio Roadster matter.

And then at home she'd received a vase of yellow daffodils, which were still on her front hall table. They were the first things she saw when she came home and the last things she noticed when she left. The note he'd sent was sweet and sexy. Everything she'd expect from Antonio.

And a part of her…okay, all of her hoped that this relationship was more than an affair. But she was afraid to believe it.

He had said that they should keep their dating

private and that it had nothing to do with the negotiations they were both embroiled in right now, but she worried that she wouldn't be able to.

Her mobile rang as she approached the restaurant and pulled into the valet lane. She glanced down at the caller ID and saw that it was an Italian number. Antonio?

She hurried out of her car and into Ladurée. The restaurant was over a century old and a famous institution on the Champs-Elysées.

"Bonjour, c'est Nathalie," she said, answering her phone.

"Ciao, cara mia. Did you get the flowers I sent?"

"Yes, I did. Thank you for them."

"You're welcome. What are you doing?"

"Having dinner with my family. I'm sorry I haven't sent you a thank-you note."

"That's nothing. Why haven't you returned my calls?" he asked.

She shrugged and then realized he couldn't see that response. "I'm not sure. I've been busy."

She realized she was making excuses and she knew better than that. "I guess I wanted a chance to get you out of my head."

"Did it work?" he asked.

"No. Not at all."

"Well, then you should have called me back. I've missed the sound of your voice."

"Have you?"

"Indeed. When will you be back in Milan?"

"Next week. I'm meeting with our board tomorrow and I should have a counteroffer for you."

"You know how far I'm willing to go," he said.

She wondered if she really did know. How far was Antonio willing to go to get the deal closed? Was he willing to seduce her?

She didn't know. She doubted seducing her would be of benefit for him.

"Why so silent?"

"I'm just thinking," she said. She was dreaming of this man who was her rival. This man who wanted something from her family that they had fought to hold on to. And she was going to try to find a way to make it work for him. Because she wanted to honor her grandfather's memory, but also because she wanted to get this deal off the table so she could see what lay between them.

"Nathalie?"

"Um…pardon me. I've got to go. My parents are waiting."

"Call me when you are done with dinner," he said.

"It will be late."

"That's okay, I'll be up."

She hesitated. But then she thought, why the hell not? She'd be thinking about him anyway.

"All right. I'll call. I only have your office number."

"I'll send you a text with all my numbers. I'll be at home after ten."

"Very well. *Bonne nuit,* Antonio."

"Until later."

He disconnected the call and she held on to her BlackBerry for another minute, standing in the crowded foyer of the restaurant trying to regain her equilibrium.

"Nathalie!"

She turned to see Genevieve waving at her. She made her way over to her sister and hugged her. "Are Mom and Dad here?"

"Not yet. I told them we'd meet them in the bar," Genevieve said, leading the way to the bar. They both ordered a glass of wine and found a seat at one of the high tables.

"What happened that last night in Milan?"

"What? Nothing. I told you I stayed in," she said.

"I followed you to Duomo and saw you leave with Antonio."

"Busted?"

"Big-time. So what's up?"

"I...I don't know. It really has nothing to do with the negotiations."

"How can you say that? He's a Moretti. Lorenzo already proved that the men in that family are all about business."

Nathalie took a sip of her drink. "I know. But Antonio is different."

"Is he really?"

"Yes, I think he is. I know that I might be making a mistake, but I think I can handle him in the boardroom and out."

"I hope you are right," Genevieve said.

Nathalie did too. And she knew no matter what, she had to be very careful that she didn't forget that with Moretti men, business always came first.

Antonio strolled down the hall to Dominic's office. Angelina was sitting at her desk despite the fact that it was well past five.

"*Ciao,* Antonio," she said.

"*Ciao,* Angelina. Is my brother available?"

"*Sì.* Marco has just gone in."

"*Grazie.*"

He entered the office and closed the heavy oak door behind him. Marco looked relaxed and happy, despite the fact that it was the beginning of the F1 World Championship race calendar. "*Ciao,* Marco. Congratulations on your win in Behrain last weekend."

He smiled. "*Grazie*. Everyone is gunning for me this year."

"I would imagine so," Dom said.

"How is Virginia and little Enzo?"

"Very good. We'd love it if you'd join us for dinner tonight."

He nodded.

"If that's settled, can we get down to business?" Dom said.

Antonio sat in the other guest chair, listening with half an ear as Dom caught Marco up on everything that had been happening the last two weeks while he'd been out of town.

He studied his younger brother and realized, for the first time since Marco had fallen in love with Virginia, that he envied his brother. Which was ridiculous. He was a bachelor. He loved his single life, yet a part of him wanted someone to come home to. Wanted a partner that would always be there for him.

He rubbed the back of his neck, knowing that he wasn't going to find that with Nathalie. He couldn't. No matter how much he wanted her in his life, his priority had to always be Moretti Motors.

"Tony?"

"Hmm?"

"Did you hear what I said?" Dom asked. "The leak is in the corporate offices. I've asked Ian to meet us after the dinner hour tonight. He has some information that he didn't want to give to me at the office."

"I don't like the sound of that," Antonio said. "He must think that the problem is in one of our offices."

"I'm not going to guess at anything. Can you join us after dinner?"

He thought about the call he'd coerced Nathalie into making. He wanted to talk to her, but canceling an important meeting for her... Well, that would be giving her too much power in his personal life and he wasn't willing to do that just now. "*Sì*, I'm available."

"*Buon.* So, where do we stand on the Vallerio negotiations?"

"I offered them a share of the profits from the roadster, and a seat on the board for the CEO of Vallerio Incorporated. They want to do profit sharing companywide for all of their shareholders. I've told them we'll consider it if it's a reciprocal arrangement."

"Is that fiscally a good idea?" Dom asked.

"I am doing some research on their profit and loss statements for the last couple of years. They are expecting a huge profit in the third quarter this year, but I haven't been able to figure out why."

"Doesn't Nathalie know?" Dom asked.

"I'm sure she does but I haven't asked her yet. She

is busy with figuring out what her board will accept and preparing a counteroffer."

"I thought you were working on seducing her to get more information," Dom said.

"It's never that easy with women," Marco said. "You must know that, Dom."

"Indeed, but this time I think it's important that Tony pull out all the stops."

"Are you giving him romantic advice?" Marco asked. "What have you two been up to while I've been racing?"

Antonio knew this was going to continue going downhill. Marco would tease him endlessly because Dom had suggested he seduce Nathalie. Antonio realized that to anyone on the outside the ploy was going to seem cold and calculated.

Still, Antonio knew he hadn't seduced her for any reason other than that he wanted her. He was attracted to her body and soul, he thought.

"Tony?"

"Dom suggested I use sex as another means of weakening her defenses."

"Did you? That's ethically wrong," Marco said.

"Of course it is. Nathalie and I are both very aware of our family rivalry," Antonio said.

"That's good. Do you like her?" Marco asked.

He shrugged. No way was he going to talk about

Nathalie with his brothers. Dom would find it uncomfortable if he mentioned that he was attracted to Nathalie in a way he'd never been attracted to another woman. And he knew that he didn't want to have to choose between his loyalty to his brothers and to Nathalie.

Was he loyal to her? He didn't like to think that she had any control over him, but he knew she did.

"Of course I like her. She's sexy and smart, a lethal combination in any woman."

Marco laughed and Dom looked uncomfortable.

"Can you handle her?"

"She's only a woman," Antonio said. Now if he could only convince his emotions of that fact.

Nathalie waved her mother and sister off as they went to the bakery section of the restaurant to buy something yummy for all of them. Her father was going to ride back to her parents' house with her. He wanted, as he'd said, to make sure she still realized that the Vallerio family had been done a grave injustice.

The valet brought her car and she got in after tipping the man. Her father sat quietly until she'd navigated out of the traffic on the Champs-Elysées.

"Thank you for all your hard work with the Moretti Motors people," Emile said, "but I don't think this newest offer of theirs is going to be one we can accept."

"Why not? I think the terms are good and that we will make the profit that we wanted to from this agreement."

Nathalie made a left turn and then glanced over at her father. His mouth was pinched tight and he looked like a very old man for a minute. "Papa?"

"I'm fine. We don't need the Morettis to make a profit. I don't want to give away the farm just to have a piece of their pie."

She shook her head. "I know what I'm doing."

"Do you? I've always been impressed by your business savvy and the way you conduct yourself, but Antonio Moretti…he's slick and smooth and I'm not sure you can handle him."

If her father only knew. She'd faced men like Antonio on more than one occasion and always come back a winner. "Papa, don't you trust me?"

"*Oui, cherie,* I trust you."

"Then why are you asking me all these questions?"

"I guess it is simply that I don't trust the Moretti men not to do something underhanded. And you are my daughter, Nathalie. I don't want you hurt the way my aunt Anna was."

She understood that. "I'm not *Tante* Anna, Papa, and I'm not going to let Antonio use me the way that Lorenzo did her. I'm more than capable of handling myself around Antonio."

"*Bien.* That's all I wanted to say. Also we cannot accept less than seventy percent of the profits from the roadster. I talked to the rest of the board already and they are adamant as well."

Nathalie turned onto the street where her parents lived. "Papa, that's impossible. Antonio has already turned that offer down."

"Then tell him he'll have to try harder to come up with a better offer than he has so far."

"I will."

Nathalie parked on the street in front of her parents' house with a feeling that her father was never going to accept any relationship she had with Antonio. And that made her a little sad because she had started to see Antonio as a man. Not the Moretti monster that her family had always painted the Moretti heirs to be.

Holding his nephew reinforced to Antonio how important it was to focus on the legacy of Moretti Motors. Marco and Virginia were obviously in love and Antonio saw no latent signs of the Moretti curse in his brother's house, but as they left to go meet Ian Stark and Antonio handed his nephew back to Virginia, he realized that he didn't want to take any chances.

He didn't want Enzo to experience what he and his brothers had when their house had to be sold and they had to move to *Nono*'s house. That wasn't acceptable to him.

He knew that meant he had to cool it with Nathalie. He had to treat her the same way he would treat any other woman he'd started an affair with. Sending flowers was okay, but one-of-a-kind nightgowns probably wasn't the right tone if he wanted to keep this relationship like all of his other affairs.

But it was too late to cancel the sexy negligee he'd ordered to be delivered tomorrow morning. Earlier he'd thought he'd seduce her further over the phone and then send her that sexy nightgown for her to wear the next time she came to Milan. But now… Oh, hell, he wasn't sure.

He followed Dom to his home, which was only three streets from Marco's. They'd all purchased homes in the same area of Milan so that they were close to the Moretti Motors corporate offices and each other. They were only eighteen months apart and had always been very close.

There was a Porsche 911 in the driveway and Antonio shook his head as he got out. Only Ian would drive a rival car to Dom's house.

Luigi, Dom's butler, let him in and directed him to the den, where Ian and Dom waited for him.

"Dom, you've got a big piece of trash in front of your house," Antonio said as he entered.

"Most people don't consider a Porsche trash, Tony."

"I can't speak to others' ignorance," Antonio said.

Ian laughed and stood up to shake his hand. "Good to see you."

"You as well. So, did you find our leak?" Antonio said.

"I did. I think it's going to shock you both."

"Nothing would shock me," Dom said.

"Not even the fact that the leak is your secretary, Angelina de Luca?"

"What? Are you sure?" Dom asked. He crossed to the bar on one wall and poured two fingers of whiskey into a highball glass and swallowed it in one long draw.

"Positive. She's been feeding information to ESP Motors. I saw the last drop myself."

"What the hell?" Dom said.

Antonio was surprised and concerned. "She's had free rein of our corporate offices. She knows everything."

"I know that," Dom said.

"What should we do next?" Ian asked. "I have enough evidence to go to the police. We can have her arrested and press charges."

"Do you have enough to prove ESP was behind it?" Antonio asked. ESP was the company founded by Nigel Eastburn, Lorenzo Moretti's biggest rival on and off the racetrack. Both men had started their own car companies after retiring. The launch of the Vallerio model had pushed Lorenzo ahead of Nigel, but in the '80s when Moretti Motors had started to fail, ESP Motors, named after Nigel and his two partners Geoffrey Saxby and Emmitt Pearson, had moved ahead. And that was why Moretti Motors wanted the roadster to be a success—to take back the pride that they'd lost when ESP had become the name synonymous with roadsters.

"If you give me another week or so, I'll get the proof. I need to make sure their guy isn't working independently."

"Who is it?"

"I believe it's Barty Eastburn."

"Nigel's grandson? That is big. Well, I'd rather take him down than just Angelina."

"She can't get off with no punishment," Antonio said.

"She won't," Dom said. The fierceness of his tone made Antonio realize that Dom was furious at Angelina's betrayal.

Eight

Nathalie was no closer to figuring out anything about her relationship with Antonio when she arrived in Milan a week later. She hadn't called Antonio or spoken to him since their one conversation before her dinner.

She was trying very hard to convince herself that she was only happy to be in Milan to resolve the outstanding issues she had with Moretti Motors, but she was failing.

She wanted to see Antonio. She was a bit mad at herself that she hadn't called him back, but after her conversation with her father she'd felt it was important to keep her distance. Now as she waited in the Moretti Motors lobby she knew nothing was more important than seeing Antonio.

As soon as he stepped off the elevator and started walking toward her, she had the insane desire to run to him.

"Good afternoon, Nathalie. Welcome back to Milan," he said. He welcomed her with a kiss on each cheek.

She turned her head toward him at the last second and her lips brushed his cheek.

"It's good to be back."

"Why didn't you call me, *cara mia?*"

She held her briefcase in one hand and followed him through the hallway to the conference room. "I…I don't know. I mean I had good reasons at first, but now that I'm here they don't seem valid."

"We can discuss that later, over dinner and drinks."

"Antonio, do you think that's a good idea?"

"Yes, I do. Did you get the gift I sent?"

"I did. I'm sorry I haven't thanked you properly." She'd put the negligee on and slept in it every night since he'd sent it. It was exquisite and since she knew the store where he'd purchased it, she also knew it was one of a kind. She'd been touched that he'd sent her the nightgown, but afraid to call him. Afraid that if she talked to him she'd forget to remain strong on the negotiations.

"You can do so later."

"Can I?" she asked, refusing to let him get away with bossing her around.

"Yes, you may," he said, with an unrepentant grin. "I've invited Dominic to join us. He has a counter-offer since we are at an impasse."

Antonio's words made her realize she needed to put all of her personal thoughts on hold and focus on this meeting. How could she tell Antonio that the Vallerio board wasn't going to be satisfied with anything less than a deal that was on their terms? She decided to be straightforward.

"I'll be happy to listen to your proposal, but I'm afraid nothing less than what we've asked for will suffice."

"Is there nothing I can do that would make them change their minds?"

She shook her head. "If you want to back down on your stance, we could move forward."

"I don't see that happening."

"So it's back to the drawing board," she said.

"Hear Dom's presentation. I think it'll make a huge difference."

"You know this isn't just about business," she said. "Almost everyone on the board is related to my grandfather and he was so angry about what Lorenzo did to Anna."

"What did he do?" Antonio asked. "Because from what we heard, she left him. Went back to Paris and never returned."

"He kicked her out, Antonio. He told her she wasn't the wife he needed to build his dynasty with."

Antonio looked over at her. "Some men don't know how to handle themselves with a woman who offers too much temptation."

"Is that a problem for you?" she asked.

"It never has been, but to be honest you do stay on my mind more than I wish you would."

"Do I?" she asked. She didn't want to talk about them, because if she weren't careful she'd fall for him—harder than she already had. It already was a very real danger because she was ready to go back to her board of directors and do whatever it took to convince them to take this deal.

"*Sì*, you do. Why is that?" he asked. He glanced at the closed boardroom door to the table and she almost blushed when she remembered what had occurred the last time they were alone in this room.

She tipped her head to one side. "Perhaps because you've met your match."

"I think I have," he said, leaning back against the

table in the exact spot where she'd sat when he'd pleasured her. "But then you must have too."

"I don't know about that. I'm more than capable of taking whatever you have to dish out."

He reached for her, his hands on her waist as he drew her closer to him. He spread his legs and less than a second later she was in his arms. Nestled there where she'd secretly wanted to be.

"This is so inappropriate for the business we are conducting."

"That might be, but I've missed you, *amore.*"

She glanced at the closed door and then leaned up on her tiptoes and kissed him. For a week now she'd gone to sleep with only the remembered feel of his arms around her and his mouth pressed to hers. The reality was so much better than her memories.

She kissed him as if this was the last embrace they'd have. In a way it was. After her talk with her father she'd known that nothing lasting could come of her affair with Antonio. No matter how much she might want something more.

That evening when he picked Nathalie up, Antonio wasn't sure he was doing the right thing, but he knew that unless he got her to see his family as something more than monsters she was never going to be able to convince the Vallerio board to soften their position.

And truly the only way to do that was to let Nathalie meet his parents. His father was as different from Lorenzo as any man could be. Giovanni had filled his life with one passion and that was his wife, Philomena. Antonio knew that once Nathalie met them she'd see that the Moretti men weren't out to crush the Vallerio family once again.

He wanted to make her see that they were sincere in their offer to put Vallerio back on the lips of car connoisseurs the world over.

"Are you sure about this?" she asked once they were seated in his car.

"Positive. I had the opportunity to meet your father and sister and now I think it's time you had the same."

"Aren't they going to be angry that I haven't convinced my board to accept all of your terms?"

"No. I doubt they will say anything to you about business. My parents aren't concerned about that at all."

"What are they concerned about?"

Antonio thought about that for a moment. "Each other. And that my brothers and I are happy."

"I can't imagine that Lorenzo's son wouldn't be as passionate about car making as he was."

"Wait until you see my parents. They have a love that consumes them."

"I still don't understand," she said. "Many men are married and still manage a company."

"But those men weren't cursed to be lucky either in love or in business," Antonio said.

"And your family was?" she asked.

"Indeed. In fact your great-aunt may have fallen victim to the same curse."

"How do you figure?" she asked.

"Lorenzo broke the heart of a girl he'd left behind in his village to go and seek his fortune, and she cursed him when he didn't fulfill his promise to her."

"What promise?"

Antonio glanced away from the road and over at Nathalie. She seemed very interested in his story. And he wanted to share it. Wanted her to understand that there was more to Lorenzo than his callous behavior might have indicated. "The promise to marry her once he had won the Grand Prix championship and started his car company."

"Promises he didn't keep?"

"No. Lorenzo needed more time to make his fortune. His parents were poor farmers who never did more than eke out an existence and he wanted better for his children."

"So he asked her to wait for him, or did he send her home?" Nathalie asked.

"He told her he couldn't fulfill his promise until

he was certain he'd have the future they both wanted. He asked her to wait awhile longer. She returned home to her village and waited."

"How do you know all of this?"

"Marco's wife, Virginia, is the granddaughter of Cassia, Lorenzo's first love. She has Cassia's journal."

"She cursed your grandfather but your brother married her granddaughter?"

"That makes us sound crazy, I know, but the curse she put on Lorenzo was also put on succeeding generations. When you meet my parents you will see they have a love that is just as successful as Moretti Motors was under *Nono*'s leadership. As successful as it will be now that Marco, Dom and I are running things."

She gave him a very queer look, then turned away, glancing down at her hands, which were laced together in her lap. "Does that mean your brothers don't expect to find the love your parents have?"

Antonio tried not to think of love. It wasn't really something that he'd craved. He had his parents' love and he had never lacked for feminine company and he had his brothers. What more could a man need?

"I don't know," he said honestly. "Love... romantic love just isn't something I've ever really wanted to have."

"Why not?"

"Maybe because of how badly *Nono* screwed it up. Virginia's grandmother cursed him, hated him so much that she wanted to make sure he never felt love again. Your great-aunt hated him so much that she turned Pierre-Henri against him.

"With that kind of a legacy do you think I'd even entertain falling for a woman?"

"But your father isn't that type of man," she said.

Antonio had often thought the same thing. But he'd seen Dom crash and burn with a love affair when he was in university and Antonio had realized whether they wanted to believe in a curse or not he and his brothers had inherited *Nono*'s bad mojo when it came to love and women.

"He's also not the businessman Lorenzo was."

"I see. Since you are good at business, it follows you'll be a screwup with women."

Antonio turned on the long winding driveway that led to his parents' estate in San Giuliano Milanese. He stopped the car in the circular drive at the front of the house. "I have never been a screw-up with women. You asked about love and that's an emotion I've never really sought out."

And it had never found him, he thought. Until now. Seeing the disappointment in Nathalie's eyes, he wanted to be the man who could give her everything she wanted. Including love.

He wanted to be able to make a grand gesture as his father had when he'd walked away from Moretti Motors.

"I guess I understand what you are saying. You haven't looked for love and it hasn't found you."

"Have you?" he asked. The thought of Nathalie loving another man made a red rage fill him. He didn't want any other man to have any claim on Nathalie. And that very possessiveness bothered him as nothing else ever had.

She shook her head. "I've always been too focused on making a name for myself at Vallerio Incorporated."

Antonio's family was warm and welcoming to her. They had dinner in the garden under the stars and it didn't take her long to realize what Antonio had meant by the love his parents shared.

The men left the table to have a cigar in the lower part of the garden. Nathalie felt a moment's panic when she realized she was going to be alone with two women she had nothing in common with—Antonio's mother and his sister-in-law.

"I'm so glad you could join us tonight for dinner. The boys are so excited about their new car, and working with your family to get the Vallerio name is so important to them," Philomena said.

Antonio's mom was short, curvy and still had ebony-colored hair. She had held her own during dinner, but it had been obvious to Nathalie that she doted on the men in her life, and hearing her call Antonio and his brothers "the boys" was something that made her smile.

"Thank you for inviting me. I'm glad to see my grandfather's name being used in conjunction with a car again."

"Marco said your grandfather was pure magic when it came to open-wheel racing," Virginia said. She was a lively woman who had an aura of earthiness about her. She held her son cradled in her arms and often bent down to brush a kiss on Enzo's forehead.

Nathalie sadly had never seen her grandfather drive. She was more acquainted with the man he'd been after Lorenzo Moretti had married and divorced his sister. The man who had retreated into his workroom and focused more on what was happening under the hood. "I never got to see him drive until today."

Dom had put together a documentary that they were going to run in their suite at the F1 races for the rest of the year. The film showed Lorenzo and Pierre-Henri in their glory days. To be honest, the film had done a lot to make her look at all the Morettis in a different way. They had honored her grandfather in a way she hadn't believed they would.

She hoped even her father realized that. If he didn't, she was now determined to convince him.

Philomena's question intruded on her thoughts.

"How long will you and Marco stay in Milan?" she asked Virginia.

"Just another night. Then we are off to Barcelona for the Catalunya Grand Prix. Actually, I'm not sure if Marco mentioned this to you but we were hoping you'd babysit little Enzo here. It's our anniversary of sorts," Virginia said.

"We'd love to. You know I had a nursery prepared here as soon as we had the news of your pregnancy."

"Thank you," Virginia said.

"I've always wanted grandchildren, but I feared my boys were never going to settle down."

Nathalie understood why. "Moretti Motors is as important to them as family."

Virginia nodded. "I think sometimes that to them it *is* family and not a business at all. And of course the curse my grandmother had placed on the Morettis hung over the boys' heads."

Not a superstitious person herself, Nathalie found it hard to believe that so many of these people were. Virginia hardly seemed like a witch, but she'd told the story at dinner of how she'd used her limited knowledge of the old Strega ways to break the curse on Marco.

The curse that Cassia had placed on Lorenzo and every generation that followed.

Nathalie thought that Antonio and Dominic might believe they were still cursed. That by not finding love they hadn't found a way out of the blight that Cassia Festa had put on them. She couldn't help but sympathize with the close-knit Morettis.

"How often do you all get together?" she asked.

"Not often enough. Marco and Virginia travel most of the year for the Grand Prix. Antonio is here in Milan, but he is always busy, and Dominic goes between the offices here and the Grand Prix races."

"Do you attend the races?" Nathalie asked Philomena as they sipped coffee. Night had fallen and the sweet smell of flowers filled the air.

"Mostly the ones in Europe and always the first and last race of the season."

"You should come to the race in Barcelona next week," Virginia urged Nathalie. "There is so much excitement and energy at the races."

Nathalie doubted she would. Her father would have a fit if she attended a Grand Prix race before they had a deal with Moretti that satisfied him. "Thank you for the invitation. Is it always exciting to watch or are you ever afraid?"

Philomena blessed herself and uttered a small prayer under her breath. "I am afraid every time Marco gets in the race car. One of the Team Moretti drivers almost died last year."

Nathalie reached over and put her hand on Philomena's. "I'm sorry. I didn't mean to bring up bad memories."

"You didn't," Virginia said. "But it is a scary profession and even though I know that Marco is a very skilled driver I am reminded most weeks that this is a very dangerous profession."

Nathalie could see that. She was worried about falling in love with the son of her family's sworn enemy, but Virginia had to worry about the man she loved possibly dying. It put a lot of things in perspective for her.

She realized that she didn't want Antonio to be in danger. Then it hit her sitting her in this garden with his mother and his sister-in-law that she was in love with Antonio.

And once that realization opened her eyes, everything else fell into place. She hadn't returned to Milan to broker a deal. She'd returned to Milan to be with Antonio. In Paris it was easy to ignore the truth and to pretend that she didn't love Antonio, but tonight under the Milan moon there were no denials. Only the truth. And she was still deal-

ing with that truth twenty minutes later when Antonio returned.

He looked at her and she could do nothing but
smile at him. The man she loved.

Nine

Antonio drove to Nathalie's hotel in Milan in silence. Something was on her mind but he had no idea what. It had been a calculated move to bring her to his parents' house, and now he was wondering what the aftereffects would be. "Are you okay?"

"Yes. Dinner was very nice."

"I'm glad you enjoyed it."

"And I think I see what you meant about your parents' love. Your father is positively smitten with your mother."

"Yes, he is."

"Funny to think that a curse would have given him that much love in his life."

Antonio turned to her when he stopped for a traffic light. "I don't think he's cursed at all."

"Do you think the men in your family are? When we talked earlier I couldn't tell if you really believed you were doomed."

"Doomed to spend my life alone?" he asked. "Maybe I did. I guess that when you grow up with that kind of love in your home and then you visit with friends, you start to see that not everyone has that kind of love."

He didn't elaborate and she wanted to ask if he had wanted to find what his parents had. She knew that she and Antonio couldn't have that. She was never going to be like his mother and stay home and give up her own ambition.

She shook her head. Realizing she loved Antonio was one thing. Thinking about marriage was another. Had she lost it? Too much needed to be resolved between them businesswise before they could ever consider anything permanent. "What is it about your parents' love for each other that you really envy...I mean want?"

"I've never really thought about it," he said. He pulled into the parking area of her hotel, where the valet took the car.

She looked at him and asked, "Would you like to come up?"

"I was hoping you'd ask me. I've missed holding you."

That little confession eased the worries she had felt since she'd first realized that she loved him.

"Me too."

They walked next to each other through the lobby. In the lobby bar Antonio saw a few associates who waved him over, but he shook his head. "I don't want to talk business tonight."

"Is this going to be awkward tomorrow?" she asked when they entered the elevator alone. "This isn't the first time we've been seen together."

"I think my family knows how I feel about you. I didn't just invite you to dinner tonight as a representative of Vallerio Incorporated."

Or had he? He was a brilliant strategist and he had to know that seeing his family would make it harder for her to stand firm on what her board of directors wanted.

He had made the Morettis human to her. He had shown her the people behind the car company and that was softening her attitude toward them.

"It was nice to meet your family, but I have to wonder if you didn't plan it that way…use it as a way to soften me up," she said once they were in her suite.

"Why would I do that?" he asked. He shrugged out of his suit jacket and draped it over the back of the love seat.

"All's fair in love and in war," she said, crossing to the wet bar and taking out a bottle of mineral water. "Would you like something to drink?"

"I'll have a beer," he said.

She handed him a bottle, and he took her hand in his.

"Listen, Nathalie, I stopped trying to find an advantage to use to get you to give in a long time ago."

"Did you really?"

"Yes. I don't want you to surrender to me. I want to find a solution that will make us both happy."

"If I said that Moretti Motors should go ahead with their alternate plans you'd be fine with that?"

He took a swallow of his beer and then looked her straight in the eye. "No, I wouldn't. I think you know that. What would make me happy is coming to an arrangement that both of our boards will find pleasing."

She stepped back from him and walked to the window of her suite. "I'm…I'm confused, Antonio. For the first time in my life I can't just focus on work."

"Why is that?" he asked.

"You made me invest more of myself in this negotiation than I wanted to."

"I made you?"

She shook her head. "Not like you forced me into it…I guess I don't really mean that. I meant that I am different this time because of how I feel about you."

He put his beer on the coffee table and walked across the small room to her. He stopped when only an inch of space separated them.

He took her water from her hand and put it on the bar. "How do you feel about me, *cara mia?*"

"I…" *I love you,* she thought. But she couldn't say the words out loud. Though he'd claimed to have softened his stance on the negotiations, she couldn't hand him the powerful weapon of her love to use against her.

She shook her head. "I care about you, Antonio."

He drew her into his arms. He hugged her close to his chest and whispered soft words against her temple. She felt safer in her love with his arms around her.

Antonio claimed Nathalie's lips with his and didn't let her go until they'd reached the bed. He'd had enough talking. He was never going to be able to say the right thing to her. The thing that would make her forget that he was a Moretti and she was a Vallerio. That was always going to be between them.

Earlier tonight Dom had been very blunt that he wanted the Vallerio deal closed. He wanted Antonio to pull out all the stops. Antonio couldn't tell his brother that he wouldn't do it. That he was falling for the tall French redhead who was just as strong as he was in the boardroom and in the bedroom.

But now he was in control. And it was important to him that he make her understand this as well.

In three strides he was to the bed. He set Nathalie on her feet and peeled back the covers of the bed. He toed off his loafers and reached down to remove his socks. She still had her shoes on. He bent down and lifted her foot, carefully removing one high heel and then the other.

He stood back up. She looked exquisite in her sapphire wrap dress, like a male fantasy come to life. The neckline plunged deep between her breasts, revealing the creamy white tops of each one, while the hemline ended high on her thigh.

The only light in the room spilled from the city lights outside the window. Darkness enveloped them in a cocoon, as if no one else existed but the two of them. Antonio intended to make the most of their privacy.

He lowered his head and with his tongue, traced the edge where fabric met skin. She smelled of perfume and a natural womanly scent that he associated only with Nathalie. The scent of her skin had haunted him during the week they had been apart. Now he closed his eyes and buried his face between her breasts, inhaling deeply.

Shifting slightly to the right, he tasted her with languid strokes of his tongue. Her skin was sweeter and more addicting than anything he'd ever tasted. He followed the curve of her breast from top to bottom; the texture changed as he reached the edge of her nipple.

The velvety nub beckoned him and he pushed the fabric of her dress out of the way. He wanted to see her.

"Stand here."

He crossed the room and flipped on the light switch flooding the room in light. Nathalie stood where he left her, her red hair hanging around her shoulders in long curls. Her lips looked full and lush, wet and swollen from his kisses. Her breasts spilled from the fabric, full and white and topped with hard little berries that made his mouth water.

He crossed back to her side in less than two strides. "That's better."

"Is it?" she asked.

"I want to see you, Nathalie. The real you, not the dream that's been haunting me."

He didn't give her a chance to respond. He might be playing the fool, but right now he didn't care. He already knew he was compromised where she was concerned. She had a power over him that he could only hope she never realized she had. And he had a new goal—one that had absolutely nothing to do with Moretti Motors.

That goal was to get as deep inside her body as he could.

He lowered his head once more to the full globe of her breast, scraping the aroused nipple with his teeth. She shuddered in his arms. He used his hand to stimulate her other nipple, circling it with his finger and scraping his nail across the center very carefully while at the same time using his teeth on the first one.

She moaned his name, undulating against him. Her hands swept down his body and she unzipped his pants. His erection sprang into her waiting hands. He wanted her to grasp the length of him, but instead she only teased him by running her finger up and down the sides of his shaft.

He suckled her nipple deep in his mouth and slid his hand up under her skirt, where he encountered a sexy thong. He caressed her sticky curls through the lace, and her touch on him changed, became more fevered, more demanding.

He slipped his finger inside the crotch of her panties and into her humid opening. She moaned and lifted her leg to give him deeper access. The moan was nearly his undoing. He couldn't wait much longer to take her.

He turned and lay back on the bed, pulling Nathalie on top of him. She braced her hands on his chest and leaned up over him. Their groins pressed together. She bit her lower lip and rotated on him. It felt deliciously hot and he wanted nothing more than to let her rock against him until they both came. Later, he thought. Right now he needed to be inside her.

He pulled her down to him and rolled until she was underneath him again.

"Do you have to be on top?"

He smiled at her. "It's a male thing."

"Why?"

"Because you are too strong. I want you to know that you are ceding to my will," he said.

He didn't want to say any more, but for once he wanted to feel he was really in control. In control of their lovemaking and in control of this woman who gave away so little.

He tore his shirt off and tossed it across the room and then kicked his pants down. He reached for the bodice of Nathalie's dress and tugged until the fabric ripped, leaving her body bare.

He slid his hand down to her panties.

"Stop."

He did, glancing up at her. She reached underneath his body and pushed the panties down her legs. "I like these and don't want you to tear them."

He chuckled. "I wasn't going to rip them."

He bent his head and followed the path of her skimpy underwear with his mouth. Some of her wetness had rubbed against her thigh and he licked her clean. Then he rose over her.

He bent her legs back against her body, leaving her totally exposed to him. Leaning down, he tasted her pink flesh, caressing her carefully with his tongue until her hips were rising against him and her hands clenched in his hair. He slid up her body, holding her hips in his hands, tilting them upward to give him greater access.

He grabbed one of the pillows from the head of the bed and wedged it under her. Then draping her thighs over his arms, he brought their bodies together. Nathalie reached between them and grasped him, guiding him to her entrance.

"Take me," she said.

He did. He entered her deeply and completely, stopping only when he was fully seated within her. He felt her clench around him. He knew she was doing it intentionally and smiled down at her. He lowered his head and took her mouth, allowing his tongue to mimic the movements of his hips. Soon he felt close to the edge. It wasn't going to be much longer until he climaxed in her arms.

She rotated her hips against him with each thrust and soon she was gasping for breath and making those sweet sounds of preorgasm. He reared back, so he could go deeper, her feet on his shoulders.

He held her still for his thrusts and she tilted her head back, her eyes closing as her orgasm rushed over her. It was all he needed to send him over the edge. He felt the tingling at the base of his spine and then emptied himself into her.

Knowing she'd said too much earlier, Nathalie didn't wait for Antonio to say anything now that they were in bed. When he made love to her she felt like a woman. Not the Vallerio daughter or the Vallerio Inc. corporate shark, just a woman.

His woman.

"Do you want to see the negligee you sent me?"

"I'd love to see it," he said.

The light was still on and she went to the wardrobe where she'd hung her clothes earlier in the day. She drew out the gown.

It was a Carine Gilson gown. The exclusive lingerie couture was one of the most expensive in the world. "How did you know I like Gilson?"

"I noticed your bra the first time we made love," he said.

"Most men wouldn't have noticed."

"I'm not most men. Put on the gown. I had to rely on my imagination when I ordered it."

She did as he asked. The sheer gown fell to her knees and she stood in front of him boldly, allowing him to feast his eyes on her. The gold fabric made her skin look even creamy in the light, and the black designs on the side and at the hem added a hint of elegance.

"Come here," he beckoned from the bed. She couldn't help but notice his erection and inwardly she smiled, knowing she had the power to make him hard.

"Turn around."

She did as he said and felt his hand on her thighs, teasing up under the hem of the negligee, then caressing the crease in her buttocks. She shivered with awareness.

Reaching behind her, she found his erection and encircled it with her hand, tugging on it once and then letting go as she stepped away.

Suddenly he came up behind her, his arms coming around to grasp her breasts. He nipped at the shell of her ear. "Gotcha."

She shivered. He plucked at her aroused nipples with his fingers while his mouth continued to play at her neck. Sensation spread throughout her body.

His erection nestled between her buttocks through the fabric of her gown and she shifted a little, rubbing him between them.

One of his hands slipped down her body. He lingered at her belly button, and then slid lower, parting her nether lips. He didn't touch her, just held her open so that the fabric of her gown brushed against her clitoris. She moaned.

"Please," she gasped.

She felt like a prisoner to her desire and to this man. She tried to escape from Antonio's grip but couldn't.

He chuckled in her ear. "You're mine."

Deep in her soul, those words sounded right. She ignored that feeling and focused instead on the physical. She reached behind her to his erection, taking him in her grip. But he pulled his hips back, not allowing her to touch him.

"Antonio," she said.

"Sì, cara mia?" he asked.

"I…" She couldn't think, couldn't speak. She just wanted him inside her. Now.

"You can say it. You need me."

"I do."

"Say it please," he said. He rubbed the fleshy part of her labia with long strokes of his fingers. First one side and then the other. But she ached for more. She shifted again, trying to bring his hand where she wanted it, but he wouldn't be budged. She shoved her own hand down her body, but he caught her before she could bring relief to herself.

"Impatient?"

"You have no idea," she muttered.

He chuckled. Finally he touched her, just a light brush of his fingertip. She reached for him but again he canted his hips away from her touch. "Antonio, no more games."

"Agreed. Lie on the bed on your back."

She did. He pushed the fabric of her negligee high to her waist, parted her legs and moved between them. "Part yourself for me. Show me where you want my tongue."

She did as he said and felt his breath on her. She knew he was seeing her swollen with need and hungry for his mouth. He lowered his head and exhaled against her sensitive flesh.

Her thighs twitched and she wanted to clamp her legs around his head until he made her scream with passionate completion. She felt his tongue against her, lapping at her with increasing strength. Then she felt the edge of his teeth and she screamed with pleasure.

He thrust two fingers inside her, rocking up against her g-spot while his mouth worked its magic on her. He feathered light touches in between shockingly rougher ones that brought her quickly to the edge of orgasm. Still she fought it off, not wanting to end it too quickly.

He added a third finger inside her body and stretched them out when he pulled back and then thrust back into her body. Everything inside her tightened and her climax rushed through her.

Antonio put his hands on her thighs and pushed her legs back against her body before entering her so deeply she felt impaled on his length.

But he stopped there. She opened her eyes and met his gaze. "What are you waiting for?"

"You."

She shifted onto him. Holding his shoulders, she lifted herself off him and then slowly slid back down.

"Faster," he urged.

"Not yet," she said.

She tightened her muscles around him, milking him as she pushed herself up his length and letting him slip out of her body.

He grabbed her hips and pulled her down while he thrust upward. He worked them together until she felt every nerve ending tingling again and her second orgasm rushed over her just as Antonio screamed with his own release.

The sex was phenomenal, the best she'd ever experienced, but as he turned off the lights and took her in his arms and she relaxed against him she realized

that the real power that Antonio held over her was
this. The sense of rightness she felt in his arms as he
held her gently and they both drifted toward sleep.

Ten

The next two weeks were the most intense of his life. Antonio felt more alive than he ever had before. He was exhausted from traveling between Milan and Paris but he thought the fatigue well worth it.

He had ensured that Nathalie and Vallerio Inc. would accept Moretti Motors latest offer. And tonight he was going to propose to Nathalie. From the conversations they'd had about love and that fairer emotion, he sensed that she was in love with him and he felt deeply pleased by that.

He couldn't admit to loving her. He was hedging his bets on the curse that had been a part of his life for so long that he couldn't just admit it. He wouldn't compromise all that he and Dom and Marco had worked for by admitting he'd fallen for Nathalie Vallerio, but he did need her in his life.

"Antonio, do you have a minute?"

He looked up from his computer screen. "Sure, Dom, come on in."

Dom came into his office and closed the door but not all the way. He stood there in the middle of the room, and for the first time Antonio saw that Dom wasn't confident. Not the way he'd always been.

"What's up?"

"Nothing really. Nothing important, I just wanted to let you know that Angelina will be continuing as my secretary."

"Are you sure that's a good idea?"

"Well, I have decided to use her to leak false information to Barty Eastburn. If he wants our company secrets, then he'll get them."

"She agreed to do that?"

"Yes."

Antonio signed off his computer and stood up, walking around to where his brother was. "Good. The Vallerio Roadster is almost ready for rollout. I think we've finally come up with terms that both sides can live with."

"What did you give them?"

"A partial share in the profits from the roadster and a seat on our board. We will be getting a seat on their board as well."

"Did you find out what their anticipated revenue will come from in the next quarter?"

He'd asked around and the Vallerio family was playing this one very close to the chest, but near as he could tell they had filed for new patents and would be releasing an updated carburetor design. A more energy efficient one. "It has something to with engines."

"That's good. See if we can get the exclusive rights to use it on our production cars for the first year."

"I will. I haven't broached the subject with Nathalie yet."

"Why not? You spend a lot of time with her."

"How do you know that?"

"Do you honestly think that I wouldn't pay attention to what you are doing? There is a woman involved and I don't want you to fall like Marco did."

Antonio shook his head. "Dom, it's time you stopped worrying about the curse. I think that Marco did break it. He's still winning and he seems happy."

Dom ran his hand through his hair and sighed. "I don't believe it. We haven't launched the new roadster and until it is successfully launched, we can't afford to take chances."

Antonio clapped his brother on the shoulder. As the oldest, Dom bore more responsibility than any of them. He was the one that *Nono* had groomed for the CEO position from the time they were old enough to talk.

"We will make this work. I can promise you that."

Dom nodded. "Some days just seem longer than others."

"I hear you," Antonio said. "I've been traveling too much. I'm ready to get everything taken care of so I can start loafing around again."

"You have never spent a day loafing in your life."

Antonio had to laugh at that. "Of course I haven't, but it does sound good."

"Indeed," Dom said.

Antonio looked at his older brother. They were workaholics, both of them, and he feared sometimes that if he didn't grab on to Nathalie with both hands, he was going to end up alone. Not that there was anything wrong with living a solitary life, but now that he'd a glimpse of what life could be, he wanted more.

"Do you ever wonder if we should have just followed Papa's path?" Antonio asked.

Dom turned and looked at him, studied him really, and Antonio regretted his words. Dom probably never doubted himself, and hinting that he, Antonio, doubted himself wasn't going over well.

"Never mind."

"No, I can't just dismiss this. If you are thinking along these lines, it can only mean one thing," Dom said.

Antonio shook his head. "It doesn't mean anything. Seeing Marco and Virginia together just made me curious."

Dom narrowed his eyes. "I was curious once, Tony, and I got burned. I didn't need a curse to harden my heart. I did it myself when I realized just how vulnerable a man can be to a woman. And most women can use that to their advantage."

Antonio knew that Dom's ex-lover had betrayed him in the worst way and that his brother would never risk his heart again. But he thought of Nathalie and the burgeoning feelings he had for her. They included trust, he thought.

He already trusted her and even if he never said the words out loud, he knew he loved her.

"I know I suggested romancing Nathalie Vallerio, but has that turned into something more?"

Antonio looked at his brother, straight in the eye, and told the biggest lie he ever had. "No, Dom. It's nothing more than an affair."

Nathalie backed away from Antonio's office almost running to get away from what she'd just heard. She refused to cry, but somehow her eyes didn't get the memo and tears burned the back of her eyes. She blinked rapidly trying to keep them from falling. She made it to the elevator and then had to stop.

She pressed the call button.

What was she going to do? She had taken back to her family the deal that she and Antonio had worked out. She'd compromised on things, believing that he was dealing with her fairly and that he was going to stand up and be the man she'd fallen in love with.

She should have remembered the lesson her great-aunt had learned the hard way…that Moretti men had only one true love and that was Moretti Motors.

She sniffed and blinked some more, but the tears were pooling in the corners of her eyes. She had no tissue to wipe them away. She never cried. She just wasn't the type of woman who would ever break down like this.

She heard the rumble of Antonio's voice and was horrified by the thought that he might catch her crying. She walked down the hall to the toilets on this floor.

She went inside and startled the woman already in there. She was clearly crying, her face red and splotchy. "Angelina?"

"*Ciao,* Nathalie. I'm sorry you've caught me this way."

It was funny but seeing the other woman's distress made her forget about her tears. At least for this moment. And that was all she needed. When she was alone she would deal with the heartache.

"Are you okay?"

"*Sì,*" Angelina said. "I wish I were one of those women who cried pretty."

Nathalie laughed. "Me too. Luckily I don't cry often."

"Unfortunately I do," Angelina said. There was an aura of sadness around her today.

"Do you want to talk?" Nathalie asked.

Angelina shook her head. "Not unless you know some way to keep from crying in front of others."

Nathalie thought about something her sister had read in a psychology journal a few years ago. To be honest she didn't believe it worked, but it always made her and Genevieve laugh when they mentioned it and laughter was a great mask for sadness.

"I did hear something, though I've never tried it," Nathalie said. "Don't laugh but if you tighten your buttocks, it's supposed to make you stop crying."

"And start laughing?"

"Well, it always has that affect on my sister and me."

Angelina laughed and then took a deep breath. "*Grazie,* Nathalie."

"You're welcome."

Angelina left the bathroom and Nathalie stood in

front of the mirror, trying to hold on to the laughter she'd shared with the other woman. She pushed her emotions down deep inside and tried to bury them, but it was hard for her to do.

She'd never been this vulnerable to a man before. And she didn't like that. She didn't like the fact that Antonio Moretti had done this to her.

She remembered what they had said in the beginning and realized she couldn't really get mad at him. She'd agreed that all was fair in love and war. It didn't matter that the circumstances of their relationship had changed for her. They'd laid down the ground rules at the beginning of their negotiations.

She was the one who had forgotten them. It was a mistake she couldn't afford to make again.

Breathing deeply, she left the ladies' room with a confident stride. Walking down the hall to Antonio's office, she practiced what she'd say, how she'd pretend that everything was normal until she got out of here.

She debated leaving now, not seeing him again. But he was expecting her and she had to use the new knowledge she had to her advantage. Something she wouldn't be able to accomplish if she left now.

Antonio's secretary, Carla, was at her desk this time when Nathalie came into the office.

"Is Antonio ready for me?" she asked after exchanging greetings.

"*Sì*, go on in."

The moment she pushed the door open and stepped into his office she knew this was a mistake. When Antonio turned to face her from the far side of his office and smiled at her, she wanted nothing but to confront him.

To demand he tell her to her face that she meant nothing more to him than a little affair to make the negotiations easier.

But she bit her tongue. She channeled her anger into a need for vengeance. Or at least that was what she told herself. Inside she realized that she'd trade vengeance for one more night in his arms.

Antonio was still distracted from his conversation with Dom. He wanted to get away from Moretti Motors and forget about his family for a little while. That was the past and Nathalie was his future. He didn't know how but he was going to convince Dom that there was no harm in falling in love.

He had spent a lot of time the last two weeks trying to make sense of everything, and having Nathalie here with him now made him realize that if he couldn't find a balance between Moretti Motors and Nathalie... Well, he'd have to choose between them, and Nathalie offered him something the car company couldn't.

She offered him a life beyond work.

He walked over to her to kiss her, but she turned her head so that his lips grazed her cheek.

"Are you okay?"

"Yes. Just had a long flight from Paris and I don't feel that your office is the best place for kissing."

"The boardroom is more to your liking?" he asked, teasing her.

She flushed and he saw an expression cross her face that he couldn't identify. "I guess so."

"Did your family agree to the terms we worked out?" he asked. They'd both spent long hours trying to make sure that the deal was fair for both sides.

"We can talk about that later. I'm here for a date with my main man."

"That's right. Pleasure first and then business," he said, but he could tell that something wasn't right with Nathalie. She never talked like this and he wondered if she wasn't having doubts.

Doubts about the deal or about them? Or was she simply tired? It was Friday evening and he'd asked her to come to Milan because he was going to propose to her. He wanted to do it at the house on Lake Como. He thought returning to the place where they'd first made love would be a nice touch.

In fact he'd planned for them to have cocktails and hors d'oeuvres in the boardroom first. "Will you come with me to the boardroom first?"

"Why?"

"I have planned a surprise for you, *cara mia.*"

He escorted her out of his office, glancing over at Carla. She nodded to him, letting him know she'd set up everything as he'd asked her to.

When he opened the door of the boardroom he saw flowers on the sideboard, a champagne bucket at the end of the table with a tray of food. And most importantly a slim gift-wrapped box as well.

"After you," he said.

She entered the room and then stopped. He stepped in behind her and locked the door so they wouldn't be disturbed.

"What is this?"

"Just a little predate."

"Antonio," she said, "you didn't have to do all of this."

"Yes, I did," he said. "Have a seat while I pour the champagne."

He held out one of the chairs for her and she slowly came to sit down. He put his hands on her shoulders and leaned over her to kiss her. This time she didn't turn away, but he noticed she was blinking a lot. "Is this okay?"

"Yes," she said, her voice a bit husky.

"Open this while I pour the champagne."

He handed her the box. He hoped she liked the

strand of Mikimoto pearls he'd gotten her. The creamy color of the pearls would look exquisite against her skin.

She held the box in her hands and stared up at him. "Why all of this?"

"To celebrate. Now that we aren't adversaries in the boardroom anymore, we can concentrate on our relationship. I see this day as a new start between us, *cara mia*. Open your gift."

She opened it slowly and he heard her breath catch as she stared down at the ocean-inspired strand of pearls. The pearls were offset by blue sapphires.

"This is beautiful."

"It is nothing compared to your beauty," he said.

He reached around her and took the pearls from the box. "Lift you hair up."

She did as he said and he fastened the necklace around her neck, bending to drop a kiss underneath the white gold clasp. She put one hand at the base of her throat where the pearls rested. He turned the chair around so he could see her eyes.

A sheen of tears glistened there and he knew this was a moment he'd remember all of his life. Having Nathalie here with him made him feel he'd been given the keys to the kingdom. And it was a kingdom he'd never thought to belong in.

That was what he wanted from her love, he

thought, what he needed from it. This acceptance and the desire to be with this woman for the rest of his life.

He knew that their marriage and engagement would not be easy, but he had a strong feeling that they could make it work.

He tipped her head back and kissed her, trying to show her with his mouth all the emotions he felt, all the words he couldn't say.

She parted her lips for him, her tongue thrusting past the barrier of his teeth. Her hands wound around his neck, drawing him closer to her.

He leaned in, put his arms around her waist and lifted her out of the chair and spun around so that he could lean against the table and hold her in his arms.

She pulled back and he saw something in her eyes he'd never seen before. He wasn't sure what emotion it was, but he knew it wasn't love.

"What is it, Nathalie?"

"I'm just trying to figure out something."

"What?"

"Are you giving me this gift as a thank-you for what I did to help Moretti Motors with the Vallerio Roadster? Or…"

"Or?"

"As a sop for your conscience since you romanced me around to your way of thinking?"

Eleven

"I didn't give you this for either reason. These are engagement gifts."

"There are more?" she asked, so afraid to believe what this man was telling her.

"Yes. I want you to be my wife, Nathalie. It has nothing to do with Moretti Motors."

"Really?" she asked.

"*Sì*. Sit down here. Listen to me. Over the past six weeks while we have argued and talked and become lovers, I've come to realize how much you mean to me. How much I need you in my life."

"How much?" she asked again. It was odd. She

should feel like crying now, but instead she felt oddly detached. It was almost as if she were watching the events unfold instead of actually participating in them. "Enough to give up the Vallerio name on the new roadster?"

"Why are you asking me that? You know that our affair has nothing to do with business."

She stood up and paced away from him. "No, Antonio. I don't know that."

"What is going on here?" he asked.

"I heard you talking to Dom earlier. I heard you tell him that I was just a romance."

"Merda."

"Cursing won't change the facts. And all of this is so lovely, but really it is over-the-top for the kind of affair you and I have...at least according to you."

"Nathalie—"

"Don't. Don't try to explain it to me, Antonio. I can't do this. I thought I could have it all. A man who cared for me...really cared about me and my family's respect, but I can see now I was wrong."

"What do you mean? The Vallerio and Moretti deal is done, just waiting for signatures," he said, walking over to her. He took her shoulders in his hands. "And our relationship is just starting. I couldn't tell Dom what I have only just figured out myself."

"What is that?"

"That you mean more to me than any woman ever has before."

He let his hands fall to his sides and she knew he was telling the truth. She did mean more to him than another woman, but for her that wasn't going to be enough. She wanted to be the love of his life. She wanted him to be enamored of her the way Gio was with Philomena. And that wasn't ever going to happen.

She could tell from the moment he mentioned marriage that he wasn't talking about a love affair and she knew that was what it would take for her not to grow bitter.

"That's not enough for me, Antonio," she said.

"Why not? We are both new to this relationship stuff. Give me time to get better at it."

She shook her head. "I can't."

"I don't understand, Nathalie. I have everything here that a woman could want. I will give you everything you need."

"Will you?"

"If it is within my power, it is yours," he said.

She wondered if she was being too hasty. Maybe she had misunderstood what he'd said to Dom. This boardroom certainly made it seem that way.

"What if I said all I really need is your love?" she asked quietly.

She felt the air go out of the room, as Antonio

stared at her. In that instant she had her answer and the tears started to roll down her face. She didn't try to stop them, knew that asking a man for his love and getting silence wasn't something that tricks could combat. She reached up behind her neck and took off the pearls and put them on the table.

"I think that answers my question," she said, walking to the door.

"No, dammit, it does not," he said.

"Yes, it does. Because without love, all of this is hollow. You'd think a man who grew up surrounded by the real thing would know the difference."

"You'd think a woman who spent her entire adult life in the business world would know a good deal when she sees it."

"I want more than a good deal from the man who asks me to marry him."

"I didn't mean that," he said.

"What did you mean, then?" she asked.

He raked a hand through his hair. "I don't know."

"What do you feel for me, Antonio? Is it only lust?"

He shook his head. "It is so much more than that."

"That's something at least. I think I made a mistake by starting an affair with you while we were adversaries."

"No, we didn't make a mistake. You and I we were drawn together from the very first."

"That doesn't mean we were meant to marry," she said. "We both wanted to win and I guess in the end I gave in because— Well, the why doesn't matter anymore...but I almost gave in on some important points for Vallerio Incorporated."

"Are you backing out of the deal we brokered because I can't say that I love you?"

He made her feel small and petty when he said it that way. "No. I'm backing out because we decided we don't need the money we'd make from the roadster."

"Fine. Walk away from the deal if that's what you feel you must do. But remind your board of directors that I treated you fairly and it's only your wounded pride that has you running back to Paris."

She had no rebuttal for him. She just unlocked the boardroom door and walked away as quickly as she could. She didn't want to think that she was using pride to protect her broken heart. To be fair, nothing could protect her broken heart. The pain there was already too intense for her to control.

Antonio glanced around the now empty boardroom. He had no idea how things had gone so wrong. Granted he had never proposed to a woman before, but he wasn't sure that he could screw it up that badly.

"What happened in here?" Dom asked from the doorway.

"Nothing. I…I had some— I asked Nathalie to marry me."

"What? I thought— Never mind that, are you okay?" He stepped into the boardroom.

"Yes, Dom. I know what you are thinking. I had it all under control this afternoon and now I'm afraid I may have messed everything up."

"The deal with Vallerio Incorporated on use of their name?"

"Yes. But more importantly my relationship with Nathalie."

"Which is more important to you?" Dom asked.

For once Antonio didn't stop to think about what answer his brother would want to hear. Instead he spoke the truth. "Nathalie is. And I let her go, Dom."

"You had to. You know that Moretti men don't make good husbands."

"How do we know that? Dad's happy and so is Marco."

"Yes, but they aren't cut from the same cloth as we are. We crave success the same way *Nono* did. What are you going to do? Would you choose Nathalie over Moretti Motors?"

Antonio thought about it. There was no way that he could pick between the two of them. And suddenly he realized he didn't have to. Without Nathalie in his life he didn't care if Moretti Motors was successful. "I can't choose."

"Then that's your answer," Dom said.

"What is?"

"You love her."

"I know I do. I was hoping that by not saying those words out loud I would be able to protect us from the curse. I'm sorry, Dom."

Dom shook his head. "I'm sorry, Tony, sorry that you feel like you have to apologize for falling in love. I was wrong to put you in that position."

"You might not feel like apologizing when I tell you that she's probably going to convince her board not to accept any deal with us."

Dom shrugged. "If that's what she has to do and if that's what you have to agree to in order to prove you love her, then we will find another way."

For the first time since everything went awry with Nathalie, he felt a ray of hope. "Yes, we will."

"I guess this means the curse is still in affect," Dom said.

"How do you figure?" Antonio asked.

"Well, if she's going to take the rights to the name…"

Antonio thought about it for a minute. "You know, I don't believe that's what the curse was about. I think the real curse is the fact that we would deny ourselves love to make the company successful."

"Really?"

Antonio shrugged. "I don't know for you, but for me I think that is the answer."

"What are you going to do?"

"Figure out a way to win Nathalie back."

Two weeks later Nathalie was back in Milan. Her sister and parents and the entire board of directors of Vallerio Inc. were in attendance as well. They'd taken the company jet and Nathalie was so ready to be alone by the time they got off the plane. She was tired.

Tired of sleepless nights and countless recriminations about the last time she spoke to Antonio. She'd tried to get out of this meeting, but Moretti Motors flatout refused to talk to anyone else from Vallerio. And so now they were all here for a big announcement from Moretti Motors. Something that demanded every one of them attend.

She'd tried to find out what was going on, but no one would share any details. Even Genevieve, who normally couldn't be shut up, just sat quietly next to her.

She had confessed to her sister that things had gone wrong with Antonio, but hadn't been able to tell her that she'd let him break her heart. She was a sadder but wiser woman when she entered the Moretti Motors building with her family.

Angelina greeted them all. "If you would all follow me to the garden. We have a special presentation before we go up to the boardroom."

"What presentation?" Nathalie asked.

"That's fine," Emile said, preempting her. "We will give you the time you need for the presentation."

"We will?"

"Oui, ma fille."

She shook her head and followed the rest of her family through the building and out into the courtyard. In the center of the courtyard was a canvas-draped car. She suspected it was the Vallerio Roadster coupe, though she doubted seeing the car would convince her board to go for the deal that Moretti had offered. But she'd have to wait and see.

There were several seats in the courtyard and Angelina directed them all to sit down. "Signore Moretti will be right with you."

"Merci," Emile said.

Nathalie found herself sitting between her father and her sister, tired and heartsick. Sitting here in this garden, she remembered the first time she'd been here and how it had been the start of her affair with Antonio.

She had hoped that her anger would be enough to

inure her to the love she'd felt for him, but it wasn't. And it saddened her to think that a man could use her and she'd still love him, but there it was—the truth of the matter.

"Thank you for joining us today," Dom said, stepping out of the factory and walking toward them. "I know that we have yet to reach an agreement for the use of Pierre-Henri's name on our legendary roadster and that very fact might be on your minds, but my brother has something very important he must do before we can go back to the boardroom."

She noticed that Philomena, Gio, Marco, Virginia and little Enzo were standing behind Dom. Why were they here?

Dom came over to her. "Will you come with me?"

She shook her head. "Why?"

"To make up for the trouble I caused," Dom said.

"What trouble?"

"Making my brother believe that he couldn't have the woman he loves and not disappoint me."

Woman he loved? Did that mean Antonio loved her? She stood up, putting her hand in Dom's. "Where to?"

"Right here," he said, leading her to the center of the courtyard right next to the canvas-covered car.

"Nathalie."

She turned to see Antonio striding toward her.

"Thank you, everyone, for coming today and for allowing me to do this in front of you," he said, speaking to their assembled families.

"As you are aware, our families have some mis-understandings between us. And because of that we haven't always communicated well with each other. I allowed that to ruin something precious to me."

Antonio turned to her. "I allowed the past to have more power over me than it should. I love you, Nathalie Vallerio. And I don't want to live without you."

"Antonio—"

"Shh. Let me finish, *cara mia.*"

He dropped down on one knee in front of her. "Please do me the honor of being my wife."

She stared down at him for a long moment and then drew him up to his feet. "Did you mean it when you said you loved me?"

"More than anything else in this world."

"What if my family won't agree to letting you use the Vallerio name?"

"That is why I'm asking you to marry me now. There is nothing that can change my desire to have you as my wife," he said, drawing her into his arms.

Nathalie looked at Antonio. She wanted to believe that he was sincere, but how could she be sure this wasn't the Moretti charm? The same charm that

Lorenzo had used on Anna. Was she simply being fooled because…because it was what she wanted to hear so badly? She realized she wanted Antonio's love. Not because it would end a family feud but because her life was so much better with Antonio in it.

She knew then if she was going to be happy for the rest of her days she needed Antonio and his love.

She hugged him tightly to her. "Yes. Yes, I will marry you."

Her family congratulated her and everyone agreed to go to the Moretti family home in San Giuliano Milanese after the meeting to celebrate.

They went into the boardroom and after a lot of haggling, Moretti Motors had the rights to use the Vallerio name on their roadster. They also got the rights to the new engine that her father had designed.

Everyone seemed happy with the way things worked out and when they went downstairs after the meeting, Emile and Gio both placed a temporary nameplate on the Vallerio Roadster. To see the sons of two men who fought and had grown to hate each other standing side by side felt right to Nathalie.

She hoped that with the bitterness of the feud in the past, both of their families would go on to much greater things.

"Are you happy?" Antonio asked, holding her

hand in his as they walked through the gardens at his parents' house.

"Happier than I ever thought I could be," she said. "What made you change your mind?"

"Nothing," he said.

She pulled away. "Nothing? Antonio, are you doing this on a whim?"

He pulled her back into his arms and kissed her. There was so much passion in that embrace that she knew without a doubt he loved her.

"I knew I loved you before you walked out. I had thought that confessing my love would doom it, but then I realized that by hiding it I was cursing us to a life without each other."

"Are you sure you love me?" she asked, unable to believe she was really going to get to spend the rest of her life with Antonio.

"Positive, *cara mia*. And I'm going to make sure you never doubt it or me again."

"How will you do that?" she asked, though she already felt his love surrounding her.

"By telling you of my love often, by paying attention to the little things that make you happy, by making you feel like the center of my world, because that is what you are."

"And what will I do for you?"

"You've already done it. You brought color to my life and made me realize that business wasn't the only thing I could live for." And he kissed her to seal the deal.

* * * * *

Don't miss the thrilling finale of Katherine Garbera's
MORETTI'S LEGACY *mini-series,*
The Moretti Arrangement, *available in July 2010*
from Mills & Boon® Desire™.

0_NOCTURNE_INTRO

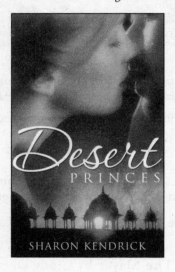

"You've been warned twice. Stop prying into Anne Trulane's death."

After someone comes to journalist Laurel Armand and claims her sister Anne was murdered, Laurel's determined to get the truth.

When a copperhead snake is left on her doorstep, Laurel realises that the warning means she's close to discovering an answer that someone doesn't want her to know...

Available 4th June 2010

www.millsandboon.co.uk

millsandboon.co.uk Community

Join Us!

The Community is the perfect place to meet and chat to kindred spirits who love books and reading as much as you do, but it's also the place to:

- **Get the inside scoop from authors about their latest books**
- **Learn how to write a romance book with advice from our editors**
- **Help us to continue publishing the best in women's fiction**
- **Share your thoughts on the books we publish**
- **Befriend other users**

Forums: Interact with each other as well as authors, editors and a whole host of other users worldwide.

Blogs: Every registered community member has their own blog to tell the world what they're up to and what's on their mind.

Book Challenge: We're aiming to read 5,000 books and have joined forces with The Reading Agency in our inaugural Book Challenge.

Profile Page: Showcase yourself and keep a record of your recent community activity.

Social Networking: We've added buttons at the end of every post to share via digg, Facebook, Google, Yahoo, technorati and de.licio.us.

www.millsandboon.co.uk

2 FREE BOOKS
AND A SURPRISE GIFT

We would like to take this opportunity to thank you for reading this
Mills & Boon® book by offering you the chance to take TWO more
specially selected books from the Desire™ 2-in-1 series absolutely
FREE! We're also making this offer to introduce you to the benefits of
the Mills & Boon® Book Club™—

- **FREE home delivery**
- **FREE gifts and competitions**
- **FREE monthly Newsletter**
- **Exclusive Mills & Boon Book Club offers**
- **Books available before they're in the shops**

Accepting these FREE books and gift places you under no obligation to buy, you may cancel at any time, even after receiving your free
books. Simply complete your details below and return the entire page
to the address below. You don't even need a stamp!

YES Please send me 2 free Desire stories in a 2-in-1 volume and a
surprise gift. I understand that unless you hear from me, I will receive 2
superb new 2-in-1 books every month for just £5.25 each,
postage and packing free. I am under no obligation to purchase any
books and may cancel my subscription at any time. The free books and
gift will be mine to keep in any case.

Ms/Mrs/Miss/Mr _____ Initials _____

_____

Surname _____
Address _____

_____

_____ Postcode _____
E-mail _____

Send this whole page to: Mills & Boon Book Club, Free Book Offer,
FREEPOST NAT 10298, Richmond, TW9 1BR